THE HAUNTING OF STRATHMOOR HEIGHTS

David Gatesbury

Strategic Book Publishing and Rights Co.

Strategic Book Publishing and Rights Co.
12620 FM 1960, Suite A4-507
Houston, TX 77065
www.sbpra.com

ISBN: 978-1-62516-778-1

Book Design: Suzanne Kelly

Thank you Stan and Marge

A special thanks to Nancy Pike for her support

CONTENTS

INTRODUCTION

For those of us who believe in and hold fast to the idea of an afterlife, we can agree that whatever awaits us beyond this present life will be far different than anything we can imagine. Even the strictest atheist will often take an abrupt change in attitude when death is at his or her door.

In our attempt to comprehend what comes after this present existence, we've formed a ceaseless fascination for ghosts. What are they, and if they are a restless spirit, what keeps them bound to our world?

There are many theories to this natural phenomena and what it suggests. Scientists in the field of the paranormal have formed various opinions for these manifestations.

The first theory is that an individual's soul is restless because he or she has left some earthly commitment undone. Until this obligation or particular task is accomplished, the soul must carry on.

An additional theory suggests an abrupt, untimely death may cause one not to understand that his or her time here is done. Not fully realizing he or she is dead, the soul lingers on, bound to a familiar or unfamiliar environment, carrying on what it perceives to be as a normal routine.

Strong evidence suggests a dramatic event—hostile or violent and usually linked to this individual's death, but not necessarily—might bind the spirit of a person to a particular place. When certain circumstances or atmospheric conditions arise or are repeated, this occurrence is replayed and/or reenacted. In the paranormal field, this phenomenon is known as a residual haunting.

All these ideas are based upon theory and conjecture, but are backed by sound reason and logic.

Whatever these images or lost souls are, they remain an unsolved, intricate part of the mystery of life....

CHAPTER 1

A FAMILY LEGACY PASSED DOWN

I remember well that day in the early spring of 1977; one of the first bright, sunny days of the year brought temperatures to a comfortable sixty-seven degrees. I sat poised behind the wheel of a tan, streamlined '74 Jaguar XKE convertible that afternoon with my long brunette hair flipping freely in the wind; the sporty Jag took to the asphalt smoothly, hugging the road as I steered in and out of a long curve.

As I was driving to my mother's estate in Newport, Rhode Island, the world seemed so fresh and reborn; heavy rains the night before helped trees and flowering plants flourish throughout the countryside—the repetition of the seasons beginning once again with rebirth and renewal. New England is one of the most beautiful regions in the country, but instead of taking in the scenery, my thoughts were distant in thinking of how I may soon be the only heiress to the multi-million dollar estate my father built up over his lifetime.

Before his death, my father sold a highly lucrative pharmaceutical company he'd established. He patented several successful drug treatments, which my mother now legally held the rights to, and these achievements alone could serve to provide financial support for a lifetime. Having acquired a master's degree in chemistry, I had designs on one day taking over the company, and it surprised me when I discovered he'd sold the business. I think running such a sizeable company for so many years had taken its toll on him both physically and mentally, and I believe he sold it so that my mother wouldn't have to deal with the headaches and decision making that came with managing a huge corporation.

Up till four years ago, the East Coast is where I spent my entire life. Somehow, it didn't seem the same since my return; there wasn't that welcoming spirit for a person coming home after a term of travel. After a lengthy cruise to Bermuda and returning home to visit friends in Cambridge, Massachusetts, I'd failed to live up to my position as daughter of Edith MacKennsey by not bothering to maintain the requisite mother-daughter communication. A phone message informed me that my mother was gravely ill; and as I started home, I carried with me a guilty, hollow feeling. Thoughts and memories of my mother often served to plunge me into a somber mood.

I'd long since reconciled any ill feelings I harbored about my mother by concluding that she was raised much the same way as she brought me up, and she did the best job she knew how. She molded me into the same type of independent individual she was—a person brimming with self-reliance. I understood that all she had done was for my own good, and I wanted to show her how I'd matured into womanhood; I hoped it wasn't too late to display love and put the past behind me.

I steered off the roadway to follow a snaking tree-lined drive. Up ahead I saw the huge Georgian-style mansion where I'd grown up. My eyes scanned the healthy green lawn and neatly trimmed hedges surrounding it: it all looked much the way as I remembered. As I drove closer, cherished memories replayed in my mind as I envisioned the many times I'd rushed out to greet my father when he'd come home from work or from a business trip; he was full of smiles every time he saw me.

Mom's gray Rolls-Royce sat parked on the circled driveway in front of the house. Her automobile had been around longer than I had. A dark blue Sedan Deville Cadillac conveniently situated at the bottom of the steps that led up to the entrance of the house belonged to George Tallin, an investment broker and financial manager for the family. I parked behind his car then glanced in the rearview mirror to fluff and rearrange my mussed hair. Satisfied, I grabbed my handbag and exited the car. The burgundy purse hung loosely from my elbow by a thin strap as I buttoned one more button on my white blouse, then straightened the slim-fitting burgundy skirt, leaving my knees exposed.

As I climbed the steps, a persistent sense of guilt about seeing my mother caused me to hesitate. After a moment's pause, I opened the door and entered the palatial entrance hall. Standing motionless for a moment, the area before me seemed somehow smaller than I remembered. Then a uniformed maid I'd never seen before approached me.

I placed my handbag on a nearby table. "Hello, I'm Claire MacKennsey."

"Claire," a man's voice broke from down the hall. It was George Tallin, who looked more distinguished than ever.

George was a handsome man who possessed an admirable continence one could never ignore. Time had given him an even more appealing look: broad shoulders, now-frosted black hair at the temples, and wearing a medium gray pinstriped suit. Turning to give him a gaze, it came to mind that I once cared very deeply for him. Having had a crush on him in my late teens, I hoped that he'd gained weight or lost a leg—anything to help diminish any feelings I might still have for him—because he was one of the few men who'd ever snubbed me. I'd held it strongly against him ever since.

As George neared, the maid turned and exited from the room. The grin on his face grew, and it somehow touched me as if rekindling those old feelings I had for him.

"You've really blossomed into quite a lady," he said, sounding warm and friendly. Ignoring the compliment, I asked, "How's my mother, George?"

His expression grew serious. "She's not in good health, and the prognosis hasn't changed."

"You'd think that with all the advancements they've made in medicine they'd be able to do something for her," I replied.

"Claire, the only way her condition can improve is with a bypass operation, but her heart is in such bad shape that the doctors have said any operation is out of the question."

3

He stepped to one side. "I think you ought to see her immediately." He gently touched my arm and led me in the direction of the broad staircase at the far end of the room. "She hasn't been herself lately, but seeing you will lift her spirits. You know, I've met few people as strong willed as your mother. She's always had what they call spunk or grit, but losing your father was something she never got over. Theirs was true love."

We ascended the stairs. As I listened to George, I never recalled him talking this way about my mother before. He spoke with genuine feelings towards her, and this was a side I'd never seen of him.

Midway on the staircase, I caught sight of a nurse starting down the stairs. She gave a friendly smile as she passed us, coming down. It suddenly occurred to me that this was probably a caregiver for the terminally ill, and I then realized just how critical my mother's condition really was.

"I've been meaning to phone her for some time," I said as we climbed the stairs. "I had no idea that she needed me, and then I received a phone message that she was ill. Was she the one who called and left a message?"

"No, I did. She didn't want you to know. She wanted you to come home of your own accord. It's important for her to believe that you've come home just to see her, Claire, and not to know that I called."

"I want to thank you for making an effort to reach me."

"I rummaged around here and found a booklet your mother had that listed your friends' addresses and phone numbers, so it wasn't a lot of trouble. You'd have never forgiven me had she passed away without your saying good-bye."

"I feel so guilty, as though I'd let her down. I guess it's been a year since I've seen her last."

"I don't mean to correct you, but she says the last time she saw you was two years ago, at school."

"She's got a better memory than I have. I feel terrible, George. I won't know what to say to her."

"Don't let that worry you." He put his arm around me and escorted me from the crest of the stairs to her bedroom door.

4

"All that time apart, I'm sure you'll find plenty to talk about. She's been grouchy lately, but I imagine her crankiness stems from growing impatience in waiting to hear from you."

Coming to her bedroom door, I stood there feeling like a coward. George took control of the situation and knocked on her door.

"Who is it?" my mother responded in a voice I knew better than anyone's.

I looked to George, hoping he'd enter her room with me. He smirked before turning and walking away.

"Who's there?" she said, her soft voice lacking the authority it once carried. Opening the door, I felt as though I was years younger.

"May I come in?" I entered the room and saw a frail, white-haired woman lying on the bed. The bedspread covered her up to her armpits, and plump pillows against a large padded headboard supported her head. Her face looked narrower than I'd recalled. She'd lost weight, and her body showed signs of deterioration.

Sighting my presence, she perked up and smiled. "Claire, darling, come in."

Her hand patted the bed, welcoming me to her bedside. She wore a long-sleeved pajama top, and extended her arms outward to greet me.

I bent over, kissed her, and then sat on the edge of the bed next to her. With this close-up view, as she stroked back my hair I noticed fresh lines and wrinkles set in her pale face.

"My, it's hard to believe how you've grown into such a sophisticated young lady. It seems only yesterday that you were my little girl. You always had the prettiest hair."

She had a serious look. "You were afraid to come in. You should be." Then she smiled and touched my cheek. "You're young and lovely and discovering what life is all about." Her eyebrows rose. "I hope you're using discretion in the people you're running around with nowadays. You may think it's none of my business, but I'm still your mother."

She took a deep breath and exhaled. "I only hope you can be at my side at the time of my passing."

"Mother."

"No, my time is coming, I'm going to die soon, and it's important that we talk. You'll never have to worry about money. George is competent at handling finances and he's arranged for most of our estate to enter into a trust at the time of my death."

She held my hand tightly, her eyes studying my every expression. "I hoped that when you'd finished school, you'd come home, and somehow, you and George would hit it off."

My eyes wavered, turning to the base of the lamp standing on her nightstand. "I don't think George holds any romantic notions about me. Hasn't he ever married?"

"No, and I've often wondered why. He's certainly a ladies' man. Over the years, I've seen him at many dinner parties with a different girl on his arm every time. I don't know if you've ever heard him play the piano, but his playing is quite elegant. I suppose you never took a liking to him."

"He's nice looking, but I think we're too different."

"Oh, you don't know him. Your father and I both knew you were infatuated with him in your high school days; he knew it too. I think he deliberately distanced himself from you to keep from getting embarrassed, but now, regardless of your age difference, you're a woman and he's a man."

With a strange glint in her eye, she added, "He's approaching forty now. By the time a man reaches that age, he should consider settling down."

"Seriously, mother, I doubt if he has the slightest interest in me. Besides, I think he's too old for me."

"Too old? Look at the age difference between your father and me. Winston was a great companion, and I have no regrets about having married him."

"I know, mom."

She looked down at my palm and caressed it gently with her fingertips. "Claire, there's something we've kept from you. For some time now, I've felt compelled to reveal something to you about your father's family."

Her eyes held a downward gaze as she continued. "Winston was born in Wales, not far from a village named Cardigan. His mother's name was Angela, and she gave birth to him late in life, as I did with you. She gave birth to another son named Daniel much earlier. There was a vast difference in their ages because Daniel was born in the first year of his parent's marriage, so I've been told. About the time your father entered the world, Daniel was approaching the age of twenty. Within days of giving birth to Winston, Angela went berserk and murdered her husband, Charles, in his sleep. She decapitated him."

I sat there in shock and disbelief but intent on hearing the whole story, telling myself she'd never make up such a story.

"Police never recovered the severed head, and Angela was placed in an institution for the remainder of her life. Your father's Aunt Irene is the one who raised him."

Curiosity caused me to blurt out, "What happened to Daniel, why wasn't I ever told that I had an uncle?"

"Only a few months afterward, shock and grief over his father's death must've driven him to take his own life."

I turned my head away, "My god, what a terrible tragedy."

"How do you think I felt when just two days before we were to be married, Winston told me this ghastly tale? But I loved him so much I wouldn't let it come between us. As far as I know, they never found the cause of his mother's illness. I imagine some rare cases are beyond treatment even today, and it's because of that story that your father and I originally decided not to bear children. Then you came along—a real surprise package. I was thirty-seven when I had you. You were the most beautiful thing your father and I had ever seen. We loved you with all our heart and never knew such happiness until you came into our lives.

"Your father often wanted to go back to Cardigan to revisit the home where his Aunt Irene raised him, but I wouldn't let him go. I was too afraid of the past. He had a few peculiarities, one being that paralyzed left hand of his. He had several specialists look at it, but there was no physical explanation for the paralysis. They all thought it was nerve damage, but from what?"

I recalled the hand he could never use. "I remember him mentioning he couldn't hold open a newspaper and consulting a number of doctors that were no help to him. I thought he'd had a stroke."

"Another strange thing, he had a nasty, terrible scar on the left side of his body. He must have undergone great pain at the time he received this injury, and yet he had no memory of how it came about."

"I don't remember any scar."

"That's because he never left the horrible mark exposed. As soon as he got out of the shower, he'd throw on a shirt; he didn't swim, and he never even got in the pool unless it was just the two of us. If you think about it, you'd remember that whenever we had guests, he'd mosey around the pool making conversation, carrying a drink in his hand, wearing one of those brightly colored flowered shirts he liked. Once I asked his Aunt Irene, who's long since deceased now, how he acquired this mark and she answered that it resulted from an accident when he was a baby. From the very first time I heard about the murder, I suspected that his mother performed some hideous torture on him. God knows, she must've had an unbalanced, twisted mind.

"The night your father died, he woke up drenched in sweat, his face was pale and off-colored, and I asked him if he'd had a bad dream, but he gave no answer. I thought he was ill, so I offered to dial for help, but he wouldn't let me. We sat up in bed for a while and he told me about a curious dream he'd had. He explained the dream by saying, 'I hear someone calling to me, a voice calling out to me very faint at first, then it's as clear as we're talking now. I can see a door, and I want to open it, but I know there's something behind it I'd rather not face. I'm urged to open the door, and yet I know something terrifying is waiting for me beyond it'."

I couldn't help but grin. "That sounds pretty strange."

"Strange, I got the distinct impression that this was a dream he'd had on numerous occasions before, and I told him that first thing in the morning, I was going to make him an appointment to see a psychiatrist. Of course, he didn't survive to see the morning; he had a severe heart attack. I knew I should've called for an ambulance that night, but he insisted he was okay."

"Why wasn't I told about his family before?"

"Honey, there were times I wanted to mention it, but you were too young to understand. He was a fine man, and I have only fond memories of your father. I hope this story didn't lessen the memory you had of him."

"No, not at all," I replied.

"I wouldn't have told you about it now, but you may be thinking of having a family of your own one day, and I felt obligated to let you know."

She put her hands to my cheeks. "You ought to put this out of your mind now. I don't think you have anything to worry about, but this information may prove useful to you in the future."

I got the impression that it gave my mother relief to tell me how my grandfather was killed, as though telling me about it took a great strain off her. It was the first mother–and–daughter talk we'd had in a long time, and I last let her know I'd be staying home for a while. Leaning over to hug her, we kissed, and seeing she was physically tired, I made sure she was comfortable and in a restful position before walking out of her room.

Life had taken on a strange new meaning, the lingering story of murder and decapitation moving me in such a way that I felt uncertainty and doubt about the future. I'd only begun to grasp the implications of this shocking and dreadful story, which made the strong statement that insanity ran in the family. If my grandmother was a crazed murderess, did it mean that I was heir to some inherent gene? Was I predisposed to one day go stark raving mad and kill somebody? The possibility of this prospect stunned me and absorbed my thought processes. I always expected to have a family of my own, but my mother had actually suggested thinking twice about childbearing. The knowledge she gave me implied I could be capable of murdering my spouse. How else was I to interpret it?

This was my family's legacy, and I didn't know how to contend with it. Throughout my childhood, I knew all wasn't right between my mother and me, and consciously or unconsciously, the wedge she'd driven between us caused me to feel like an outsider when growing up. I strived to be in her good graces for winning her love and attention, but I couldn't melt her heart; her cold, distant, insensitive ways gave me the deep-rooted sense that I was unwanted. Now these fears and flashback feelings found grounds for real concern. Because of this strange and dark story about my family's past, she made me believe she must've thought she'd given birth to a bad seed or an unbalanced child. Whether she loved me or not, she must've always suspected I was touched and possibly deranged, and even if her actions weren't intentional, they had taken me to the brink of an inferiority complex.

One aspect of my childhood fueling these thoughts and ideas was that I'd spent much of my youth acting as my mother's secretary, following her around and keeping track of her constantly changing agenda. It was sort of fun at first, but it seemed she'd prefer I carry on the role even at home, and I'd discourage it; at least at home I preferred not to be treated like an employee. There always seemed to be an undercurrent running between us, making me feel like a misfit, I have no recollection of the love and pampered affection I saw other girls getting from their moms. I knew she was capable of showing affection because I'd seen it when accompanying her to hospitals to visit neglected children who'd fallen under serious illnesses. One could detect compassion in her eyes when she cuddled them in her arms, but I never really felt loved. Perhaps now, I understood why—my mother must've thought she'd mothered an ill-fated child.

My mother couldn't help being the person that she was, always carrying herself so dignified and proper, and I never knew anyone so concerned for what others were thinking. I would've understood her much better if she'd been a conceited person, but she wasn't that way. The truth of the matter was that she was a person easily drawn into a cause. Driven by charitable events she organized and promoted, she showed herself to be a big-hearted woman with a persuasive way of winning people's trust and respect. She was an icon of society, a spokesperson for the poor and grief stricken, and a woman who wielded power by representing wealthy friends and associates of my father's who were looking to generously throw around money.

She had an entourage of jabbering females who, in my eyes, were birds of a feather—each of whom had their own stylish way of flaunting wealth. However, the sincerity in my mother's voice and the meaningful chosen words she used gave way to such articulate expressions that I never doubted her sensitivity in helping the needy and underprivileged was less than genuine. At the same time, because these social endeavors took priority over her life, I sometimes wondered if they meant more to her than I did. Now I saw things differently in that she may have bestowed so much tireless energy to these charities as a way to occupy her mind. She kept watch over me like a dutiful mother should while at the same time distancing me from her, almost as if making believe that I was merely hired help; and in a way thinking I was her acting secretary, I fit the role well.

Mulling over remembrances while retracing my adolescence, I came to terms with the fact that I grew up faster than most children, for sadly, I can not recall a time when I was naïve and pure of heart. I had few close friends in my childhood, as I didn't get along well with my peers and I'd broken off several friendships after my mother had taken a shining to those girls. As much as I tried not to let it show, it bothered me when she made a fuss over them or took a caring interest in their lives. I couldn't help throwing an occasional tantrum, and once, my mother caressed the curly, strawberry blonde hair of a girl I invited over, and within an hour, I chased her out of our house. This type of resentful behavior left me uncomfortable with myself, causing deliberation and wonder, but now I was able to grasp at least some understanding for why I acted that way.

These thoughts drew more memories to the surface. While rehashing them in my mind, I remembered learning at a young age that my parents had arranged for me to go to a prestigious private boarding school for girls. More than ever before, I thought she wanted to be rid of me and desperately begged and pleaded not to be sent away. Both my parents tried reasoning with me by explaining all the educational benefits this school offered, but all I knew was that they were sending me away. I became so depressed, distraught and emotional that my father finally relented and persuaded my mother, who'd gone to nothing but the finest private schools, not to force me into going. Now I wondered if she really wanted to get rid of me, as though the proposition for sending me off to a private school made for a good excuse to push me out of her life for a time. Maybe I reminded her that my grandmother was an axe murderer and how I could one day develop the same tendencies.

I always felt closer to my father, and the boarding school incident made me realize that, like me, he had experienced loneliness in his life too. I knew even as a child that he'd lost his parents at a young age; I just didn't know what the circumstances were. If I had any cherished memories as a child, it was through him. All this muddled thinking about my family's past made me feel as though I was beginning some strange and unpredictable odyssey with no way of knowing where it would take me. Dwelling on it didn't diminish the problem, but only served to compound an already-complex ordeal. I threw an endless array of questions at myself, causing me to imagine an ever-expanding scope of theories and ideas about my family's past. By doing so, I created my own form of self-persecution.

Seeing how this story of murder invoked wide speculation, at an open hallway junction I took a convenient chair to contemplate the situation. Sitting there, experiencing a rising, unwanted upsurge within me, I stared aimlessly while being drawn deeper and deeper into intense thought. I could already tell that learning about this murky murder was going to leave a lasting impact on me. In considering how a crime of such magnitude can fracture lives for generations, this murder in particular would leave anybody profoundly disturbed and troubled, a maliciously shocking slaying with such bloody overtones by the merciless method of delivering death. What made it especially dramatic for me was the victim and the murderer were both close relations of mine, my grandparents, and I wasn't sure how to cope with it; but I kept connecting it with my own life, partly because my mother had suggested the same. As my thoughts raced wildly, I tried convincing myself that I was taking it all too seriously, but there was no escaping the sobering thought that lying dormant in my genetic code could be a deadly sickness with the capacity to influence me into committing violent murder.

Meditating on this indelible revelation, I swung my head back to clear my hair from my eyes and viewed a framed photograph of my father within arm's reach on a nearby table. Then, in wondering what could've driven my grandmother to commit such an unspeakable act, I picked up the picture frame to gaze at it. She must've fallen so far out of the realm of reality and became so psychologically unbalanced that she didn't know what she was doing. How many ways can one define madness—psychoneurosis, schizophrenia, and paranoia describe a medley of mental disorders and diseased abnormalities categorizing deranged behavior; but they all were vague and ambiguous to me. Still, I imagined one's wants, needs, and desires turning into extremes and excessive cravings until thoughts created by the mind consumed present reality. Common mood swings getting so far out of proportion as to take one on a high euphoria, then in sweeping seconds thrown uncontrollably into sorrow, despair, and depression, excesses feeding deceptive delusions, evolving while developing a self-imposed, erroneous perception about life.

Without a record of my grandmother's medical history, there was no way to gauge the degree or perplexity of her illness and arrive at whether the condition was treatable, thus leaving the possibilities endless. With no way to learn what her prognosis may have been, I pondered whether the disease took hold by the way she had been raised—a result of environment, primarily by mistreatment or abuse. Did her mother suffer from mental illness? If she had, then I definitely would have something to worry about. But there was no way to know any of this. The whole idea that my grandmother went mad was all so very disturbing to me because I could never hope to learn what was in her mind at the time of the crime.

Gazing at the picture of my father and focusing on his facial features, I saw what I perceived to be an imperfection I never noticed before; then bringing the picture closer for my eyes to give it further examination, on the left side of his face one could faintly detect what may be a scar which few people could see or be mindful of. It actually appeared that in an effort to close a wound the skin was stretched ever so subtly, causing the left eye to have a slight squint. The scar ran from just above his ear and upwards along the hairline—that's what made it so hard to see.

Scrutinizing that subtle squint, I stared at my father's photo while imagining he must've suffered an injury as a baby under my grandmother's care at or about the time that she'd murdered my grandfather. I couldn't help asking myself how sick an individual my grandmother was, but quickly concluded that only a person with a diseased mind could harm an innocent child. That coincided with the thought that only a person with a deranged mind could decapitate a human being. My mother had described a nasty, terrible scar on the left side of my father's body too, and I thought how I never saw him around our pool unless he had a shirt on; and rarely did I see him in the water.

In the midst of concerning myself with this scar—if it was a scar and I wasn't just imagining things—I thought how it must've always been there and yet, I never gave it a thought. I could no longer look at the photograph and torture myself with these crazed ideas about my grandmother. I placed the photo back on the table, and then shifted its viewable angle so that I no longer had to look at it. I didn't need any more reminders or considerations of the madness that came to possess a grandmother I never knew, and I didn't want to tarnish the memory of my father any further.

My hair kept falling down and getting into my eyes, and I ran my fingers through strands while pushing it back to get it out of my face; then I saw George approaching me as he appeared in the hallway. He carried in each hand a glass of orange juice with crushed ice, and came in my direction with one hand outstretched as though offering me a glass. He said, "I took the liberty of fixing us both a drink spiked with a little vodka, I hope you don't mind."

Assuming George didn't know what my mother and I had spoken about; I looked up at him and asked, "What made you think I could use a drink?"

"You'd just arrived after a long drive, and usually after I've made a long journey, I can use a refreshing pick-me-up, did I guess wrong?"

"No," I replied, reaching my hand out for the cold feel of the glass, and after taking a sip, I leaned back and muttered, "You could've made mine a double."

"Did it go that badly?"

"Not really, but I suppose you're right. I'm a little fatigued, partly from the trip here and yes, partly from the talk she and I had."

George lifted his glass and took a long drink, then removed from his suit coat pocket a business card and left it on the table, saying, "I don't know if I can be much aid to you, but should her condition change, I'd like to know. As long as I've assisted the family, I think she considers me a friend, and I hope you do too."

Resting my head against the back of the chair, I crossed my legs, looked up at him, and smiled, "In case you're the least bit curious, your name came up in our conversation."

A boyish grin appeared on his face, "Oh, really."

"My mother's quite fond of you."

He finished his drink and puckered in losing the lasting taste of the juice in his mouth, and responded, "That's what I've always thought, but she wasn't exactly tickled pink with me a couple of days ago. Just before slamming down a hand of cards that beat her at gin, I had the gall to mention some of her stocks were losing money. You know, I shouldn't say this, but she's the type that would prefer to take the money with her."

"I know."

George glanced at his watch, "Well, I've got to get going." Then starting down the hallway in making his exit, he stalled while turning and twisting his upper body to look back at me, "I have an answering service so don't hesitate to give me a ring day or night."

I felt relief knowing that I had someone to talk with who knew my mother well, but I had no intention of asking him for advice pertaining to the problem I'd just been dealt. To me, the main topic of conversation between my mother and I was something personal and private, and I preferred that no one knew about it; however, the story of decapitation had a profound effect on me in that it dominated my thinking throughout the day and evening. I'd become overly conscious of it, and the more I brooded over inhibiting thoughts regarding this awful story, the tighter its hold had over me; and unable to suppress the eerie thoughts created by this wretched story, I only wished there was a way to learn the details of what transpired back then. All I kept doing was going over my mother's revealing description of a part of the family that I never knew existed before, inventing and reinventing scenarios; but without facts, what else was there for me to do but to speculate and surmise what had happened? Would I always be wondering if I'm to follow in the footsteps of my grandmother and harm someone whom I loved dearly?

CHAPTER 2

BROODING OVER THE PAST

I looked in on my mother later that same evening, and seeing she was asleep, I decided to turn in, taking my old bedroom just down the hall from hers. I'd tried thinking about other things, but the story of this grisly murder remained firmly fixed in my thought processes to make me feel depressed and withdrawn. Caught up in an event that happened so many years ago, I went to bed under the unsettling gloom of knowing my grandfather was decapitated in his sleep. Being that my grandmother wielded the fatal blow left me believing that she must've committed the horrific murder while in the throes of a psychosis or psychotic episode. While grappling with this ghastly crime, I continued to hold the strong suspicion that she may have harmed my father when he was no more than a baby.

Didn't anyone see she had the potential to harm someone? If she wasn't in control of her faculties, shouldn't she have been under constant watch and confined so such a disaster wouldn't occur? There must have been some indication that she was sinking into an unbalanced state of mind, or had she suddenly unraveled and lost touch with reality by having some kind of mental breakdown? If it had been known that she was unstable, surely family members would have sought psychiatric help for her; and if that had been the case, then this should've come out at the time of the murder—she would've been found to be not responsible for her actions. In pondering and probing her illness, I wondered if a brutal and tyrannical husband had systematically driven her mad.

As these fears and concerns weighed on my mind and ran awry, I realized how this incident was fast developing into a wrenching phobia to dominate my conscious thoughts. Just like I'd begun persecuting myself worrying about a mentally disturbed relative, did the illness of my grandmother begin in much the same way? A silent, taunting inner conflict, beginning in part because of a family history of mental illness, fueling a deviating struggle that culminated in a moment of sheer madness—resulting in a senseless act that somehow in her warped and declining way of thinking, she believed and ultimately convinced herself that murdering her husband was the only way to finding a lasting peace.

As if this type of a murder wasn't bad enough, why didn't they find the head! Deeply troubled and bewildered by what could've possessed my grandmother to commit such an irrational act, I kept waking up, picturing this frenzied act of a mad woman swinging an axe over her husband's restful body. I felt as though I'd suddenly learned my grandmother was Lizzie Borden, and the implications weren't easily swept aside. No matter how hard I tried to let these dark morbid ideas go, I couldn't channel my thoughts elsewhere; and this annoying line of thought served to mock me, sparking my own self-analysis. I began questioning even my slightest peculiarities and in a sense scrutinizing my own little quirks that might indicate, suggest, or imply mental illness. Thinking I may have some of her character traits and be much like her in many ways, I further tormented myself wondering how old my grandmother was when she first began showing outward signs of losing her mental faculties. There was absolutely no end to it.

Restlessly tossing and turning throughout the night, I frustrated over these nagging, prevailing, and unrelenting questions that wouldn't allow my mind to relax and uncoil. I found time to consider my Uncle Daniel, whom I never knew before existed, and wondered if he had suffered from the same mental illness; and if so, did it undermine his sanity and eat away at his senses to the point that it drove him to suicide? Is this insanity hereditary? I couldn't discount this possibility and while this question kept surfacing in my mind, I knew there certainly was no proof that it wasn't.

Lying in bed sleeplessly drifting in conscious thoughts, I wished I'd had another human being to confide in and convey these concerns to, but the only person whom I dared talk about it with was my mother, and she obviously believed my grandmother to be hopelessly insane. What concerned me most was that she must think I'm a candidate for doing the same thing, or else why would she have bothered disclosing the murder, as if telling me about it with a word of warning. In my restlessness of contending with these overwhelming ideas and forever-festering thoughts, I felt somewhat angry with my mother for divulging this gruesome murder. I suppose it was a story she thought must to be told and I really had no reason for being upset with her, but part of me was searching for someone to blame, and there wasn't anybody.

In the midst of my mounting hysteria, I finally had enough, as I was unable to sleep, and glancing to the window to see the faintest sign of the dawn of a new day, my thoughts went to my mother. I rose from my bed with the intention of going to her room and checking on her to see that she was all right. Carefully opening her door and looking in, I found the room dark with the curtains drawn closed. At first, I didn't see anything, but the dim gray light seeping in and around the edges of the curtains soon allowed my eyes to focus on the room's furnishings. From my position standing at the door, I couldn't make out her head or face from the bed's linen, nor did I detect the sound of her breathing, so I softly took steps closer to the bed to see if she was sleeping restfully.

My feet quietly skimming across the carpeting as my eyes scanned the way ahead, I turned my head when noticing what looked like a clump of clothes on the floor at the door leading to a connecting bathroom. Suddenly realizing it was my mother lying still on the floor, I knelt and stooped over her, touching her arm while saying, "Mom."

When she gave no response, I placed my hand to her cheek, it felt cold to the touch, and when feeling her wrist for a pulse, I didn't detect one. Without a seconds delay I went to the nightstand and turned on the lamp, reaching for the phone only inches away to dial for an ambulance. Communicating my mother's condition as best I could to the person on the other end of the line, I then gave our address. I saw my mother's hand moving in a trembling motion, and as soon as I hung up the receiver, I returned to her side.

She murmured a short succession of words that I couldn't discern, and as I brushed her hair back to see her face with more clarity, she asked, "Where am I?"

"You're home, Mom, you must've fainted trying to get to or from the restroom. Is that nurse here in the house?" Receiving no response, I started to ask again, but remembered the nurse mentioning that she needed the night off.

Seeing my mother lying there in such a condition made me feel helpless; all I could think to do was to cover her with a blanket and prepare for the ambulance so I could accompany her to the hospital.

"I need to get some clothes on, but I'll be right back," I told her reassuringly.

Dashing to my bedroom down the hall, I removed my night clothes and quickly threw on a blouse, slacks, and a pair of slip-on shoes; and a short time later we were on an ambulance ride rushing to the hospital. Seeing the grave state she was in, a feeling of dread came over me as concern and worry for my mother's frail condition bordered on anxiety. She fell in and out of consciousness, causing me to be afraid of losing her, and I held her hand clasped firmly in mine the entire way to the hospital. My father's death had been somewhat similar in that I was at his bedside, holding his hand at the time he died, and as I recalled the moment, his hand fell limp in mine, the memory brought to bear the clinching reality that I might soon be without my mother. A feeling of loss and loneliness drew my head to her arm and understanding how great the love I felt for her, I began weeping like a little child.

When we arrived at the hospital, the emergency staff whisked her out of my sight; this heavy feeling of being left all alone in the world had not yet subsided, and the only person whom I thought to call was George. Not only had he asked me to phone him if my mother's condition changed, but I sort of felt obligated in that he'd been the one person kind enough to call me and inform me of my mother's condition in the first place.

After phoning the number he'd given me, I got his answering service and left a short message. Hoping my mother's condition would improve, and expecting him to show up later in the day, I felt sure he wouldn't mind giving me a ride home that evening.

Two hours later, George joined me in the hospital waiting room outside the intensive care unit; and it wasn't too long afterwards when Dr. Bottoms, who'd been our family physician for years, came to deliver word of her condition. George and I both stood up to greet him and approached him to hear the news of how she was doing, and I asked in a caring and concerned manner, "Dr. Bottoms how is she?"

He removed his eyeglasses, rubbing his eyes before replying, "Claire, your mother has suffered a series of heart attacks. She's in a comatose state, and she may or may not come out of it. There's little we can do now except wait, but she doesn't have much time."

"Can I see her?"

"Of course, I'll have one of the nurses take you to her in just a few minutes. I wish I had better news for you, but for day's she's been on the verge of congestive heart failure, and I would've preferred she'd been in the hospital long before now, but she wouldn't have it. Now if you'll pardon me, I'll try to make arrangements for you to get in to be with her. I'll probably see you a little later when I look in on her."

When finally allowed in her room, I saw a nurse checking a chart at the door as I walked over to her bed and saw her lying before me with her eyes shut. George must have thought I looked distressed because he immediately arranged a chair so I could sit at her bedside where I remained most of the day. George kept popping in and out of the room; and at about two in the afternoon, he offered to treat me to lunch, but I declined because I was concerned she might either gain consciousness or expire. Not wanting to leave her bedside, it meant a lot to me to be with her at the time of her passing.

Some time later, when George was out of the room, I saw the fingers on her right hand flinching. I placed her hand in my left palm, and then began gently stroking and massaging the back of her hand with my fingertips. Her eyes opened slowly, and as I gently caressed the side of her face, tears began trickling down my cheeks, and I wiped them dry while attempting to smile so not to look so grim.

In studying her expression, I understood that I was losing something very precious to me. She was the nearest and dearest thing to me, and I thought that no matter how harsh and insensitive my memory represented her as, from now on I'll try focusing on the fact that she'd always done what she thought was in my best interest. We quietly gazed at each other for a while, and I found pleasure in sharing this time in her company. Then I saw her moving her mouth as if to say something but was too weak to express what she wanted to say.

"You don't have to speak," I said, trying to calm and comfort her.

She was persistent about wanting to say something to me, and signaled for me to come closer, so I leaned over, putting my ear close to her mouth in an effort to hear and understand the faint words she whispered.

"Don't..."

"Don't what?" I asked her and then moved my ear even closer.

"Don't go there," she uttered softly.

Having barely heard her words, I looked at her, and then leaned over once more for attempting to understand what she was trying to say, becoming doubtful that she herself was clear on what she was trying to tell me.

"You know...Don't go."

A little confused, I drew a deep breath and looked at her again, saying, "Conserve your strength, Mom, I'm not going to leave your side."

Less than a minute later, George entered the room; and seeing my mother conscious, he reached over to pat her hand gently, and we all smiled. He then pulled up a chair to join us; and now sensing she wanted to tell us both something, she gripped my hand and motioned for his, then placed mine over his and we all smiled again.

We then watched as she gave a twinge as if showing great pain and a second later, she fell limp, still, and lifeless—she was at peace.

"George, she's gone," and I crumpled into tears.

He leaned over, took me in his arms, and held me tight, resting his head against mine as he ran his fingers through my hair. Anxiety that had been building up inside of me for hours now poured out, for I'd lost both my parents now, and I was just beginning to understand how I'd never see either of them again in this life.

In the days that followed, I made preparations with the funeral parlor to have her laid to rest, and George was a huge help to me. He aided me by taking time from his busy schedule to assist me and provide transportation for me. Even though my mother had taken care of most of the arrangements some time ago, there were still a few decisions I had to deal with.

When my father died, my mother's health was good and she took care of everything; and with her gone, I'd become the only family survivor, and I had to shoulder the responsibility for seeing that these duties were carried out. I didn't realize how this particular segment of life drained a person, and I found it comforting to have George at my side. It became so much to bear that when my mother was laid out at the funeral parlor, I felt beside myself and it was as though I wasn't altogether there; I just went through the motions in an almost zombie-like state. I hardly knew any of the people associated with my parents, but most of them were elderly, and there were few whom I recognized and remembered. Those faces I did have recollection of meeting, it seemed like ages ago, when I was merely a child, that we'd met; and they'd changed considerably. Some I remembered having met for the first time at the funeral of my father's, but throughout the entire episode of parading strangers, I felt awkward and at the same time surprised how so many had come to say their last farewell. She must have touched a lot of people's lives, and many of them had kind words for her.

That following Friday, the first of May, the funeral procession arrived at her burial place at the cemetery. Cloudbursts repeated throughout the day, and at the cemetery, a canopy shielded us from a downpour. The gloomy weather was much like my mental state and everything else around me that day, the wearisome black outerwear and black umbrellas carried by those who'd gathered. Through my veil, I viewed the solemn, somber, and dismal faces of elderly friends and aging business associates who mourned my mother. We paid our last respects by chanting a prayer together, and then the priest said a few words before giving a final blessing over the casket, which the cemetery grounds keepers would have lowered after we'd gone. I placed a single rose on the lid of the sleek black casket, and after kissing the palm of my hand, I placed my hand flat on the lid as a final farewell gesture.

"I think you've been through enough, Claire," said George. "Shall we go?"

"I'm ready," was the drowsy answer I uttered back, and he walked me to mother's Rolls. It seemed so appropriate that we ride in her car today.

My mother's chauffer had joined us at the gravesite, but he'd already gone back to the car to patiently await our return to open the car door when we got there. He showed no emotion when stepping aside to open the rear passenger side door for me; I got in first and scooted over to make room for George.

As the driver took us back to the house, George turned to me and said, "Claire, I've been in touch with your family attorney, William Caulfield. He's had some papers drawn up that require your signature, and he's asked me to witness them. Except for a relatively generous sum of money Edith left to a few charitable organizations, you're the only heir mentioned in the will. There's some paperwork regarding the estate which needs my attention before everything can be ready, so I'll need to return to my office immediately. I've asked your chauffer to drop me off there. Will you be alright for the rest of the evening?"

"I'll be fine," I replied.

"You look exhausted. Why not take a couple of days to get some rest, we can put off signing those papers till Wednesday. Is Wednesday a good day for you? I mean, you don't have any plans for that afternoon, do you?"

"No, nothing, I'll be there."

Having appreciated all the courtesies, and comfort George had given to me the past few days, I also valued his attention. I sat snugly next to him, my arm around his; my head fell gently to rest against his shoulder, and then I came to fall asleep in this cozy, secure position. A kiss on the forehead awakened me sometime later, and I then felt George carefully squirming to work his shoulder and arm out from beneath me. As I heard the car door close, I opened my eyes; and noticing that the car wasn't moving, I caught a glimpse of him entering his office building just as the car pulled away.

As soon as I arrived home, I decided to lie down for a spell and in doing so took a long nap. The wet, rainy weather had subsided by the time I awoke in the early evening, and I had a light meal. That same night, feeling reflectively moody and melancholic, I pulled the cork from a previously opened bottle of red wine that had been in our refrigerator for an unknown period of time and poured a goblet half-full. I took a whiff from the rim of the glass to catch the aroma and then tasted its slightly semi-sweet flavor, then casually strolled about the premises with the drink in my hand. I went outside into the cool, refreshing night air, and onto the terrace to gaze at our swimming pool and the grounds about me, then pondering moving memories that sprang forth.

Minutes later, I went back inside the house; and everything around me began to speak of, or for, my mother, and perhaps even for both my parents, as well as for the love I had for them. I remembered she had a pet name for my father in that she'd often affectionately call him Mac. The moment moved me so much that I felt the need to do something in their honor. I didn't know what or even why I felt this way, but for reasons I could not explain, I came to the living room and went to the stereo console. I hadn't played the thing in ages, but fingering through her collection of long playing records, I found the one that seemed most appropriate to play. Her favorite singing artist was Rosemary Clooney and her favorite song was "Tenderly," and so I thought I'd play it for one last time. As the needle came into contact with the record, music well orchestrated with fine accompaniment filled the house, and the voice of the female vocalist seemed perfectly suited to the words and melody of this romantically touching song.

The sound served well to fit my mood in reminiscing about my parents. It spoke to me of the love they shared; and as the final line to the lyrics came across in ending the song, I felt as though the house came crashing down upon me, and I broke down and cried. The tears running down my cheeks were for my loss as well as for the disturbing and demoralizing details of the story my mother told me. Now I felt a dreaded, deep loneliness in that I'd have to dwell on our family's legacy, and live with the nightmare of thinking that I may one day inherit a terrible mental illness with potentially horrible consequences.

I had suppressed the gory description of a decapitation all throughout the time of the funeral, and as much as I hated dwelling on it, this deepening dilemma had come back to taunt me again. As all the unyielding and inexorable questions began to resurface and devour me, I never felt so crushed and devastated in my life. I wasn't bitter for having to bear this alone, but I wished I had more time with my mother to find out more about my family's dark past. At the same time, I didn't think she really knew much more about it than what she told me, nor did she want to know anything more about it.

Drying my eyes, I fast came to terms with the fact that this is a problem I may never be able to put entirely behind me. However, whether or not I'd go crazy in the near or distant future, it wasn't something I'd have to think about every conscious minute of the day. Needing time to adjust and cope with this dark secret, for now I wanted to distance myself from the prospect of marriage and having children. Reminding myself how my mother wasn't shy about discouraging the idea of childbearing, this only made me anguish and despair over unborn offspring. Without knowing the facts in this matter, how could I conceive children and risk passing down a mental illness that may destroy a family. I kept reverting to these thoughts because I know our genetic makeup plays a big part in our lives. An individual's character is multisided and complex, and there are more people leading double lives than we can guess; however, so much of our mental traits are preordained from the time of conception. While being formed in the womb, our personality begins taking shape, many of our likes and dislikes, our favorite color, perhaps our sexual preference are set in our mental processes prior to birth.

Finishing off the wine, I left the goblet on the record album cover before turning off the stereo and then switched off the lights before heading up to bed; but one thing I concluded was that this house had belonged to my parents, and it represented an important aspect of their lives. I intended selling it and the furnishings it held; the remembrances it contained for me would remain only as memories in my mind.

Before turning in, I looked into my mother's bedroom; an endless stream of questions began to resurface about the murder of my grandfather: Was it a mental disorder that brought on this woman's mental breakdown, or was my grandfather a possessively domineering tyrant who drove her to commit murder? If my grandmother wasn't mentally sound, did the injuries that scarred my father come about as a result of a mother's negligence, negligence that may have indicated the start of the initial decay of her mind, leading to the deranged individual who decapitated her husband?

No matter what, decapitation—the method of my grandfather's murder—kept leading me back to the inexplicable conclusion that she must have lost her mind, plus the fact that the authorities never recovered the head kept needling me, and just the idea of it made my skin crawl. Then there was Daniel, a young man, bereaved, and grief stricken with these awful consequences to shoulder. He must've found his father's nightmarish death impossible to bear and chose to take his own life rather than live with the scorn of public scrutiny. In those days, as

27

much as any time in history, the press would've hounded him. Who wouldn't be subjected to suicidal thoughts after such a terribly infamous thing happening?

I took to my bed that night, engaged in a rash of demeaning and degrading thoughts regarding my future. These unpleasant, meandering considerations were very depressing and not easily dealt with. I had no doubt that I wasn't the same person as I was before hearing about the murder of my grandfather. This murder mystified me to the point that it took some of the starch out of me, and since the cause for my grandmother's illness had never been established, for some time to come I'll have to contend with concerns for my own sanity. It was as if this crazy incident in my family's past placed a permanent and lasting stain on my family's history, and it hovered over me like a dark shadow; but without some record of the past, there was simply no way I could sort things out.

The last thing I thought about before going to sleep was to recall a girl whom I roomed with in college who'd at the time already made up her mind not to have children. She lived under the fear of contracting a neurodegenerative disorder called Huntington's disease that had plagued members of her family for generations, leaving some of them crippled and bedridden at a young age. I remember her presenting the question of why should she raise children, only to watch them decline in their youth to a vegetative state. Now having learned about the fateful murder of my grandfather, and knowing that mental illness runs in my family, how was I any different than she?

CHAPTER 3

A NEW REVELATION

By Wednesday, I found myself totally consumed by a murder that happened such a long time ago, and there was little possibility of finding answers to put my mind at ease. Even if I uncovered a newspaper telling all the ghoulish details from the tragic event, it wouldn't solve anything. I needed to learn all the circumstances behind the story in order to find out my grandmother's frame of mind when the crime happened, and there seemed little chance of that happening.

I left the house that morning to meet George at the lawyer's office, and within forty minutes, I met up with George in the building's lobby whereby he soon introduced me to William Caulfield. I remembered the attorney's strong Irish features from a previous occasion, and returned a friendly gaze as he shook my hand.

"I'm sorry to hear about the loss of your mother, Ms. MacKennsey," said Caulfield, "and I want to leave my card with you in case you should have any questions about the legal documentation I've prepared."

Then Caulfield remarked, "If you'll pardon me for just a few minutes, I have everything nearly prepared in my conference room, and I promise not to keep you long."

George spoke in a casual manor, "I was thinking about your father earlier today, he was quite a remarkable man. I remember him as a wheeler-dealer of types who enjoyed running the company, but it became such a gigantic conglomeration of businesses that holding it all together had become a strain on him. Believing his health was failing him near the end, he sold the company. Your mother didn't want to be chairman of the board for a pharmaceutical company, and knowing you'd be the one whose lap it would've eventually fallen into, I don't think he wanted you burdened with managing a corporation."

Caulfield returned to motion for us, and the two escorted me to a spacious rectangular-shaped conference room where he'd arranged all the necessary papers on a table for me to sign. Either Caulfield or George gave a brief explanation of each document presented before me, and I followed through with the stroke of a pen. When documentation required a witness's signature, George followed up by giving his signature and soon the formalities were over for placing me in control of all family holdings, and I'd become a major stockholder in the drug company my father had established. Some of the money from the estate went to my mother's favorite charities, as I'd already expected.

"You're the sole beneficiary of a great fortune," said Caulfield, as he handed me a manila folder containing records. "There are copies of everything in this folder and there are also copies kept here on file at the office as well. If you need me for anything, you know how to reach me."

George came to stand beside me, "Claire, I'd like you to come to my office so you and I can go through a few things connected with your mother's estate."

I gave George the manila folder before we walked out the door together, and we soon arrived at his office, located just a couple blocks away. Upon entering the confines of his private office, I saw a stack of records and old deeds lying on his desktop.

George placed the manila folder I'd entrusted him with on the desk next to the other documents and said, "The reason why I asked you here, Claire, I didn't know what you wanted me to do with all this. You and I haven't had any time to discuss whether you wanted me to manage things for you."

"Of course, I do, George, I want you to carry on in the same capacity as you always have for the family. The first thing I want you to handle for me is the sale of the house, which will mean auctioning off all of its contents and furnishings, the Rolls-Royce, everything. The money from the sale of the house is to go in the bank, less any commission you deem as fair."

George held a serious expression when saying, "You're sure that's the way you want it all handled—I'm only asking because it seems you're moving a little fast for me. You're not going to just take off on some trip around the world and leave all this in my hands, are you?"

"I don't know what my future plans are just yet, but I'm certain I want this handled the way as I've instructed you. I'm probably going to rent an apartment for the time being, so I'll be available to direct you on things you're not sure of. Anything in the nature of personal belongings, such as important papers, valuables, jewelry, and so forth, I'll either keep at the apartment, or have it placed in storage or in a safety deposit box." Then I smiled, adding, "And if I do run off I'll keep you posted on my whereabouts."

George's eyebrows rose, wrinkling his forehead, and after shuffling through some folders on his desk, he singled out one that had yellowed from age. Opening it, he commented, "I've come across this deed on more than one occasion, it's for a piece of real estate in Wales."

He placed the document in front of me, "This property belonged to Charles MacKennsey, then it fell into the hands of Irene MacKennsey, and after that it passed down to your father."

Learning about the old house in Wales perked my interest, for I knew my family migrated from the British Isles to the United States before the outbreak of World War II, bringing with them a large portion of their wealth. I looked at the papers inquisitively, "Charles MacKennsey was my grandfather and Irene MacKennsey my great-aunt. She raised my father and these papers must be connected to the house where my father grew up."

"I showed these papers to Edith at the time your father passed away and she said to leave it alone. Judging by the taxes paid on it, this must be a handsome home. It's not the real estate which concerns me so much, but I came across an unusual document drawn up with the design to block the sale of the estate, in addition to all its furnishings."

He flipped through the papers until uncovering a document attached to the deed, adding, "The caretaker, Maurice Addison, receives a sizeable monthly check drawn from a trust fund set up by Irene MacKennsey; it includes a lifetime position of employment for this Addison character."

George pointed out signatures and dates, "Your Aunt Irene made these arrangements over a half century ago, and for her to be so generous, she must've thought a lot of Mr. Addison. There's nothing here indicating his age, but he must be of a ripe old age, and the checks are still getting sent out and cashed in."

Thoughts erupted in my mind as the possibility dawned on me that there might be a person still living from the time of my grandfather's murder. Not only someone living from as far back as that black moment in my family's past, but an individual who may have firsthand information about the crime as well as my grandmother's mental condition at the time that it occurred.

Lifting the document up in my hands, the title of the deed describing the estate read as Strathmoor Heights. I spoke out loud about thoughts conjured in my mind, saying, "This caretaker may have been with the family since before my father's birth."

Now the words my mother whispered from her hospital bed came back to me, "Don't go there", for she anticipated my learning about this house still being in the family holdings and had realized I'd consider going to Wales.

I continued reading, and at the same time, said, "I'd like to get the address for this Strathmoor Heights."

"I had no idea you'd be so interested in this estate, Claire. You're not considering going over there now, are you? Because if you're thinking this Addison conned your aunt, why not let me send an investigator over there first to see if everything is on the up-and-up. We can keep everything confidential, and if we find something suspicious, we may be able to challenge this document in court. I'm not familiar with British Commonwealth law, but I can find someone who is."

"I'd rather not, George, these papers clearly detail the way my Aunt Irene intended for things to be set up. I happen to believe she was in sound mind at the time she had this document recorded, and it's not my place to question her reasons for making these arrangements."

Feeling a sense of urgency about meeting this man Addison, I lowered the document with my eyes staring aimlessly at a window. This caretaker overseeing the Welsh estate was probably my last source for gaining knowledge of the past, and I knew I must journey to Wales to learn everything I can from him. I saw great importance in finding out all I can about my grandparent's lives for uncovering facts about how my grandfather's death came about.

George handed me a piece of note paper with the address for the Welsh estate on it, saying, "Then you're not going over there?"

I placed the paper in a pouch inside my purse, "I didn't say that, it's just that this is a private matter I'd like to work out on my own. At your first convenience would you have copies made on whatever information you have on this property in Wales and send it to me."

"If you don't mind my asking, what's the big mystery, why is this house in Wales so shrouded in secrecy? First, your mother doesn't want to have anything to do with it, and now you seem spellbound by it, but you won't discuss why it interests you."

"George, I'm mostly curious because I only just now learned about the house and there's something sentimental and nostalgic in wanting to see the place where my father grew up. I'm simply going to write this Mr. Addison and let him know about mother's passing away and ask a few questions about my family's past."

George took down a few telephone numbers to keep in contact as the sale of the house progresses and then we walked to the door. "There's just one more thing, there was no mention in the will about the dozen or so people your mother employed."

"My mother employed some of those people for decades and I don't want them to think I don't appreciate the years of service they've given to the family."

33

He nodded, "Allow me a little time to draft an agreement covering the sale of the house and so forth. I'll also put together some figures based upon a few weeks' severance pay, taking into consideration the years of service for each employee, and arrange it so this funding will come out of the sale of the house."

"Excellent."

Then George's expression changed as he moved a little closer, "You, know, Claire, it goes without saying that I thought of your folks as more than just business associates. If you're ever in need of friendly companionship or just someone to talk to, I'm available."

"I appreciate your concerns and I'll hold that thought, George."

I saw this gleam in George's eyes and sensed he was uncomfortable, but I couldn't pinpoint what the problem could be.

"In a few weeks, I'll have some free time, and if you like, I can accompany you on a trip to Wales, that's if you're determined to go there, and I sense that you are. Actually, I could use a vacation, and frankly, I don't like the idea of your going over there by yourself."

Changing to a more casual tone, he added, "Claire, we're not strangers, I've watched you grow up and mature to a lovely woman. I guess what I'm trying to say is, I'd like to see more of you—I have tickets to a stage play tonight, and I've made dinner reservations...What do you say?"

I looked him in the eye, "It's an awfully nice invitation, but why now?"

"Well, I haven't seen much of you these past few years, leaving me few opportunities to make an approach like this. I've always been very fond of you, but there was a time when our friendly relationship was mistaken for something more. You were quite young then, not even out of high school yet, and I was old enough to understand that I had to cut it off before things got out of hand."

I couldn't help grinning, "I guess I came on a little strong at the time."

"I think you know me well enough to know that I'm not after the money."

"Of course, and while I'm very flattered, I've also come to think of you as a kind of a big brother, but maybe some other time."

"I didn't expect you to jump at the idea, but we're going to be spending a lot of time together in the near future with the sale of the house anyway, so why not mix a little pleasure with business."

"George, I want to thank you again for calling and letting me know my mother was ill, I'd never have been able to forgive myself if I wouldn't have been there for her. She and I weren't as close as some mother and daughter relationships, but I loved her very much."

George opened the door, saying, "I'll walk you to your car."

We strolled to the elevator together, and entering its confines, he said, "I'd like to give you something to think about between now and the time we meet again."

"And what's that?" I had my purse open to gather up the keys to my car and closing it, I turned to him.

George took me in his arms and kissed me ever so gently on the lips, and I melted. He continued to hold me close, and the elevator stopped for allowing another passenger to get on, but neither one of us paid any attention to the individual keeping us company on the way down.

He tried kissing me again, but I resisted and scooted away from him, "I think I got the message."

We didn't speak a word walking to my car, and then George took my keys from my hand to open the car door for me, "I'll be stopping by in a day or two to drop off some papers."

I sat down in the driver's seat and he dropped the car keys in my open hand, then I thanked him again before driving away. I couldn't fool myself about how I felt about George, I knew deep down inside I wanted him, and his kiss warmed me, while stirring emotions within me. He was a guy who had my heart from almost the very minute I met him years before, but for now, I was glad I shied away from seeing him. I knew enough about dear old George to understand that he had a lot of experience with women, and if I rushed into things or appeared too anxious, it could never work.

If George hadn't kissed me, the last thing on my mind would've been romance, as for now I lacked any inclination to pursue a long-term relationship with someone. My focus soon turned to this Welsh mansion called Strathmoor Heights, as the prospect of meeting its caretaker was enlightening, giving me hope for learning about events surrounding my grandfather's death. Caught up in wanting to find out all I can about this terrible murder, I couldn't think about anything else, and it was as though my life was on hold. However, for the first time since learning about this dark and dreadful family secret, I believed I had a serious chance at finding out details about the past. For the sake of my own mental well-being, I had to pay a visit to Wales to find out everything I can about circumstances surrounding this awful tragedy that happened so long ago.

CHAPTER 4

THE MANSION

That same day, I sent a special delivery letter to the Welsh caretaker, Maurice Addison, who watched over my father's childhood home. I made mention of my mother's passing and expressed an interest in seeing the Welsh estate referred to as Strathmoor Heights. Refraining from asking a lot of questions, I kept the letter short and simple and waited patiently for a reply.

After about ten days, I received a short correspondence telling me that I'd be welcome, and this only served to fuel my excitement and curiosity; I could hardly wait to see this house and talk with this fellow Addison. I thought my Aunt Irene had probably employed him long after my grandfather's death. There just didn't seem like much chance that he would've been around longer than that, but I felt very hopeful that he could have some knowledge of the gruesome killing. He must've held a position of trust with my Aunt Irene, and maybe she'd taken him into her confidence by divulging information pertaining to the murder. I also had the idea that authorities in the area or an old established newspaper may have kept records and eye witness accounts reported at the time. Most important of all, I held the strong desire to dispel the image I had of my grandmother, that she was some sort of raging homicidal maniac that had to be kept isolated and locked away. Until I learned more about the past, these unpleasant thoughts and ideas would continue to plague me. There was no way to shake the idea that if she became a deranged psychotic killer in her adulthood, then so might I, and I simply didn't know how to go on with my life without having made every possible effort to learn more about this killing.

As soon as George had a closing date for the sale of my parents' property, I scheduled a plane flight for London, England. I'd always wanted to visit Great Britain, for when traveling abroad it helps to visit a country where we at least speak the same language. However, I didn't anticipate seeing many of the sights in London or anywhere else for that matter. This was to be a journey to discover my roots and attempt to investigate a chilling tragedy that overshadowed my present life as well as my future. I wrote Addison once more to let him know when I'd be coming and that I'd be at the Queen's Inn in the city of Cardigan in Wales at 3:00 p.m. on the twenty-fourth of May. I mentioned that I'd find some means of transportation to get me from there to Strathmoor Heights and asked him to send me directions on how to get to the estate from Cardigan. Addison was quick to acknowledge my communication, letting me know that he'd pick me up the next day following my arrival at the Queen's Inn, and he'd bring me to the house.

George offered to drive me to the airport, but I declined, believing it might work to my advantage to avoid seeing him for awhile. He came on to me rather suddenly, and I didn't want to rush into anything for giving me time to investigate my family's past. From my own experiences with romance, I acquired the belief that true love required nurturing; there were many elements to building a lasting relationship. Marriage took a lot of giving on one's part, and I didn't want to later be the only person who gave. If George was at a point in life where he was seriously considering settling down I didn't mind eventually seeing him on a steady basis, but I didn't want to just become another fooling-around partner or plaything of his. It was no secret that he had a reputation with women, but I didn't want to get involved with a man who just wanted to have fun. If I knew old George as well as I thought I did, I wasn't the only heartthrob who had designs on him.

By making this trip, I was accomplishing two things: I'd learn all I can about my predecessors and at the same time leave George to simmer. I liked the idea of leaving him hanging, as this was the only way I could get back at him for treating me so snobbishly in my teens—a taste of his own medicine. If he really did care, then his feelings should easily out last the term of this separation.

Finally arriving in London, England, I spent the night at a hotel there, and in the morning, I made arrangements to rent a car, which I was to later leave at the Queen's Inn in Cardigan, located on the west end of the island country. The drive to Cardigan was an interesting one and I thoroughly enjoyed the scenic landscape. Soon finding myself in the dreary municipality of Cardigan on the twenty-fourth, I proceeded to find the Queen's Inn, and this hotel turned out to be one of the more cheerful aspects of this town, accompanied with a restaurant and pub.

I was to meet with this caretaker, Maurice Addison, the next morning between 10:00 and 10:30 a.m. here at the hotel; until then I took time to explore some of the nearby shops and it came to be an entertaining experience. I had dinner later and turned in early but naturally had difficulty sleeping; I felt far too excited to sleep because of my anticipation of both seeing and exploring this Strathmoor Heights, the place where my father grew up. I really didn't know what my expectations were, but I felt anxious and hopeful for Addison to be helpful and that he and I got along well. Not knowing if there'd be other people residing at the house, for all I knew, he may have his family staying with him, and this might make for a difficult situation, leaving me feeling rather awkward about our meeting. I probably should've wrote to him and asked him a lot of questions ahead of time, but I refrained from doing so because I didn't want to come on as being too inquisitive.

At precisely ten o'clock the next morning, I occupied a small space in an entrance enclosure to the lobby of the Queen's Inn. I didn't understand why he couldn't be more precise in his telegram about the time we were supposed to meet, but I had the patience to wait. A few minutes later, while watching through the window glass of the lobby, I saw a bulky, black, four-door automobile pull up in front of the inn, driven by a crusty white-haired man in a dark suit, wearing a derby. The elderly gentleman removed himself from the car with care; then he opened the back door and, using a hand brush, began brushing off the back seat. When he'd finished, I watched him put the brush away, and he approached the door in his out-dated dark suit, a conservative bow tie in the collar of his white shirt; his eyes appeared friendly. Entering the entrance enclosure, he removed his hat as a gentleman would.

"Pardon me," he began in a distinctly clear but smooth, gruff voice, his hat dangling from his hands, "but are you Ms. MacKennsey?"

"Yes I am," I answered respectfully, and smiled. "You must be Maurice."

"It's a pleasure to make your acquaintance. I knew your father when he was just a pup, a fine lad he was...I'm a bit disappointed, though, that he never wrote to tell me he'd had such a lovely daughter, but he was a busy man for sure."

"You knew my father well?"

He smiled, "Oh yes, I knew him from when he was just a baby till he grew up to manhood. Of course, I was a good deal older than him and still nothing but a servant in the house, but I guess because we lived on such an isolated estate, we managed to form a sort of friendship, a young boy needs companionship, and I enjoyed his company. After finishing with the chores, we'd get away, go fishing most of the time and just roamin' about the countryside while doing things that boys like to do. Ahhh, but we've plenty of time to talk about that."

It would've been difficult to guess this man's age, but thinking he knew my father from the time he was an infant gave me the impression that he may have been with the family even before the murder of my grandfather. Not wanting to ask too many questions at first, I refrained from bringing the matter up.

His eyes wandered until they caught sight of my suitcases. "These must be yours."

"Yes, I didn't know how long I'd be staying. They're rather heavy, maybe I can get some assistance from the desk." I motioned towards the lobby, but stopped when I saw him shaking his head.

"Don't trouble yourself, miss, I'll take care of them."

He placed his hat on his head and caught hold of the handles of two suitcases to lift them and lug them out to the car. Watching him labor, I knew they were heavy and becoming concerned he might hurt himself, but he was quite determined.

Deciding to lend a hand, I lifted the last bag and followed behind him. He stopped behind the automobile to place the bags on the ground, and it was plain to see that the sight of me carrying a bag visibly perturbed him. He motioned for me to stop, and then said in a low cranky voice, "Look here, miss, I can't permit you to carry luggage or do chores. You're the lady of the house and that's simply the way it is."

I left the suit case rest on the walk, and after he'd finished loading the baggage in the trunk, he opened the door for me. I wasn't used to that sort of service, but I didn't want to say or do anything to upset him any further.

Within a few minutes, we were on the road out of town, and even though I'd found this man to be likeable, I reserved judgment. Addison had a quiet way about him, and he seemed easy going, partly because of his age. I knew so little about him, and if we continued to carry on as lady and servant, there wasn't much chance at learning about who Maurice Addison really was. Hoping he wouldn't fight me on talking about the past, I wasn't sure how difficult it was going to be to get him to talk for uncovering his character and persona.

All the while driving, he refrained from speaking a word; and wanting to initiate conversation, I wondered if it might interfere with his driving skills. I thought he drove capably, so I commented, "Maurice is a popular French name."

"Yes, madam, I suppose so." he replied in a smoothed-out tone of voice, glancing in the rear-view mirror at me. "It's a common name, but now that you mention it, my mother was French."

"Oh, really." I then gave the interior of the car a look over, and asked, "What kind of a car is this?"

"She's a '57 Mercedes-Benz, madam."

"It seems to be in extremely good condition for its age."

"I do my best to keep it well maintained. Polished the machine up for you yesterday, but she's dirtier than she looks though, a lot of road dust on her."

He took a second glimpse in the mirror at me, "Before we go any further, may I give my condolences for your dear mother. I saw her only a few times before she and Winston moved to the States, but I thought her a very charming lady and a fine person."

"Thank you."

"May I also add that I miss your father...Hold many special memories of him. I guess in my mind, he'll always remain young."

"I understand my Aunt Irene raised him, I would have liked to have met her. If it won't be bothersome for you to talk while you're driving, maybe you can tell me about her, what kind of a person was she?"

"Your Aunt was a lady in every sense of the word, and a sensible person who had a mind for business. When I met her, she was approaching her midlife, but I understand that when she was younger she was very outgoing and more athletically active than most of the women of her time."

"Was she ever married?"

"No, she never married."

"I have to admit that I'm very much looking forward to seeing the house my father was brought up in."

"If you'll be patient a little longer, I promise you won't be disappointed."

Conversation diminished during the course of the ride, mainly because Maurice didn't act very talkative. Though I felt comfortable in his company, I think he wanted to concentrate on his driving, so I left him alone. In a way, I thought I needed to be cautious because I wasn't quite sure about his position with the family, and I didn't know what secrets he held about my family's past.

I soon directed my interest to the still, fertile lowlands of Wales as this misty emerald green countryside bore rolling hills and a patchwork of fields bordered by trees, hedges, and short stone walls. In no time, the car began climbing as we moved upward and into scenic highlands, and I saw heather covered mountains in the distance. My eyes caught sight of a few charming stone cottages on the hillside; and when crossing a brook by means of an old stone bridge, the car had to stop to give time for a flock of sheep to cross the road, and the car idled while the shepherd maneuvered his small herd. Seeing how Maurice was losing patience, I thought this must be an occurrence that happens to him all too often on this road.

The sheep were a dingy white but had black faces, and rolling down my window, two of them came over to stick their noses in. I let them smell my hand, saying, "They're darlings, aren't they?"

At the moment Maurice nodded, one of the sheep snatched his hat and I hurriedly left the car to retrieve it. I had to enter the fold or flock to catch up to the one that held the hat in its mouth, and luckily, I got it free without damaging it. I briefly inspected it to make sure of its pristine condition before returning it to him, and he mumbled something about the sheep in a grouchy manner, but I pretended not to hear.

We were soon moving again, and the sight of clumps of mature trees grew more frequent with less open fields; but the ride itself was becoming less enjoyable because the road narrowed, turning more rugged and bumpy. Beginning to question Maurice's handling of the automobile by the way he swerved to avoid potholes, I saw a truck approaching from the opposite direction; and as it neared, there was this growing concern and apprehension that there might be a collision. I wanted to caution him but remained quietly alert of the situation; at the last second, he got over, and I breathed a sigh of relief.

"It won't be long now." With that, the automobile changed course—turning-off the main road, and moving up into a densely forested area.

Gravel kicked off the bottom of the vehicle, pinging as the rear tires pushed for climbing a steep incline, and the one-lane road had pitch for water drainage to gullies on each side. Sunlight broke through the treetops in spurts, dancing in and out of my eyes, and I was fast growing tired of this rough ride. Just as I'd begun to get carsick, the road suddenly leveled off, we broke into a remote clearing, and I saw this graceful weeping willow tree standing by itself in a meadow.

Up ahead, two giant elm trees stood in the foreground before a colossal house—a magnificent fortress strong structure built by skilled stone cutters. The handsome home held much character, and it seemed it would stand for eternity in this peaceful, tranquil serene setting where the wooded isolation helped to almost make it something out of a marvelous fairy tale.

After the Mercedes came to a halt, I stepped out of the car and stretched; having been confined in the car for so long, my body seemed slow in regaining movement and normalcy. Still left in captivating wonder by this sprawling huge mansion, I studied its architecture with detail, and then my eyes sketched over the dark green ivy-covered walls and steep slate roof. From the angle where I stood, I could see not only the front of the building, but the side wall facing southward too. The window's upper panes of glass were ornamental stained glass done in diamond-shaped patterns, and I said, "I never knew a place could be so beautiful."

Overly anxious to feast my eyes on the interior of this stately grand manor, in an uncertain instance, I thought I saw through the sun's glare in a second-story window a shadowy figure, when something nudged my leg. Looking down, a shaggy-haired collie wagged its tail at my feet; she'd come to greet both Maurice and myself.

"Shannon, don't pester the lady," said Maurice, in his gruff tone.

Maurice was insistent, but the collie didn't seem to care—I'd made a friend. I think she and I both knew that Maurice may have seemed cranky at times, but he was actually an old softy with a big bark.

I knelt down to pet her. "You certainly are a pretty lady."

"She's mischievous, is what she is, but it can get lonely out here, though, and for that it's nice having her around," he explained.

Looking back to the second-story window again, the shadowy figure was no longer visible, and I squinted as I stared up at the window, saying, "How many other servants are there here, Maurice?"

"None miss," he said, pulling the three suit cases out and setting them together. "I'm here by myself."

Surprised by his answer, I had to say, "That's funny, I thought I saw someone in that second-story window."

"Must have been mistaken, miss," and he looked up and then shook his head. "Perhaps, you saw the reflection of these trees in the window glass."

I looked at him strangely while considering that it would be only he and I staying at the house, "You stay alone here?"

"Only for a few hours every Wednesday, a maid comes to help with the cleaning and chores. There's a great deal of upkeep on a house this size. I hope you won't find your stay here to be a boring one, but with an old man and his dog, you can't expect much."

I turned back to the animal, but she'd gone. "Don't you have any friends, besides Shannon, that is?"

"Not really," remarked Maurice, "most of those from my generation are all gone, and I haven't much appetite for meeting people anymore. I'm quite satisfied with my life here—prefer the privacy and solitude. I guess I've become what could best be described as a hermit."

Maurice picked up two suit cases then made his way towards the red granite steps leading up to a wide stone arched entrance that provided a shaded air space before tall mahogany doors, which followed the shape and contour of the archway. Wanting to help him, I showed restraint and walked quietly with him.

Maurice placed the luggage down long enough to unlock and open the door, unveiling the interior of a unique home, untouched by time. He allowed me to enter the reception hall first, and the house seemed to beckon me as I crossed the threshold onto a sparkling white oak parquet floor. I felt as though I'd stepped back in time, and above my head, a supporting beam of lumber, over a foot square, bridged the hallway;

and supporting this beam were bold spiraling columns standing vertically on each side of the hallway.

A medieval suit of armor stood in a corner like a lone sentinel, and examining it, I asked, "Is it real?"

Maurice lugged the suitcases into the entry hall, taking a deep breath before replying, "Yes, miss, you'll find a treasure load of relics and antique furniture here. Your grandparents collected pieces from all over the world, and your Aunt Irene had impeccable taste in what she added. The house is more of a museum than it is anything and much the same as it was the day your father left."

The hall opened at a wide doorway where it flowed into the sunken living room which had much depth, partly because of its towering cathedral ceiling. This lavishly decorated room had elegant furniture, including two cream-colored couches with soft scrolled prints sitting adjacent to each other. Centered between them was a dark cherry wood coffee table on a colorful elaborately designed hand-woven Persian rug with fringe before an enormous stone fireplace. On one side of the fireplace stood the father of all grandfather clocks, and on the other side stood a prominent white headless statuette. Nearby, between the fireplace and the base of a jumbo staircase, a sleek shiny black grand piano sat catty-corner; an ornate brass candelabra resting on the piano held five candles, the fifth stood elevated in the center above the others.

The interior of this fabulous house and its furnishings worked on me like a tonic and looking forward to see more, I uttered, "It's positively enchanting."

Off this entrance hall, but opposite the wide doorway to the spacious living room, I viewed the library; and a monstrous moose head with bold protruding antlers overlooked the room from the wall above the mantle and fireplace. The room held a coffer ceiling and hard-backed books of a wide variety of sizes and shapes covered two walls; two ladders erected to ride on rails side to side made the reach and accessibility for books simpler and easier. A bulky, broad desk angled diagonally in a nearby corner was accompanied by a comfortable chair and a tall standing floor lamp; centered on one of the walls but spaced out from it was an oblong table with wooden chairs situated at each end as what I'd describe as a reading table, a tall decorative black iron table lamp capped off with a colorful mosaic of stained glass for a shade in its middle. Over in front of a window sat a pedestal table teamed with a pair of chairs; the table supported larger-than-normal-size black-and-white chess pieces on a checkered marble game board, and arranged off to a side along a wall was a cozy broad burgundy padded leather chair with a table-floor lamp.

Maurice passed through the living room and began ascending the mammoth staircase as I returned to the living room; and this time actually entering it, I gained sight of the wide second-story balcony above. Just then, I caught sight of a fascinating life-size bust portrait of a mystifyingly handsome man, medium complexion with wavy black hair.

As Maurice kept climbing the stairs and neared the balcony at their crest, I asked, "Maurice, whose portrait is this?"

He paused long enough to say, "That's your grandfather, miss, Charles MacKennsey."

Standing there studying the portrait, I continued admiring this man's countenance whose benevolent face and eyes showed wisdom and goodness.

"Maurice, I'd like you to tell me about him," I said out loud, only to then notice that he'd gone from the stairs and balcony up to the second floor. With Maurice no longer present, my eyes turned back to the image of the man in the painting, for I hadn't expected him to be such a handsome gentleman, and I gazed at his features for some time.

CHAPTER 5

INSTRUMENT OF DEATH

As soon as Maurice returned down the stairs, I repeated the question, asking, "Maurice, what can you tell me about my grandfather?"

He came toward me, saying, "What is it you wish to know about Master Charles?"

"Anything you can remember...What sort of a man was he?"

He joined me before the portrait, "I'd describe him as a very unusual man, but the kind of person most people feel comfortable being around. I'd say he had a way of bringing out the best in a person. He had his serious side too in that when he found something that interested him, he'd go to great lengths—even extremes—to learn about it in depth."

Maurice gazed at the portrait as he continued, "I think it goes without saying that he was a handsome gentleman. It was his wife, Angela, who insisted he have this painting done. I know for a fact that he didn't want a portrait of himself, but she always had her way with him."

It became obvious to me that Maurice must have known both my grandparents quite well, and as he spoke, I listened intently to every word while wandering over to the piano. The candelabra's image reflected off the pool of black, top surface of the huge playing piece, running my fingertips across its sleek, smooth exterior.

I saw sheet music above the key board and curiously picked it up to read the title of the song out loud, "'The Band Played On'."

Maurice followed me, "Your grandfather loved music and was an excellent piano player...that was their song. He was also a great magician."

"A magician," I raised a brow as this talk of my grandfather aroused my curiosity further.

"He was accomplished enough that for a brief period he rivaled the great Houdini, performing astonishing acts, but he never gained the worldly notoriety that Houdini had, and to some extent, their lives paralleled. They were both fascinated with the afterlife and communication with the dead, and they both died tragically before their time, but magic was just one aspect of Charles' life."

He looked at the piano as if reminiscing, and smiled, "Your grandparents loved to entertain and hold parties. They knew how to have such a good time and they made such a distinguished couple. It doesn't seem so long ago when laughter and singing filled this very room. On countless occasions, friends and guests gathered around this piano as he played it—all fine, charming people—I can still see 'em singing together as he'd play."

Moving around to the piano seat and keyboard to stand next to me, he continued to ponder the past, "They usually ran with people much wealthier than they were. They had many American friends and periodically they traveled to the United States. I don't know what the term is nowadays, but because they liked to travel abroad, I suppose he and your grandmother were what you'd call part of the jet set of their time."

Listening, I leaned on the piano and clasped my hands together.

"Charles had a pleasant nature, a personality one can't help but to like, and a knack for being comical at the most opportune time, mostly poking fun at himself when he'd reach the punch line...He could steer a crowd, that he could.

"I can recall a time when he was wearing a dark suit when entertaining a few guests who'd shown up unexpectedly with their teenage daughter, doing some card tricks to pass the time. With the wave of his hand, he spread the card deck out in a line, and no matter what card he pulled from the deck to flip over it turned out to be the ace of spades. The young girl said insistently, 'They're all the ace of spades,' but when Charles flipped over the entire set of cards, it was seen as a regular deck.

49

"Charles then quickly pointed out that the one card missing from the deck was the ace of spades, which was true.

"With a slide-of-hand, Charles pulled from behind the girl's ear the missing ace of spades, by which the girl then claimed, 'You had that card tucked up your sleeve.' Which he'd either simply palmed the card or he did pull it out from his sleeve.

"The girl said demandingly, 'I'm convinced you pulled that card out of your sleeve,' as though expecting Charles to admit to it. Charles response was to act somewhat ticked as he removed his evening coat, carefully folding it before setting it aside, and then unbuttoned his shirt sleeves, and said, 'I assure you, I have nothing up my sleeves.'

"She then guessed, 'You changed decks, and then you took that one ace of spades from your sleeve.'

"Charles said, 'A magician never divulges the secrets of his trade,' for which the girl replied, 'Won't you at least tell me whether you had that ace of spades up your sleeve?'

"He said, 'I'm considering adding a talented young lady to my stage act, would you be interested?'

"The girl had an expression of awe at his offer, and Charles rolled up his sleeves before looking her in the eye, saying, 'I'm looking for a person who has no objection to being sawn in half!' And everyone broke out in laughter.

I read in Maurice's eyes how he missed those days with my grandfather and I tried to imagine the room with him entertaining people while playing the huge instrument.

He looked down and shook his head a little, "Those were great days—the best days of my life. I started working for your grandfather when I was just a boy, must have been no more than eleven when he brought me here.

"I'll never forget him, miss, just like I'll never forget the day he took me in, not as long as I live...It was hard times when I was an orphan living under deplorable conditions, and I took as much of it as I could before going off on my own."

"I thought you came here with your mother. You'd said she was French, so I naturally assumed."

"That she was, so I've been told, but I have no memory of her. It had been said that she was the French servant of a wealthy landowner, and that she couldn't keep me, so I was turned over to an orphanage."

His eyes squinted as he continued, "I still haven't forgotten the place where I grew up—a regular house of correction, not much more than a stable, and run like a prison by a coldhearted malicious bunch. A skinny runt of a kid I was, having to fight to stop the others from taking my food. I came to live in the streets in the poorest part of town like a pitiful, dirty-faced pauper, enduring harsh cruelty and indignity. Maybe some people can't help being the way that they are, I'm sure living in that sort of environment can make a person cruel and callus, but people can take advantage of you when you're just a kid fighting to stay alive. They'll use you and manipulate you, God help the person who has to depend on the mercy of others.

"One evening, I got caught stealing food and took a terrible beating as punishment for it, and the next morning, I began aimlessly wandering the streets, a malnourished dirty, barefoot beggar in rags. My spirit broken and my stomach grumbling, I think I'd come to the conclusion that if I didn't get away from the deceitful people I'd come to live around, I wasn't going to live much longer."

Maurice took a moment to ponder the past, "I remember limping in the direction of a street corner when I saw a carriage and a well-dressed man leaving a shop with his arms full of packages going to it. The rig's driver came down to assist him, and as one of the packages fell to the sidewalk, I snatched it up and began running. I didn't get far before the driver caught me by the collar, so I dropped the package and fought like a wild animal to gain my freedom but couldn't get free from his hold.

"The driver spoke angrily, saying something like, 'You want me to whack him a good one before I let him go?'

"The owner of the carriage quickly caught up to us and said, 'No, no harm's been done.' Then the driver pulled me by the shoulder to turn me toward him, and I tried biting his hand so he'd let go of me. I then made a mad dash to get away, but when

51

I didn't hear their footsteps chasing after me, I stopped to look back, and both men were just standing there looking at me. The owner of the carriage held no anger or hostility for me, seeing an unthreatening kindness in his eyes as he smiled. He reached in his coat pocket and brought out a paper bag, and said, 'If you really want something to chew on, you're welcome to a piece of taffy.'

"Because my belief in people had come to be so misplaced by misfortune and trickery, I wondered if these men were trying to lure me back to give me a beating. Experience had taught me to beware, but this man had a calm, understanding manner, and a look in his eyes that made me believe I could trust him. I slowly and cautiously walked back to them and he handed me a chunk of taffy, and his next words to me were, 'When was the last time you had a real meal?'

"I can remember munching on that taffy, chomping away as I said, 'I don't know.' He asked me my name, and he gave me his, and in the little time we spoke he must have gathered I was all alone in the world. I sensed a certain sincerity about the way he treated me, as though making me feel I was more than just a piece of garbage, and the next thing I knew, I was climbing in that carriage with him. I didn't know where we were going or what I was in for, but as bad as things were, I hoped that by tagging along I'd latched on to something better than what I'd had.

"The gentleman who owned the carriage was your grandfather, and as things turned out, I can never repay him for his generosity. He saw to it that I received tutoring and some semblance of an education, and through patience and understanding, he made me feel that I belonged to this household. He gave me a purpose, and the feeling of being wanted; he restored my faith in my fellow man, reaffirmed my trust in human nature, and gave me my life. I've never forgotten his kindness, and if it was pity, he never let me think so...It's funny how I can recall so clearly something that happened all those years ago, but just try asking me what I had for breakfast this morning."

"It sounds like you've had a rough life."

"In some aspects, that may be true, but overall, it's been a good life."

"How about my grandmother, what do you remember about her?" I watched and listened for his response.

"A beautiful lady she was—the belle of the ball...I heard she came from a poor family too, but I can't say...miss, I can understand your being curious about your family, but I don't think we need to cover the entire family tree all in one day. There will be plenty of time for conversation during your stay but, before it gets too late, I'd like to get that last suit case in and put your things away."

"Yes, you're right." I stood upright, "It looks like I'll be spending days in exploration here. I don't know where to start."

"She's a grand old stately manor, all right. Have yourself a look around but don't get lost. The third floor is the ball room, one big wide-open space."

He moved in the direction of the entrance hall to retrieve the last suit case, and then stopped to say, "As soon as I've put your things away, I'll fix you something cold to drink, as after that ride, you must be thirsty."

In his own humble way, Maurice made me feel welcome, but even more important was that I'd begun to trust him. He was my only link to the past, and I felt assured that I'd learn from him important details regarding my grandfather's death. Taking one last minute to gaze at the portrait of Charles MacKennsey, I wondered what happened that fateful night when he died, as thoughts about my grandmother's illness still took priority over my thoughts. Quite eager to hear what Maurice can recall about that incident, what puzzled me now was how he described my grandparents as such a happy couple, so what made everything go so terribly wrong for them?

Surveying the living room, I thought to myself this was their world, their home, and these walls held the secret behind a man's fate. More than ever before, I was determined to learn the cause of this terrible tragedy.

Resuming my tour of the residence, I returned to the reception hall, and found out that the furthest and most distant doorway from the entrance to the house opened into the dining room. The most spectacular aspect of the room were the sturdy, exposed overhead beams, erected in an unusual design—resembling a large A—to support the steep gable constructed roof in this section of the house. The ceiling's vertex was accentuated by exposed dark beams anchored together by giant bolts—a skillfully engineered piece of architecture. Hanging from the suspended cross-member beam—the cross-member required to complete the A—a brilliant crystal chandelier hung over a massive dining room table. The walls of this room were dark, rough-cut wood panels rising eight feet from the floor, and above this rich molded paneling was a shelf supporting silver dishes standing on end, each with their own engraving of scenery; rough swirled plaster finished the remaining four feet of wall space. All furniture, including a tall cabinet and chairs to seat twenty, were of fat, brawny-legged furniture. A fatherly-sized chair fit for a captain or a king headed the set; and located at the end of the room, behind this chair, was a stained glass bay window, constructed from rustic red, gold, and green leaves; these fall colors cheerfully enriched the room and gave it life.

My attention drew to a large portrait-size coat of arms made of brass in an elaborate design and in the shape of a ferocious lion standing on its hind legs; the beast's jaws were open as if in attack form, and the animal held in his right paw a staff. The left paw supported a broad shield with an emblem symbolizing royalty. Reposed beneath it was an ornate Tudor style, throne like chair, having demonic dragon's heads with flaring nostrils for armrests as though from a Gothic period.

Moving along, I entered the kitchen; and if the history of the house was true, from what Maurice had said, there must have been huge meals prepared here. The kitchen held organization with a sturdy round oak table centered in its middle, providing good arrangement for the cook who could circle the table and find most cabinets within arm's reach, including the pots and pans, which hung from a bakers rack above this table.

In one corner of the kitchen, I found two doors in an alcove area, one was for a pantry or storage closet, and the other opened to descending stairs leading to a dark cellar. When a third open doorway off the kitchen came into view, I discovered it gave access to a servant's staircase leading to the second floor. Not that it mattered much, but my intention was to return by the avenue I'd first taken to access the living room from the entry hall for taking the jumbo staircase to reach the second story. Wishing to avoid using the servant's stairs for now, the purpose for this was that I merely preferred seeing the layout of the house by how one should see it for the first time. It actually made little difference, as I'd eventually make use of the back stairs anyway, but I had my mind set on following through this way.

Before leaving the kitchen, I stopped to look out the window behind the sink and saw it was nearing dusk. Out back, beyond a circular courtyard, I viewed a plain-looking brick-constructed, two-story stable. A structure as big as a house, it had four windows on the second story and a set of tall, bulky arch-shaped doors with broad black hinges on the ground level; the doors when opened would have easily allowed entrance for a car or a large carriage. A carport connected on one side of the building gave enough space to adequately park a car, but for now, it was vacant.

Believing I'd covered the first floor, I took my time backtracking to the living room. Returning from the opposite direction I'd just come from allowed me to see things from a different approach, and I was just as taken by the arrangement of the furnishings, even seeing things I hadn't noticed before as I'd first made my way to the kitchen.

Upon returning to the living room, I stopped to gaze about while gaining a sense of pride in my family's ancestry; having lost track of time long ago, I began to wonder why I hadn't seen or heard from Maurice, and I started up the main staircase to reach the second floor. At the halfway point on the stairs, I sighted a long-handled battle-axe hanging slanted diagonally on the wall, and it stunned me. Actually startling me wasn't so much the sight of this medieval axe, but that its counterpart was missing—it was one of a matching set that, when paired together, completed an X; looking closely, one could see the hangers for the missing axe. My eyes carefully traced the space the twin of this weapon had occupied, and I immediately associated it with the murder of my grandfather! Somehow coming to the realization that this missing instrument of death was the weapon used to decapitate him, I backed off, turning my eyes to the wide blade of the hanging axe occupying the wall, and then scampered up the rest of the stairs.

I paused at the top of the stairs to ponder if what I thought was true—if the missing axe was the murder weapon, thinking how there must be an explanation for why things have remained untouched for all these years. Even the white headless statuette was a bold reminder of what happened here, so I couldn't understand why my Aunt Irene would leave things situated the same as they were after such a gruesome murder had occurred in the house.

CHAPTER 6

A GHOSTLY MANIFESTATION

Standing at top of the stairs on the second floor, I turned to face a long running corridor where rose colored carpeting in a floral design covered the floor. The wide corridor ran nearly the entire length of the house and gave access to over a dozen rooms. There were some modest furnishings in an occasional half-round table on the left and right supporting a lamp, vase, or some other ornamental object; at one end of the hall was a window with curtains draped back. I began strolling down the hall, admiring pictures hung on the walls, and just as I noticed an attractive crystal swan on one of the tables, I heard a disturbance from the end of this walkway and looked to see what it was.

Maurice appeared from a doorway at the end of the hall, and no longer wearing his derby, he exhibited neatly combed, thinning white hair. Carrying a tall glass of lemonade on a tray, he'd apparently come up the back stairs—the servant's staircase leading up from the kitchen.

"I meant to catch up to you in the kitchen, but I'm not as quick as I used to be," he said, slightly out of breath as he handed me the glass. "How do you like the house so far?"

"It's a magnificent home," I replied.

"By the way, yours is the second room on the right when you come up the main stairs."

He motioned for me to follow and led me to a room bearing a replica of a fourteenth-century Henry VIII bed with a tall flowing canopy supported by four posts.

Sipping lemonade from the rim of the glass, I asked, "This wasn't my grandmother's room, was it?"

"This was your Aunt Irene's room, miss. I thought you wouldn't mind taking her room since she's the person primarily responsible for raising your father. Like her brother, Charles, she had a big heart. She was a spinster who desired a family and him a baby who needed the love of a mother, and they were fortunate to have each other." Maurice smiled, adding, "She deserves credit for your father becoming the successful man that he was, instilling in him the motivation to make something of himself.

"On the ride here you asked if your Aunt had ever been married and I answered no, but I'd like to expand that answer by saying she'd twice been engaged to be married. The first man she was supposed to marry drowned in a boating accident. A few years later, she had a whirlwind romance with an aviator. He wasn't a daredevil or stunt pilot, but there were serious risks in those early days of flight, and just a few days before they were to be wed, he died in a plane crash. These two twists of fate influenced her life in such a way that she became very superstitious and never became engaged again, which is quite sad because she was an attractive woman. As a result of these misfortunes, your Aunt Irene developed eccentricities, and by that, I mean that most of us want to avoid change in our lives, but she took it to an extreme fixation. The death of her brother, Charles, only made matters worse in that she believed that by altering any of the furnishings in this house, she would be, in an essence, flirting with fate. I can never recall a time when she'd even enter Charles or Angela's bedrooms, much less go as far as to suggest changing anything in their rooms. Those rooms were always kept locked up and were strictly off limits to anyone and everyone, except for a rare dusting and change of linen."

Maurice took a deep breath, and continued, "I didn't want to start talking about your aunt's private life when we were in the car because of the lengthy time it would take to explain how she avoided making changes here in the house. Over time, and after you've had a look about the place, I knew you'd be curious as to why the house was arranged the way that it is. You may have already seen something that struck you as odd, presuming you know how your grandfather died?"

"My mother told me," and I nodded.

"Your Aunt Irene never spoke about what happened to her brother, the only times she brought up memories of him was to reminisce about their happy childhood or to talk about some of the parties she attended here. She was very fond of her brother, and losing him was deeply heartfelt; she mourned over his death a long time.

"I remember an afternoon when she had some lady friends over, and when one of them made curious mention of her brother's murder, she demanded that they all leave at once. In seeing how it disturbed her to touch on the topic of his death, they were all very apologetic, but she still insisted that they go and then went up to her room; and I escorted the guests to the door. The incident distressed her a great deal, I think she was hurt and felt a little betrayed since these were people whom she knew well and should've known better. She'd experienced enough tragedy for one lifetime, she had no problem talking about any other tragic events in her life, but she felt bitter about Charles's unexpected death. After all, no one knew why Angela committed the murder, so what good could it serve to speculate, except to fuel more gossip, which she resented more than anything. She rarely had guests after that.

"The very minute Irene became the sole guardian of your father, he became the most important thing in her life. As much as she tried to protect him from finding out about how his father died, eventually it was something she revealed to him at a young age for concern he'd learn about it through another person. He did much of his schooling abroad, and it's not likely people he met at school knew anything about it, so it wasn't something that burdened him growing up."

He strolled slowly over to a big hutch, opening its doors to display how neatly he'd hung my clothes.

"If there's anything you can't find, please be sure to ask. The bath is just across the hall from your door. In it, you'll find a linen closet, and I left some toiletries there. However, I'm afraid you won't find much water pressure—the lines are quite corroded."

"I'm sure everything will work out fine, but if I do need assistance, which room is yours?"

"My living quarters are above the carriage house out back, madam."

The idea of staying in this house alone momentarily stunned me—I'd never expected it.

"I can see you're upset about staying in this old house alone, and it's only natural that you would be. I suppose I could've made other arrangements, but like I already mentioned earlier, I'm such a hermit, and I've never slept in this house before. The way I live, it just wouldn't be suitable or proper for a young lady, such as you, to stay in the carriage house, but it was a terrible oversight on my part, miss. I'll put together a knap-sack and take a room just down the hall so you won't be made uncomfortable."

Not wanting to stay in this house by myself but unable to ask this elderly gentleman to go any further out of his way than he already had, I said, "You've gone through too much trouble already, Maurice. That won't be necessary."

"Are you sure, miss, it'll be no trouble, and I think you'd prefer that I did."

I touched his arm gently, saying reassuringly, "I'll be all right."

"For some reason I pictured you to be a woman a little older than you are, and I didn't anticipate it to be an inconvenience or a problem. I apologize for being so inconsiderate, I'm afraid I've lived alone up here for far too long…Well, if you no longer have a need for my services, and you're sure this situation won't annoy you; it's been a rather long day…I've prepared a broth for you down in the kitchen. It's simmering now, but I'll check it once more before I leave, and I'll make sure the house is secure before going…Are you sure there won't be anything else?"

"Just one thing, it would mean a lot to me if you'd call me Claire."

"If that's what you'd prefer, I'll try, but old habits are hard to break. I'll be saying goodnight, then."

There's always the unexpected, I thought; however, things were for the most part going quite well. After all, I held the strong belief that I'd soon learn details about my grandmother's mental condition before she committed the murder, and that was the most important thing to me. I wanted to get a broader understanding of the person that she was. Like I didn't already have enough to think about, I now learned that my Aunt Irene had strange tendencies and superstitions, but what Maurice told me about her gave a reasonable explanation for her oddities. Not only had she lost two men she was engaged to marry, but her beloved brother was murdered and decapitated in his sleep, and naturally, these tragedies had a great impact on her life.

Deciding to take a bath, I discovered a fireplace in the bathroom; and when going to draw water in the tub in an area of aged ivory-colored ceramic and porcelain, I never saw such unusual fixtures. The deep tub stood upon four brass claw legs. The faucet handles on the tub and oval pedestal sink matched them, and when adjusting the slow running water a bit to the hot side, I spilt a perfumed liquid forth; and it immediately began bubbling up.

For a few minutes, I shuffled back and forth between what was now my bedroom and the bathroom as I tried to get myself organized. I placed some personal things handily out on the sink for when I'd finished bathing and set aside some other items that I'd need in the morning, arranging them somewhat in the order as they'd be required. The porcelain counter showed wear and had lost its sheen from the use of abrasive cleansers in areas most commonly used, the same with the sink. There came a strange moment when standing at the mirror that for just for a second, at a glance, I thought I saw another image in the mirror of someone standing behind me. When my eyes quickly shifted back to the mirror, I saw no one; and I even turned around to see if someone was there, but there wasn't anyone present.

Looking back at my own reflection, I shrugged off the odd sensation that I was being observed and paid notice to how the mirror had aged. Its ability to show one's refection had some-what diminished because whatever element that allowed it to mirror an image had deteriorated with time, showing cracks and a foggy appearance especially around the perimeter. However, the mirror was ornate in that a few inches inside the outer rim held an etched or imprinted leaf design, and this lent to the idea that the mirror must have been of a high quality in its day.

Gathering up my sleep wear, fluffy white slippers, and a small hand bag, I returned to the bathtub, undressed, and sank into the sultry hot water. My body easily conformed to the tubs shape, and in the rising steam, a perfumed fragrance filled the air.

After soaking for twenty minutes, I rose from the tub refreshed, dried off, and slipped into a sky blue brushed night-gown with a matching blue robe; then the slippers came on. Stopping in front of the sink and mirror, I paused because some of the things I'd placed on the counter appeared rearranged from the original order I set them down in, and it made me think for a moment. I felt certain that I'd put my comb and hairbrush in a particular spot so they'd be handy for me, and now they were not where I'd left them. The thought that they may have some-how been moved gave me a rather queer feeling, and stopping to think, I told myself, *Now I'm not going to start driving myself crazy imagining things.*

Concluding I was tiring from a long day, I realized I could've unconsciously used the brush and moved things around while I was looking in the mirror. I told myself reassuringly, *I may have mislaid these items without even giving it a thought.*

All the while in the back of my mind, I had reservations about staying in this old house by myself, but I refused to start manufacturing wild thoughts and ideas, and began thinking about my appetite. Deciding to use the servant's staircase Mau-rice had used earlier, located at the far end of the hallway from my room, I found a landing there leading to a staircase. The stairs were rounded and sort of pie shaped in how the staircase was built to conform to a turret jutting out from the house. There were not only stairs leading downward, but I also saw another set of stairs that gave passage up to the third floor, and I then remembered Maurice mentioning there was a ballroom located on the third floor. I hadn't explored that third floor as yet, but knowing I had weeks ahead of me to see the house in its entirety, I was in no hurry to go up there.

On the way down to the kitchen, I smelled the aroma of the broth Maurice prepared; and passing a tall, narrow window, I saw that the sun was setting and barely visible on the horizon. I soon came down into the kitchen and found that he'd left a light on for me; the broth steamed from a pot, and when turning off the stove, I noticed that he'd also left out a large bowl and spoon with a napkin on the counter. After a brisk stirring with a ladle, I dipped it into the broth and filled the bowl, then used the napkin to protect my hands from the hot bowl while maneuvering it to the nearby round sturdy oak table where I sat down. Desiring a taste of it and apparently hungrier than I'd thought I was, I had to allow the soup to cool to a tolerable temperature, and then I completely finished it off. Resting back in the chair for a minute to allow the meal to settle, I became aware of the quiet stillness holding the house and it gave me a sort of uneasy feeling. Ignoring it, I rose up to rinse and wash the dishes and dried them off; and looking out the kitchen window once more to view the carriage house where Maurice stayed, I didn't see any lights from the second story there, so I figured the old fellow must've already turned in for the day.

By now, it had grown quite dark outside, I found the light switch to the stairs before shutting off the kitchen light, and then started making my way upstairs by the light from two wall fixtures hung at different intervals on the winding stairway. Coming to the narrow window where I had seen the sun setting when at first on the way down, it was now dark enough outside that the window glass vividly mirrored my image, and I wasn't long in continuing my ascent. At the second-story landing, I opened the door to gain entrance to the hallway corridor; and attempting to find the switch for the hallway lights, I saw two light switches on the staircase wall but neither one worked for the hallway. One worked the lights I'd just used when coming up from the kitchen and the other controlled the lights leading up to the third floor; and I could not see beyond the turn in that set of stairs to confirm what was up there. Now thinking the light switch controlling the second-floor hall lights must be inside the hallway on the wall, I reached in and felt the wall, sliding my hand up and down while trying to locate it.

In fumbling for the light switch, an awful cold draft took hold over me, causing me to shiver; and withdrawing my hand from the wall, I used both hands to close and secure the opening in my robe. That's when I noticed my breath in the air, and in a matter of seconds, it grew increasingly colder; the light on the staircase blinked, then went off and stayed off! The bitter cold taking hold over me now motivated me to enter the hall in search of my room, but noticing a faint, eerie glow nearly three-quarters of the way down the hall caused me to stop, stiff, and still. I initially thought it to be the slightly wavering reflection of a dim flash light beam, but it now appeared to be a mysterious, blurry luminous mist, a mystifying cloud or vapor floating toward me!

The crawling misty vapor advanced at a steady pace, giving me a spine-tingling sensation, and unable to take my eyes off this supernatural entity, I awed at the sight of it. I wanted to retreat, but the best I could do was to take one big step backward; then my legs locked!

Frozen like stone with my shoulder blades set firmly against the wall, I stared wide-eyed, my conscious mind telling me this was some incredible hallucination; but what I saw as a shifting form began to look more and more like a humanlike figure! In only a second, I clearly saw the outline of a shapely woman with a thin waist line, wearing a flowing gown that bulged from her hips as she gracefully swayed and sashayed in my direction. Coming even closer, she had an unworldly aura, which accentuated and pronounced her glowing shape; the transparent image and outline of this vision had this prominent and distinctive glitter. Her face was so bright that I had difficulty making out fine details of her facial features, but she was beautiful; then she turned and walked right through a closed door as if it wasn't there!

Suddenly a brilliant flash of light burst forth from another source, and I thought my heart would burst; then realizing that the stair lights had come back on, and I stood there momentarily shaken and dumbfounded. My composure slowly returning, my wobbly legs and knees felt as though they were made of rubber, but what made me fully realize it was over was the rising warm temperature. What I witnessed evoked strange sensations within me, and placing my palms against my cheeks, I thought, *What an extraordinary experience—no one would ever believe me, for I wouldn't believe it myself if I hadn't seen such a strange entity with my own eyes.*

Looking at the hallway wall next to the door off the stairway, I saw the light switch for the hallway lights was located much lower than normal, and that's why I had so much trouble locating it when reaching for it minutes before.

"There you are," and after turning on the hallway lights, I switched off the lights for the stairs, closed the door, and started toward my room.

Still shaken and nervously excited, this feeling soon grew to an exhilarating fever that made me giddy. Having experienced a deeply moving spiritual sensation that had left me brimming with emotion, the vision of a ghost touched me from within.

Before turning in, I tried to familiarize myself with the light switches and learned there was a light switch for the hall at the top of the main staircase and another conveniently located next to the door to my bedroom; so after turning off all the lights, I didn't have far to go before reaching my Aunt Irene's comfortable bed. I slid beneath a velvety feathered-quilt, and it wasn't until I became snug and cozy that I realized I wasn't the least bit sleepy—what I'd just seen left a chillingly profound and lasting impression.

I shuddered to think this prowling ghostly manifestation was my grandmother—forever cursed to nightly stalk these rooms and corridors. Concluding that the room I saw the manifestation go into must have been hers, I pressed in my mind the geography of its location with how far away it was from the servant's stairway; having the intention to have Maurice confirm whose room it was the following day. I tried blocking the incident out of my mind, but it was useless; and I wondered what could keep a person's restless soul bound to this earth. Surely, the murder must be what holds her here, but there must be more to it than that—what was the motive for this ghastly act that took the life of my grandfather? I felt my mind sinking into that never-ending speculation, pondering what drove her to commit murder, but then forced myself to push aside these escalating questions to think about other things, and the night wore on.

CHAPTER 7

AN UNEXPECTED VISITOR

Lying in bed awake for some time, I'd begun looking back on how life had changed so drastically over the past few years. I thought about the people whom I'd been gallivanting around with through my college years and how we'd grown apart for going our own separate ways; all the others had tied the knot and were making families of their own, and yet, I was the last single one out of the group. Although they still enjoyed my company and made me feel welcome when I'd visit, I couldn't help the assumption that I was imposing. It wasn't at all the same as it used to be, as life's responsibilities had taken away our free-spiritedness.

Throughout the college years, my girlfriend Rachel and I had nothing but fun. I guess it's true to some extent that we were teasers, but it was never intentional. We were popular, and even though we'd make it clear that we didn't want to get serious, it frequently happened that the males did. Even those who weren't looking to settle down, sooner or later they'd try to take control of the situation—typical male domination—but we remained elusive and carefree.

After college, Rachel and I wanted to stay single and play the field; we kept our independence and shared an apartment for a while, and then I started seeing a change in her as she became seriously involved with a very influential man in the banking business. It seems all good things have to come to an end, but I didn't want our friendship to die; so after they married, I kept our old apartment but managed to tag along with them whenever I could. We were like sisters, to say the least, and when she gave birth to a baby girl, I was there to lend what assistance I could. However, it all abruptly ended one night when her husband tried cornering me in their swimming pool to get a kiss. Rachel had gone to put the baby to bed, but she saw it all and still accused me of coming between them. Though it wasn't my fault, I still shared some of the guilt because I knew the pregnancy had strained their marriage, and he'd mistaken my kindness for making a play for him. Feeling terrible about what happened, and recognizing that I'd simply stayed on too long, I'd do anything to change what occurred, but there's nothing I can do to repair that friendship.

Now I had to make a life of my own, and that wouldn't have been a problem except for my having learned that my grandmother was an axe murderer; this was a great stumbling block for me, an obstacle which would not allow me to imagine what lies in the future. I'd lost all the dreams I'd ever had about having a family of my own, for it crushed a part of me that once yearned for the prospect of having children. I'd always taken this aspect of life for granted—that one day, I'd bear children—and it seemed sadly funny that something I'd never given much consideration to I now wanted so desperately; this caused me to think I'll never see the day when I'll hold my own newborn child cuddled in my arms.

I've never taken a serious outlook on marriage, mainly because the right person hadn't come along yet, and I felt cynical because there were so many fortune hunters out there. I'd met enough of them in the little time I'd traveled. The extravagant life I'd been living grew tiresome, and I longed for lasting satisfaction and happiness if I could find it in this world. I didn't know if I'd ever discover the magic of love, prove myself worthy of the trust and love of another, or experience the miracle of child birth. At this point in time, it didn't seem likely these things would happen.

Just as I realized I was getting sentimental and a bit melancholic, I remembered poor darling George, the loyal friend of the family whom I'd left behind. I always admired him and thought him a polished individual. It overwhelmed me to think he wanted to get romantically involved. Even though I didn't think money was an influencing factor because he had enough of his own, I still couldn't help but wonder; maybe it was just a female's nature to be suspicious of such things. George had traits I desired in a man, and except for the day he expressed having feelings for me, he was always cool, calm, and collected. I've never seen him as off-balance as I did then, and instead of showing respect for his emotions at the time, I left him hanging.

Thinking about George brought me to take up with a pen and notepad to write him a letter, first describing the house, I then mentioned how Maurice Addison was cordial and friendly. Writing a few lines to him helped me unwind and served to take my mind off the spirit I'd seen in the hallway. It also pushed back bothersome things connected with this house and the fact that the murder of my grandfather was committed here. Besides, I believed this communication might keep me in George's thoughts. I wanted to reveal the story my mother told me and why it was important to learn the facts leading up to that fatal night when my grandfather was killed in his sleep. Instead, I held back, merely writing about this fine house and characterized the man my grandfather was. Ready to sign off, but wanting to let him know I was thinking of him, I paced and while strolling by the window I saw a person or thing outside the window ledge! I dropped to the floor!

Startled, I remained in a squatting position, scooting in the direction of the headboard of the bed, and bracing my back against the wall, I placed my hand over my heart.

Oh, my God, I thought, *he must've seen me! What do I do now—crawl over to the door?* Then I concluded that if I moved away from the wall I'd leave myself exposed out in the open, and looking about, I had nothing to use for self-defense.

I'd seen something at the edge of the roof line—a dark shadow in a strange configuration—but I could've been mistaken about what I'd seen. With this idea, I chose to move closer to the window and get a peek at what or who was out there. My eyes widened as I awkwardly tilted my head to peer over the windowsill, and a drifting cloud allowed moonlight to unveil a squatting gargoyle. This beastly stone lookout had pointed, webbed wings, a head turned to one side resembled that of a bald eagle, and the scaly, curled tail of a serpent.

Easing away from the window ledge, I sank until my bottom rested on the floor with my back to the wall and breathed a sigh of relief. Now seeing humor in how I'd nearly scared myself to death, I smiled and said, "I've got to get some sleep."

Turning my attention back to the letter, I wanted to sign off with a brief but vivacious ending to stir his desire for me, but I couldn't think of a thing. I simply ended it with "Thinking of you and missing you" before signing the bottom of the page.

From the moment I first saw George, there was something about him that played on my heartstrings and stirred a strong desire within me. There was no sense in denying that I loved him; I guess I always have. As far back as my high school days, I fell under the spell of his charms and, in no time, became totally enamored with him. I got the impression that he liked me too, but because I was only a teenager at the time, he must've realized the embarrassment of dating a girl my age. He chilled out and began ignoring me to discourage advances during a period when I was infatuated with him. Because our relationship wasn't moving as fast as I wanted it to, I practically threw myself at him. It turned out to be a disastrous ploy that I still regret even now.

My parents were throwing a party at our house, and I'd dressed up in what I thought to be the most gorgeous evening gown I'd ever seen and had my hair done up, leaving a lock or a curling strand of hair hanging loosely, which I kept pushing back all night long. The young slender creature I was at eighteen, I believed I looked rather ravishing and alluring; I even got a few looks from our male guests, young and old alike. Even though I noticed George had brought a date, I kept trying to get his attention. Keeping an eye on him, whenever his date strayed away, I'd come over to him and try to warmly make him feel welcome.

He'd been politely cordial all evening, even introducing me to his date; but for the most part, I felt he'd given me the cold shoulder. I believed that the reason he avoided taking our relationship any further was because of my parents, and I resented their interference, for I thought myself old enough to have a relationship with a man. My parents must have known that I was crazy about him, but never once did they say anything to discourage it.

As the evening wore on, I spent some time with people my age, but my thoughts never left George, and seeing him constantly in the company of his young lady friend annoyed me; I'd begun to feel downright jealous, and besides, in my youthful vanity, I thought myself prettier than she. I'd gotten the chance to get my hands on a glass of champagne, and in trying some of it, I found it to be sweet tasting, and snuck a second glass when I had the chance.

Later, I saw George standing all alone next to our swimming pool and quickly finished off the remainder of champagne in the second glass before catching up to him. The lights in and around the pool set off a romantic glow, and I approached him in a shy, genial and unassuming way, saying, "George, are you enjoying yourself?"

"I'm having a wonderful time, Claire."

In the moment we stood together, we made small talk, and I thought George looked very handsome and enterprising in the dark suit he wore and complimented him on it, saying, "You look very distinguished in that suit."

"Why, thank you, and I don't mind saying you look very lovely tonight—you're the prettiest girl here."

"You really think so?"

"I thought I saw you speaking to some young men a little while ago. They looked like drones gathering around the queen bee. Is one of them your boyfriend?"

"I don't have a boyfriend, George. I don't think any of those boys are my type, and anyway, I've been saving myself for somebody else."

"Oh, anyone I know?"

"I don't want to mention his name out loud, but if you'll allow me to, I'll whisper his name in your ear."

He bent over as if to lend me his ear, and I caressingly placed my hands on his cheeks, turning and adjusting his head so our faces would meet; I closed my eyes and kissed him ever so gently on the lips.

George unexpectedly brushed me off, pushing my hands away as he backed up a step, and even though he hadn't actually pushed me, I momentarily felt off balance. I took one short step back to gain footing and catch myself, my eyes bulging as I found nothing beneath me, and I fell backwards into the pool! I plunged completely into and under the water before I was able to bring my head up to hear a thunder of laughter. Treading water and never so shocked and embarrassed in my life, I saw George's date appear at his side, carrying two glasses of champagne; and she looked surprised by what had just happened while handing him a glass. George stood there, speechless, with the most awkward expression on his face, but then taking on that boyish smirk that grew on his face.

Swimming to the underwater steps to make my exit from the pool, I rose out of the water sopping wet with water draining from me as I marched angrily toward the house. My soaked hair drooping in a mess and the dress I wore probably ruined, I was prepared to sock the first person who made a remark; but except for the endless laughter and peering eyes, no one said a word to me. I saw my parents on the terrace, they both noticed me dripping wet while wearing my mad-with-anger expression, and neither one spoke a word. My mother wore a stunned look, and not knowing what to say, she just stood there with both eyes gaping wide.

The incident my mind recreated brought back some of the emotions I felt at the time, but now returning to the present, I could look back and find some humor in it. I don't think I said a word to George for a year after what happened.

Now ready to bed down and go to sleep, I knelt in prayer, asking our Heavenly Father to grant me the courage and guidance to see this through, and in His goodness and wisdom to forgive my ancestors for whatever faults they may have had.

Closing my eyes, I also asked God to help me learn answers to the secrets surrounding this murder, for I needed to learn all I could about the past in order to be certain of my own destiny. It meant so much for me to know the truth in whether or not my grandmother was a mad woman with homicidal tendencies— what could have driven her to commit this horrible murder.

It had been a long day into night, and now I had to make a decision about whether to leave my bedroom door open; but courage was the very thing I'd just asked for in prayer, and knowing to accomplish what I'd set out to do here, I would have to be brave enough to leave the door open. I must leave the door open to face what lay ahead because if I wasn't willing to unlock and leave open my bedroom door, I wasn't ready to bear the truth. The door hadn't been an issue all evening; in fact, I hadn't even given it a thought until now, but at this moment, I found myself fighting an inner conflict about whether to leave it open. I'd never thought of myself as a timid person, and finally ready to make a committal, I got up and opened the door, then returned to the bed and slid under the feathered quilt where finding warmth and comfort there, I eventually fell asleep…

I awoke in the middle of the night from a sound or disturbance; the hall light was in my eyes, but I caught sight of a dark fleeting blur moving from the door!

The light went out!

Frightened, I jerked myself up into a sitting position, my eyes concentrating on the open black space beyond the doorway, my heart pounding—I dare not move or make a sound.

The floor creaked, and a sudden electrifying chill climbed my back, followed by the sensation of needles and pins to the scalp like my hair was standing on end—I wanted to scream but couldn't, and a voice shouted from the back of my mind, *THE DOOR! CLOSE AND LOCK THE DOOR!*

I leaped from the bed to slam the door shut, bracing it while twisting the key in the lock, and it latched.

Unnerved, my heart raced as I breathed hard, and I heard a crash—glass shattering on the hall floor outside my door. Placing my palms and ear flat against the door, I heard footsteps quietly descending down the stairs. Bewildered but finally able to take a deep breath, I sat at the edge of my bed until sunup, wondering who this person might be—it certainly was no spirit that came to my door, and I didn't think it was Maurice.

CHAPTER 8

THE RED DRESS

I don't know when it was that I dozed off, but the following morning, I overslept. Sunlight shown bright through the bedroom window, and without a moment's hesitation, I dressed casually, putting on a white blouse, faded blue jeans, and sneakers. Still on my mind was the visitor that came to my bedroom door in the middle of the night; the fleeting form of a dark figure still left me a little skittish and unnerved. Now the sun-drenched world brought the promise of a new day and helped to quell my fears, and in the motion of dressing myself, I took time to gaze out my window at the sentinel perched at the edge of the roof. The gargoyle appeared far less threatening and sinister in the light of day, and now that I was aware of its presence there, I was certain to give it a greeting every morning.

Moving out into the hallway to investigate and see if I could find what made the sound of broken glass in the middle of the night, I was disappointed to find nothing, nothing except at the table where I'd remembered seeing that crystal glass swan; now a empty forest green flower vase had replaced it. Examining the floor where the carpet stopped and the bare hardwood was exposed, I discovered small fragments of crystal glass. I assumed Maurice, being the type that turned in early, must also be an early riser and, perhaps, thinking I'd broken it, cleaned up the mess and replaced the broken piece with this vase.

Coming to the door where I saw the ghostly image of a woman dissipate last night, I saw the door still closed; and curiosity, plus a thirst for knowledge about my family's past, prompted me to try the door handle. Finding it unlocked, I opened it and saw a room tastefully done in a scheme of red and pink colors, accentuated with soft lilacs. The blanket covering a broad bed had a cheerful pattern of pale pink roses; the wallpaper was a deep rose with a dark, almost black scrolled pattern. The painting of a woman hanging on a wall inhibited me from further motion, and I was certain that both the person's image in the painting and the person who previously occupied this bedroom was my grandmother. Gazing at this lightly complexioned brunette, she was very beautiful, as Maurice had said; and her penetrating eyes had much depth and mystery to them.

A patch of sunlight pierced tied-back frosty white curtains hung at the location of french doors, and just outside these doors, I saw a balcony; and the foliage from the fat, overgrown branches of an oak tree blocked out most of the sunlight. Located on an outside wall, closely set between the french doors and the room's corner, a wide vanity held tall mirrors and shapely perfume bottles. The housekeeper who came on Wednesdays kept the room and its furnishings dusted; even the overhead brass chandelier was free of cobwebs. Being the vain woman my grandmother must have been, she would've preferred it this way.

Turning my attention to a merry-go-round jewel box centered on top of the vanity, I opened the colorful antiquity and became disappointed to find it empty. Closely examining the underside of the lid, I had difficulty reading the fine lettering etched on it, but then spoke out loud what it said, "1904 World's Fair."

"Hmmm," I unconsciously sounded in studying the underside of the lid where I located a key for the musical mechanism. After cranking it, I closed the lid and then heard a catchy jingle as the top rotated; and placed it on the vanity counter to get the full effect of it's functioning top piece, watching with amusement as the horses circled while performing their up-down motion like a real merry-go-round. Faintly familiar with the notes it played, I tried thinking of what turn-of-the-century songs I knew, and I smiled in recognizing the tune, "Why, it's their song, 'The Band Played On.'"

Deliberating whether to go through her personal things, I considered that by doing so, I might be able to learn something about her state of mind back then and took it upon myself to commence a search. In the top drawer of her vanity in the midst of a variety of trinkets, I found interest with a picture of a young man in a small silvery frame. It may have at one time sat upon her vanity, and gawking for a moment at his dark wavy hair and sideburns, I assumed he must be her eldest son, Daniel; I returned it to its place.

From another drawer, I turned up a shoe box containing a group of letters bound together by a red bow; and with my expectations brimming with romantic notions, I selected the first letter I saw for reading its contents, finding it tattered by time with lines and creases:

> *Dearest Angela,*
>
> *When I first kissed you, I learned how truly wonderful life can be, and when you're in my arms, I know a peace and serenity I've never before experienced.*
>
> *Since we've met, I find myself acting as a bungling fool—can these unsettling feelings be love and I'm falling helplessly to it?*
>
> *When I'm with you, you're my blushing bouquet, I'm high on a cloud, and all I can see is the glitter in your eyes. Yes, you have me under your spell. I know I'm bewitched because I melt whenever I hear your voice.*
>
> *But, darling, I've never been as happy as I am now. You're all I've ever wanted, and you're everything.*
>
> *With all my love,*
> *Charles*

All of these heartwarming, intimate love letters were from Charles to Angela, and she must have relished them. My grandfather was devoted to her, a romanticist whose writing told of an undying love. He must have written them during their happiest years, never even the slightest hint of the nightmare fate had in store for them. After giving them a quick glance over, I retied the bow and placed them back in the drawer the way I'd found them, leaving them for someone else, possibly another generation, to find at another time in the future.

Standing in a corner was a tall double door hutch made of oak, and the brawny cabinet with short, curved legs drew my interest; the left door was open just a pinch, and certain my grandmother would have no objections, I decided to open it. Having anticipated the hutch to be empty, I was awed to find an entire wardrobe hanging inside, dresses galore neatly partitioned one side, and my nostrils caught the scent of cedar. A tall mirror hung from the inside of one door, and a variety of shoes hung from their heels on the backside of the other door.

A very large odd-shaped box situated on a shelf above the hanging wardrobe drew my eye and curious as to what was inside it, I pulled it out and sat it on the bed. Removing the top of the box, I searched through soft tissue lining the inside until producing the most stunning hat, having a wide rim that waved high from the front and around to the back. The scarlet head cover was simply elegant with its white bristled feathers, and I momentarily lost myself rummaging through the dresses before pulling out the hat's matching garment; it was easily located once I spotted its bright, lively color, and I thought it the most attractive of the bunch. It had a ruffled collar and sleeves adorned with very fine silky white lace, and the stylish detailed embroidery of yesteryear made me smile. However, I also thought that the dress looked rather gaudy and ostentatious, and in thinking this, I didn't believe that the dress suited me well; at the same time, I wondered where or for what occasion such a showy dress ought to be worn.

Flirting with the notion to try the dress on, I stood in front of the mirror while holding the gown up in front of me; it showed that my grandmother and I were relatively similar in size. Then having this irresistible urge to try it on, I no longer saw its color as displeasing, but now something about the look of the garment seemed to influence me into believing that it was oddly appealing to the eye.

Looking at my grandmother's picture, I made a pleading gesture, "I have to try it on. May I?" The motionless face gave no answer but remained still, and trying to make her understand that I'd never take what I presumed to be her most prized dress, I said, "I promise to return it." Believing I was thin, I soon found myself battling to squeeze into this lavishly beautiful gown, as it surprised me how much I had to suck in my tummy to fit into it. I must've fought with the dress for five minutes, and the persistent effort I'd made in wrestling with its snuggly tight-fitting waistline left me breathless. It became an exhausting task, but I finally won out and succeeded in fitting into it; then I had to become a contortionist in order to secure its backside.

Tired and drained from struggling with the dress, I now felt strange and rather peculiar, as if in the process of putting on the dress I'd slipped into someone else's skin. I blamed this odd feeling coming over me for the fight I'd just gone through getting into the dress; however, now gazing in the mirror at how it appeared on me, the scarlet gown looked stunning with its white lace and ruffled, frilly collar. Before I knew it, I was putting on rouge, maybe a little heavier than I usually would have, dabbing behind my ears a touch of a potent perfume that gave off an exotic fragrance. There was no jewelry so taking an old red ribbon from a drawer, I tied it behind my neck, leaving a band of red in front.

Wrapping and balling my hair up, the hat gave the final touch, and giving it a slight tilt, I lifted a brow, saying, "Now there's a Gibson Girl, if I ever saw one."

Not wanting to bother with trying on shoes, as I couldn't see my feet anyway, so while remaining in a standing position, I managed to slip my feet into my sneakers. This strange feeling surged over me again, and looking at my reflection, I didn't like the strange sensation it left me with—it was as if I was somebody else, and I'd gone through a transformation.

While still in my grandmother's room, I turned my attention to a door that gave access to the connecting room; and going to it, I gripped and turned the door handle, but then paused. I was somehow certain that this next room was my grandfather's bedroom; and in a weird, strange way, it was like I could feel his presence beyond the door. I held my breath as I resumed turning the handle to open the door, releasing a stale, musty odor; and with the door partially opened, I saw a dull, dreary room with a mammoth four-post bed. A sudden ominous feeling prevailed over me as I uttered to myself, "This is where it happened."

Alarmed by the awful scene that once was, these strange sensations continued to taunt me as I respectfully closed the door; and backing slowly away from it, I decided to never to cross this threshold again.

I left my grandmother's bedroom wearing her gown, while carrying with me the oddest feeling, and I couldn't shake it as I ventured down the hallway in the direction of the servant's staircase. When passing the next door, I thought to myself that this must be the hallway door giving entrance to my grandfather's room, and I stared at it while quietly passing it by. I soon came to the end of the hallway and stepped out onto the stair landing, then began my ascent up the stairs to the gymnasium-size ballroom Maurice had made mention of. Bright sunshine came through a row of tall oblong windows, reflecting off a dusty but highly polished wood floor, and at the end of this wide-stretched floor space, I saw a stage area. Pretending to hear music, I began to dance and whirl about until this strange, queer feeling swelled within me again, coming on stronger than ever, overwhelming me until my knees weakened. I became faint and light-headed while overcome by hot and cold flashes; the sunshine faded and the room turned dim, dark, and black.

From out of the darkness, I heard distant voices and laughter; these sounds became louder and distinctly clearer, mimicking a fairly large gathering. Music commenced, softly playing a bouncy but popular turn-of-the-century song, "In the Good Ole Summertime". Beginning to sense movement all around me, I dimly saw line, shape, and movement as the wall lights brought on their soft glow. The windows remained dark as night and through a misty haze, I saw people—as there were many couples swaying in a swaggering style to the song's rhythm.

Puzzled and baffled, I could no longer tell if what I was seeing was real or an illusion—the faces of these people were pale, and dark circles around the eyes gave them the look of death! The men were dressed in dark conservative suits or tuxedos, most had sideburns and mustaches, and a few displayed the handlebar mustache. The ladies were all dressed in glamorous gowns in a variety of styles, but all were basically soft, light, drab colors of the same period with ruffled fringe and long skirts bulging from the hips down. Those guests not dancing mingled in groups while sipping from champagne glasses, standing at or near a line of tables displaying a variety of dishes; a large heart-shaped cake was the main exhibit at the middle of the table. The band members occupying the stage were all well-dressed males, and dangling from the ceiling were clumps of colorful balloons.

As the song ran down, in my observation I noticed how my presence drew everyone's attention, especially the women, whose unfriendly looks made me feel as if I didn't belong here. Four ladies in particular huddled while sharing words and giving an unwelcome stare, and I easily understood that their conversation pertained to me. Then it dawned on me that maybe it was the dress and not me which they found offensive—its loud color, perhaps, suggested the wrong thing. A growing discomfort loomed over me, and I started looking for an exit, but something held me bound to that spot; then the band cranked up another melody—this time playing the merry-go-round song "The Band Played On."

From the corner of my eye, I saw an approaching figure and turned to see a man with dark wavy hair and sideburns coming towards me wearing a grin on his face. I had the oddest feeling I recognized him, but in my confused state of mind, I couldn't be sure of where or when I'd seen him before. He bowed as if making the gesture that he wished to dance with me, and without thinking, I accepted. I actually liked the lively tune, but my dancing partner's expression turned grimly serious as he took me in his arms and looked at me with a dark stare. I no longer wanted him to hold me, but there was no time to rationalize for I was already swinging in his arms to the beat of the music.

After the band played an instrumental verse of the song, a man stepped forward on stage and gave it lyrics as he sang:

"Ca-sey would waltz with the straw-ber-ry blonde,
An' the Band Played-On.
He'd glide-cross the floor with the girl he a-dored,
And the Band Played On.
But his brain was so load-ed it near-ly ex-ploded,
The poor girl would shake with a-larm.
He'd ne-ver leave the girl with the straw-ber-ry curls,
And the Band Played On."

The vocalists singing ceased, but the band went on playing their instruments, and as the musicians stepped up their beat, my eyes became locked with my dancing partner's; we raced with the song's accelerated pace and I saw in his eyes a look of threatening doom, but I couldn't break away from his hold! We kept circling on the dance floor; and turning my eyes away from his cold, bizarre stare, I struggled uselessly to get free, and then those strange people surrounding us began closing in, converging while balloons floated down from the ceiling! The spinning and whirling I did in his arms made me dizzy and nauseated until everything blurred, and then faded to black.

Lying motionless on the floor, when my eyes refocused, I thought the man I faced had aged incredibly, but I then quickly recognized Maurice kneeling over me.

Wearing a worried look of concern as he examined me, he spoke in a caring voice that sounded far away, "Are you all right?"

Hardly having the strength to reply, I felt flushed, and perspiration covered me from head to toe. I looked to a nearby window and the sun's strong reflection off the floor nearly blinded me.

"Just relax, you'll be fine in a minute," Maurice said calmly.

Removing the handkerchief from the pocket of his jacket, he dabbed my forehead to wipe away perspiration. "All heat in the house rises up to this level, making it nearly unbearable up here on the third floor... You look pale—the sooner I get you downstairs, the better."

Life continued flowing back into me, and attempting to sit up, I noticed he held in his hand a wide-rimmed dingy white hat; and it occurred to me that this must be the hat I had worn, but it had changed to a plain eggshell color! I looked at the dress I wore, and it, too, was no longer the bold scarlet I'd seen it as before, for it now appeared to be the same dingy white color as the hat!

"The dress," I declared, glaring at it, astonished and awed by how it lost all its color.

"You needn't be concerned about that old dress. It's not likely to ever be worn again."

"I could've sworn this dress was red before."

Maurice didn't seem to hear me as he held the material of the gown in his hand, "This gown is more of a fall or winter garment, though very stylish for it's time, the material is too heavy, and they were worn too tight. You're a very petite young lady and fortunate to have a lean, slender waistline, but it must've fit snuggly on you to restrict your breathing. In my day, there was nothing more important to a woman than her figure, and it was common for females to wear a corset, also quite common for them to pass out during the summer months."

"In the good ole summertime," I muttered under my breath.

"Come now; let me help you up...The fact that you haven't eaten anything yet doesn't help matters either, and if I keep breakfast any longer, it'll be supper."

Rising to a standing position, I brushed off the gown; and remaining amazed by its color change, I asked, "Maurice, do you ever remember my grandmother wearing a scarlet dress?"

He looked at me funny, "Scarlet—sort of a loud-reddish color, she was a dresser, all right, but I don't ever recollect her in any dress that shade of color...I'll say this much, though, wearing that dress you certainly hold a striking resemblance to her."

We took the stairs down to the second-story landing, and Maurice said, "Why don't you find something more comfortable to wear than that stuffy old dress, and then we'll see about putting some meat on those bones...Can't have you faintin' all over the place now, can we."

Returning to my grandmother's bedroom, I gazed at my image in the mirror above her vanity, and placed the hat back on. I thought the drastic change of color in how the hat matched the eggshell color of the dress unbelievable, when only a short time ago, I saw them both as a scarlet red color. The only thing that had any true color was the red ribbon I'd tied behind my neck, and after undoing it, I placed the ribbon back in the drawer where I'd originally found it. Perplexed by this phenomenon, I removed the hat and tossed it on the bed, staring at it while letting my hair down, wondering at the same time if I was beginning to lose my senses—the scarlet color seemed so bright, vivid, and genuine—like the strange ballroom scene I'd experienced.

Stunned by this event with the dress, I momentarily dwelled on the thought that I no longer had that weird sensation I'd had before when first putting the dress on. Rehashing the strange and mysterious episode in my mind caused me to recover the picture of the young man from the top drawer of Angela's vanity, and I looked at it curiously with the idea that he was my dancing partner. Remembering the fear I felt when looking into his eyes, I studied the eyes of the man in the picture. I didn't believe that I'd actually, physically, experienced this event, but that the incident was more of an illusion or hallucination involuntarily conjured up in my mind, and that it may have even been the recurrence of an event which happened years ago. Whatever meaning or significance it had, I didn't know, but the experience certainly left me disturbed, and that may have been what the incident was intended to do. In a way, I believed this was the case; and the more I thought about it, the more I didn't like the idea of temporarily losing touch with reality. I only hoped that it didn't happen again.

Having the fate of my grandmother still on my mind, and understanding how mental illness can be passed on through the bloodline, I couldn't help wondering if this may be the beginning of my worst fears—that my mental faculties were becoming unstable or unhinged. As much as I didn't want to believe it, I had no understanding for how or why I experienced these occurrences.

CHAPTER 9

WHERE THE MAGICIAN RESTS

After changing back into my white blouse and faded blue jeans, I felt more like Claire MacKennsey; however, the incident on the third floor remained fresh in my thoughts. Pondering that strange scene with all those people and a dance partner that refused to let me go made me wonder how long I'd been unconscious up there on the third floor. I had no idea how I could've thought that the hat and dress were red when they were simply a dingy white color. As much as I didn't want to allow these deceptive delusions to bother me, the fact I'd begun to imagine things made me worrisome. The very thing that drew me to this house in the first place was the belief that my grandmother was criminally insane, and after this incident, I was starting to wonder if I was losing touch with reality. I never had an experience like that before where my mind was fabricating things that did not exist.

Finally putting these thoughts aside, I felt as though I'd regained my composure and started downstairs to see what meal Maurice had prepared.

Upon entering the kitchen, I saw Maurice putting together sandwiches made up of a variety of thinly sliced lunchmeat and cheeses arranged on bread.

"Make yourself comfortable, Claire," he said. "I had to scrap what I made for breakfast, I hope you like cold cuts."

Instead of taking a chair, I strolled over to the window where I viewed the courtyard, and paying notice to the fact that he called me Claire gave favorable indication that we were forming a personal relationship. Remembering the sound of breaking glass in the middle of the night, which must have been the crystal swan shattering, and knowing that a vase had replaced it, I chose not to bring the matter up just yet. Not wanting to seem unsociable, I commented, "I can't get over the unique architecture of this house."

Surveying the area beyond the courtyard, I spotted stone steps leading up to a pathway, which I'd overlooked the day before. The path led through a beautiful flower garden encircling a green house—a glass building with stone columns at each corner, sunlight reflecting off the glass on one side.

"I don't know if it's true or not," began Maurice, "but I heard the house had been both designed and built by Charles' grandfather, a ship's captain. It's been rumored he was a bit of a shady character, dealing in illegal contraband, smuggling while importing raw materials from the African coast. It was through the distribution of this merchandise that your family's wealth stems from. He had the house built over a cave and reportedly used its honeycombed hollows to stash loot. I've yet to stumble upon an entrance to the cave, but Charles once described exploring the passageways of a cavernous place connected with the house."

Amused by this story of a cave beneath the house, I looked at Maurice, hoping to hear more about it.

"You don't see that pesky dog out there, do you? She's been out bummin', coming home later and later."

I glanced outside and saw no sign of her, "No, I don't see her."

"Guess I'll have to start keeping her in until she straightens out her act. I don't want her wandering off and getting lost."

"Are you the botanist with the green thumb?"

"Why, yes," he said, modestly. "I find enjoyment in making things grow. It takes a great deal of my time, but it's quite rewarding."

"I see a variety of flowers. You must be very proud of them."

"In a sense, they're like family to me. I talk to them, and believe it or not, it helps them to grow and flourish...One of the main reasons why I took up the hobby of gardening is because this is such a dull, dreary, and dreadfully lonely place. I hope your stay here isn't going to be too terribly boring."

"What species of plants are kept in the greenhouse?"

"Greenhouse…My dear, that's your grandfather's resting place, a mausoleum."

I turned to the window, aiming to see the glass shell's interior, but the distance along with the sun's glare made it impossible to see inside it.

Maurice stopped what he was doing long enough to come to my side, "You know far less about this house than I'd expected. I'm certain it's unorthodox in the States, and it scarcely happens nowadays here, however, in your grandfather's day it was fairly commonplace on the European continent for these older, upper-class estates to have family burial plots. I assure you, he wasn't the first or the last to be buried in such a manner."

I nodded, and although surprised to find out that my grandfather's resting place was here on the estate, I wasn't going to let it traumatize me. "I've heard of it before, but I didn't anticipate running into it here," I commented as I went over to a chair and plopped down into it. However, somewhat uncomfortable with this thought, I asked, "Maurice, I don't like surprises, so are the remains of anyone else kept here on the premises?"

"No, only your grandfather is buried on the property. He loved Strathmoor Heights, and it had been stipulated in his will that he be laid to rest here."

Maurice set a glass of milk down in front of me and then joined me at the table, placing in my reach a tray full of sandwiches with bite-size slices of cheese scattered around the edge of the tray.

Keeping me company while he nibbled on a sandwich, Maurice asked, "Are you feeling any better?"

After chewing and swallowing, I said, "A little, I think getting something in my stomach is going to help. I'm glad you came up to the third floor, who knows how long I would've been lying up there. I hope I didn't have a seizure or anything of that nature."

"I think it was the heat and perhaps that dress restricted your ability to breath. I noticed that you'd overslept, and when I didn't see you by noontime, I thought I'd better look you up to make certain you were okay. I suspected you were exploring the house, and that's why I ventured up to the third floor."

"I had the most difficult time getting into that dress, and I'd begun having some of the strangest sensations even before going up to the third floor. I imagined the craziest thing—I thought that dress and hat were red."

Maurice got up from the table, "I need something to drink." He went over to a cabinet and opening it, he produced a long-stemmed bottle of wine.

"I sometimes have a glass of wine with my afternoon meal, would you care for a glass?"

"Yes, I'll have a glass of wine with you."

While Maurice uncorked the tall bottle and filled two narrow goblets with red wine, I sank my teeth into my sandwich and chewed, then washing it down with the remainder of the milk he'd first given to me.

Maurice bought over a glass of water for me, placing it down in front of me as he joined me, once again, at the table.

I finished off the rest of my meal before handling the wine goblet, swishing the wine around while giving it a moment to breath. I then raised the question, "Did you sweep-up some broken glass upstairs in the hallway this morning?"

"Yes, I did, a swan—a piece collected by your grandmother, or was it a present from your grandfather to her, I'm not sure anymore." Maurice scratched his head while chewing on a slice of cheese.

I sipped a little of the semisweet, fruity-tasting wine, "Something woke me in the middle of the night, I heard the swan shatter and then I heard footsteps on the stairs. Can you give any explanation for this?"

"I've heard many strange sounds in this house which I can give no explanation for, and probably the most incredible thing I've ever encountered was the sound of a woman crying. I can't remember what I was doing in the house at the time, but I do remember it was raining that day; the sound of her whimpering filled this house and it seemed to come from every corner. This house holds many secrets from the past about your family, and it once held a special happiness, but it also has a dark side with a terrible sadness...I don't know if dreadful sorrow can linger on in a house long after its residents have gone, or if a house can shed such a thing as sadness and anguish, but if you could've heard it, it was like the house itself was crying."

Finishing off a slice of cheese, he then asked, "I hope you don't mind my asking, but what exactly brought you here, was it curiosity about this old place?"

I leaned back in my chair, "I've come to learn what I can about my grandfather's death. More than anything, I wanted to know what caused him to be murdered in such a way."

"The fact that you spent the night in this house shows you're very determined to gain this knowledge." The elderly cavalier raised his glass to his lips and sipped down wine while collecting thoughts and memories documented in his head, "I'm going to tell you all I can so you needn't stay here any longer than you must… In the years I spent here before your grandfather's death, I witnessed a man and a woman in a wonderful marriage. Surely, they had their ups and downs like any couple, but for the most part, they were very happy together...

"It was your grandfather's obsession with his magic that was the main cause for their squabbling—it took him away from her and eventually devastated their social life.

"Angela was a stunningly beautiful woman who thrived on the attention of men but she undoubtedly loved Charles very much. A woman in her full bloom, possessing the beauty she had, and now beginning to see she's losing the looks that used to turn men's heads, you know it's going to be disheartening to come to the realization that she's no longer in the spring of life. She must have been nearing forty when their world began crumbling, and it's at that age a woman begins to see she's no longer in the prime of life; that's when she needs her man's company all the more. Losing the attention of her husband took its toll on her—she'd drink and fall into depression.

"Your grandfather had always taken his magic seriously, but his ability to hold an audience spellbound was no longer enough to satisfy him. Deeply dedicated to the art of magic, he wanted to perform an act of wizardry never before accomplished. He, like Houdini, realized physical conditioning was crucial in performing escape magic, and he also understood he'd one day be too old to perform such death-defying ruse.

"Charles had out done himself in that he'd found the ultimate challenge—his idea was to be buried alive in a casket for three days with no water, food or air supply—outdoing any previous magical feat ever attempted before. The oxygen of an air tight casket could support a man's life for only a short number of hours, so he'd done careful planning and preparation, and Angela frowned on the idea from the beginning.

"Your grandfather and I had grown quite close, and from time to time, he confided in me what methods of trickery he'd use in performing his magic. Charles was somewhat of an inventor, and I learned from him how he'd both designed and built a flat metal casing to hold enough pressurized air to outlast the time he'd be contained in the casket. He'd concealed the metal casing in a false floor in the base of the casket and when the scheduled date for the magic act came around, newsmen were on the scene to witness his burial, and dignitaries made a thorough inspection of the coffin. They proceeded by handcuffing Charles and then sealed him inside the coffin; it was nailed shut then wrapped in heavy chain, held in place by eye screws and padlocks.

"Nearly fifty hours after the time they buried him, Angela awoke from a dream she had about Charles suffocating in the casket, and she insisted they raise the coffin; orders came to resurrect the casket, and upon its opening, Charles body was found lifeless. The authorities immediately transported him to a nearby hospital where doctors pronounced him dead, but over an hour later breathing commenced. Medically speaking, it was a miracle, but Charles shied away from reporters covering the story and after a short time of recuperation, he emerged from the ordeal a different person—something happened to him when he was in that casket that changed his life. Afterward, he separated himself from all who knew him, and he became deeply involved in the study of the occult.

"Between then and the time of his death, I had few opportunities to talk with Charles, but one day I took a meal to his room and interrupted his study of three old textbooks. Stopping long enough to have a meal, he confessed that while buried he discovered the metal case he'd made to hold his oxygen supply in the coffin had developed a leaky valve; and thinking this had occurred long before the act commenced, he realized he couldn't rely on his air supply to sustain him. In his isolated confinement six feet underground, surrounded by perpetual darkness, he remained calm while going over his predicament—he'd lost precious air and his oxygen would run out long before the casket would be unearthed.

"He quickly concluded his only chance of survival lay in a type of meditation he'd learned while traveling abroad and on an extended trip to Delhi, India. On this trip, he traveled northward to the Indian-Nepalese border to where at some kind of secluded monastery in the Himalayan Mountains, he spent time with a kind of prophetic mystic who taught him a series of exercises in yoga for which he gained the discipline to promote control of the mind and body. Through these exercises, he discovered he could reach another plane of consciousness that brought him to a new level of peace and tranquility he'd never known before. Impressed by what he'd learned, after leaving India, he continued the study and practice of yoga, and while confined in the casket, he now turned to this form of meditation in the hope of saving himself. Focusing all his mental concentration, he attempted what he described as a self-imposed hypnosis in order to bring himself under a trance or state of hibernation, thereby slowing his bodily functions down for conserving air.

"Claiming to have accomplished this, Charles insisted that through meditation and mental concentration, he'd brought himself under a transitory spell that raised his consciousness to another level, and that was the only thing that kept him alive. He also told me how he had a out of body experience, whereby his spirit or soul journeyed across time and space, and explained how while in this transient state he made a visitation through a world of the dead—seeing both friends and relations who'd been deceased for years. Now, after this astonishing achievement of surviving the magic act of being buried alive, he felt an obligation to form a lasting link of communication with those who've passed on to another plane of existence, one he hoped he could periodically tap into. It became an endless obsession with him to contact the dead, and he spent what little time he had left on this earth committed to repeating this perplexing accomplishment... Now you know what I meant when I said that his and Houdini's life paralleled, as in their later years, they were both determined to contact the dead.

"Charles soon afterward formed an association with a rather mysterious older gentleman named Thornwell who delved in mysticism and the occult. This Thornwell fellow had met with several spiritual mediums prior to meeting Charles in an effort to contact his deceased daughter who passed away after acquiring a childhood disease. Thornwell commonly had haunting visions of his daughter in his dreams. He was convinced that she was trying to communicate with him, and he believed that she was not at peace in the afterlife. I distinctly remember Thornwell as being tall, having sadly serious large eyes, a long face, bushy gray eyebrows, and a mustache; he may have been Scottish-born.

"Your grandfather and Thornwell made a relentless effort for weeks trying to make contact with the dead. I remember them once making a hastily prepared trip to Istanbul to acquire a copy of an ancient Tibetan funerary text translated to English, described as a book of the dead to serve as a guide in the afterlife. Upon their return, they vigorously redoubled their efforts, doing strange exercises or rituals by candlelight long into the night; I'd put my ear to the door on a couple of occasions to hear them mumbling chants that may have been prayers. The strain Thornwell put on himself finally caused his heart to give out, but his death only inspired Charles to keep trying, and he became more determined than ever before to go on with his work.

"Charles carried on the experiments he'd started with Thornwell as if possessed by the devil, he was a man caught up in something he didn't completely understand, and yet, he couldn't let go of it, becoming quite reclusive. The mental exhaustion was beginning to take its toll on his health, but he told me several times that he was on the verge of a breakthrough. I suggested he give it a rest, asking him what good will it be to achieve this if success kills him— like Thornwell, but he wouldn't listen. Angela pleaded with him to stop these all-night vigils he'd gotten caught up in and threw fits of anger to persuade him to quit, but he just stayed locked up in his room. When her efforts failed, she returned to drinking heavily and became very depressed.

"We soon learned that Angela was expecting to give childbirth, then gossip started that she had a lover, and I thought she'd started the rumor to get her husband out of his room so she could win back his attention. It did disrupt his work for a spell; however, the scandal caused such uproar that from then on a cloud of suspicion and mistrust filled the house. I could read in Charles face that he was worried about whether he was the father of the child, at least that's what I suspected was bothering him.

"When your father was born, there were complications, partly because of Angela's age and the fact that she hadn't given childbirth in so long. Charles' worries turned into genuine concern for the newborn child and I offered Charles what support I could—I didn't believe that Angela ever had an affair, and I told him so. I don't see how she could've been seeing anyone, she hardly left the house during that period and there were few times that they'd have visitors. Surely, if a man had been calling on Angela, I'd have seen something to justify the claim—I was here in the house most of the time doing chores, and little went on in this house that I didn't see. I do believe a few of the ladies they were sociable with were jealous of her, and maybe they were the ones who spread all the talk. The shameful rubbish I'd heard people saying at the time was nothing more than that—pure rubbish.

"Whatever happened the night Charles died has always been shrouded in mystery, though I saw Angela the following morning when the police carted her off, and one side of her face held a bruise, but that didn't really explain anything about what occurred. Police later surmised that Angela had told Charles something concerning her with another man, and he struck her in a fit of jealous anger; after he'd gone to bed, she went into a crazed rage and delivered the fatal blow; the weapon used was a halberd axe which hung from the wall over the staircase.

"It was the method by which he was murdered and the fact that the severed head was never recovered that led authorities to believe that Angela wasn't competent to stand trial. Later, more stories about Angela's peculiarities began to surface, things which I believe were directly related to her loneliness, depression, and drinking. It's true that I had seen a change in her, but nothing or at least no symptoms to make me think her capable of such a hideous crime. She and I used to have cordial conversations, but she hardly spoke a word to me for weeks prior to that night. Still, these stories served to reinforce the theory the police had, and with the absence of the severed head, psychiatrists unanimously agreed that she had to be put away."

"Do you think Angela had some sort of mental breakdown?"

"Anything's possible, I think she was under great strain to get back the attention of the man she loved, and maybe she did, as they said, go insane. If that was the case, then I still say she was the good person I thought she was because you have to take into consideration that she had no control over her actions at the time she committed the murder, and she did not understand right from wrong at the time. To this day, I have difficulty believing what happened in this house—how people I knew so well could fall into such a terrible tragedy."

"What do you think became of the missing head?"

"I'm afraid that's something we may never know."

I sat there collecting thoughts about the past while trying to understand how everything had gone so terribly wrong in my grandparent's lives, and for Charles to have died in the manner that he had. Contemplating all I'd learned thus far, there plain and simply didn't seem to be enough information for me to come to any conclusions. As much as I wanted to learn what happened that night so long ago when my grandfather lost his life, I felt stifled and the answers were proving elusive.

CHAPTER 10

THE SHRINE

Sitting at the table with thoughts of the past churning in my head, it seemed I'll never learn what happened the night of my grandfather's death, it then occurred to me that I had such a vague impression of the uncle whom I'd heard so little about. Wanting to learn everything I can about my relatives, I asked, "How about my Uncle Daniel, what do you remember about him?"

"Ah, yes, how can I forget old Danny...Up till now, you've heard the past through one person's discriminating viewpoint," and Maurice placed his hand against his chest. "I'm obliged to say that I can't speak of Daniel MacKennsey without leaving the impression that I didn't like him because I didn't, I found him extremely repulsive, and he and I had little in common."

I recalled the photograph I'd seen in Angela's vanity, which prompted me to ask, "In Angela's room, in one of the drawers of her vanity that is, I found a photograph in a silver frame of a young man with black wavy hair and sideburns, was that him?"

"Why yes, she did keep a photograph of him on her vanity, and I believe it did have a silver frame. The description you gave of dark wavy hair and side burns certainly describes him well, so I'd say it probably is a picture of him you'd discovered."

Maurice appeared grim, awkward, and uncomfortable, "Madam, I don't know if it's a good idea for me to speak badly of someone who's no longer with us. It might be best if I keep my opinion of your uncle to myself, it may interfere with our relationship."

"It would mean a lot to me to hear the truth, Maurice. Please, I want you to tell me about him."

Maurice nodded, "If anyone in the family had a mental problem it was he. I don't mean to imply that he was mentally unbalanced, but he was a particularly ornery, arrogant, high-strung individual—very cruel and insolent when it came to me and most of the other servants. Everything to him was a game, and he enjoyed taunting people by the way he imposed his authority.

"He was a few years older than I, quite egotistical and profane, using his size and position to ridicule and needle me. One thing I really resented was how his mother never corrected him or objected to the abuse and degradation he dealt to others, sometimes tormenting me right in front of her. Knowing the kind of malicious, contemptible person he was, I doubt if it would've made any difference, and maybe that's why she never got involved; your grandfather tolerated him, but they quarreled often. Being the unprincipled person he was made him a difficult individual to confront and reason with. He was irresponsible and mischievous, and I suppose most young men are hard-headed like that in one way or another, but sooner or later, they mature and grow out of that stage of life, but he never made any attempt to mend his ways.

"He ran with a spoiled, callus, vindictive bunch with a sadistic reputation that was much like him, but I won't talk down about those who aren't here to defend themselves."

Maurice looked down as if reflecting on the pages of his life, "There was once a young maiden named Anna whom I fancied, and even though she liked me, she'd seen hard times in her youth and her dream was to marry into nobility. She worked here as a maid, and in Daniel she saw her future.

"There came one windy evening when Daniel went horse-back riding, he got caught up in a violent thunderstorm and became thrown from his horse. He suffered a serious back injury and twisted his leg in his fall, his injuries were very painful, and it took a long time for him to recover. I thought the experience might make a better man of him, but it only made him a worse tyrant than ever before. Angela couldn't stand seeing her son in pain, and against the physician's orders, she gave him more pain killer medication than what the doctor prescribed, which in turn led to morphine addiction.

"During the period he was bedridden the evil in him intensified, and he entertained himself by ridiculing and persecuting people in perverted ways. He amused himself by toying with Anna, taking joy and pleasure by showing her attention, and then by humiliating her. She meant little or nothing to him, but knowing she meant a great deal to me, just for spite, he used and exploited her, stripping her of her honor and dignity. In midwinter, when Daniel's condition was showing signs of improvement, Sir Charles and Angela went away for a visit to London; it was then that Anna found out she was pregnant, and on one of his drunken nights, he threw her out in the cold. When I learned what happened, I seriously considered killing him."

He refilled his glass, then lifted it in his hand, "She should've known better, but it's all done and in the past. I later learned that she lost his baby."

Now understanding why Maurice had good reason not to speak of the past, and how personal these memories were for him, I said, "You loved this girl, didn't you?"

He stared from his chair as if in thought and remembrance of her, "Yes, I suppose I did, but she made her choice and unfortunately it was a bad one...Sometimes I think of her, she's probably long since passed away by now, it was such along time ago."

He began to take a drink from his glass and paused as a thought came to mind, "I remember seeing Daniel on the morning after the night your grandfather died. He must've been out drinking the night it happened and he appeared dazed by the news of his father's death, perhaps all those times he'd given Charles a hard time came back to haunt him, that's the way it usually goes...One last account of Daniel was that he wanted your grandfather's body cremated, but Irene wouldn't stand for it. You see, Daniel never could fully accept the death of your grandfather; he was plagued by hallucinations of his father and that, in part, may have been what drove him to commit suicide— he hung himself from a beam in the library."

Dispirited by the image Maurice gave of my uncle, I downed the last of the wine in my glass, and then stood and walked over to the window. I breathed a sigh while digesting the information he'd just given me, it saddened me to find out Daniel was such an unprincipled person.

"I apologize if I've told you something you'd rather not have heard; I really didn't want to tell you those things about your uncle…It's a beautiful day, Claire, a good opportunity to take a walk and familiarize yourself with the grounds around the house."

"Yes, I think I shall, Maurice, I'll be back a little later."

He got up from his chair and reached in his pocket to bring out keys on a key ring, and began fumbling with them. "I didn't know how long you'd planned on staying, but I wanted to give you keys for both the front and back door, so that during your stay here you'll have the ability to come and go as you please."

I took the keys and placed them in my pants pocket before going out the door to stroll across the courtyard in the bright sunshine. I saw Maurice watching from the window, and I thought he might be concerned that I may be angry with him for having told me these things about my Uncle Daniel, but I wasn't, not at all. I was actually wanting to reach out to Maurice and express how genuinely sorry I was for all the mistreatment he'd endured from my uncle.

Taking the necessary steps to gain a closer look at the mausoleum where my grandfather rested, I gave more thought to the story of how this house was built on top of a cave. While moving in the direction of the four-sided glass-faced structure, I saw the way ahead, a stone path cut through an abundance of flowers— all kinds, all colors—a maze of prismatic spectrums harmonious to the eye. A home for the buzzing bees, these carnations were bedded in florid patches, engulfing my sight as I passed between them; and at the center of the maze, I reached the glass-encased stone coffin—it altogether seemed like a shrine.

Rounding the structure slowly, I saw a paper-thin coating of dust covering the inside of the glass, dulling my vision of its interior; and engraved in the base of a white stone sarcophagus and printed in big, bold lettering was the name MACKENNSEY.

Maurice's interpretation of the night of the murder didn't help much in shedding light on what happened, but it made me pause to think about the apparition I'd encountered in the hallway last night. Convinced it must have been Angela's spirit I'd seen, I believed her ghostly presence roams the hallways of this house. Feeling very strange when first putting on Angela's dress, I asked myself if in her spirited form she could somehow be aware that a mortal was meddling in what had formerly been her private life. If this was possible, then she might try to frighten me into leaving or divert me from learning all the secrets of her life—like the ballroom experience I'd had. There were probably things she preferred left unknown by others—like her motive for murder, if she had one.

I wondered if this woman's crying that Maurice described hearing that one rainy day was hers. In pondering these things, I asked myself what keeps her bound to the present; is it the happy memories, or can it be that she punishes herself for taking her husband's life, creating her own prison here, or could there be some other unfinished business making her troubled spirit linger on in this house? A misguided entity caught in the past, a past overshadowed by the murder of her husband by a horrifyingly ghastly method. If there is a force in existence here bent on concealing the past from me, I was as determined as ever to uncover the answers I'd come so far to learn, even if it meant facing this walking death that lurks in the night. Learning the facts of that fateful night is the key to my peace of mind, but if I was to win this test of wills, I knew it wouldn't be easy. There'd be obstacles to overcome, and even though I felt this strongly about it now, I knew I may later feel different, as much depended on what the dark nights ahead would bring.

Although I hadn't really learned anything more about Angela's state of mind on the night of the murder, I suspected there had to be more surrounding my grandfather's death than what I'd accumulated thus far. For one thing, what did Charles learn which caused him to fly into a rage and strike his wife the same night his life ended—had Angela simply said something to provoke him like the police thought? Was it really Angela who delivered the death blow or did she have a lover who could've wheeled the fatal stroke? However, if she did have a lover and he really did love her enough to kill for her, how could he allow her to face the consequences alone? Last of all, why didn't the police find the head?

The missing head was the most thought-provoking element in this mystery, and there was no question that whoever committed this murder must have been the one that removed the head from the crime scene, but why? This took me back to thoughts about my grandmother's insanity, as she'd have to be out of her mind to have done this. Could she have buried the head outside the house here someplace? If that was so, why, in her jumbled way of mixed-up, twisted thinking, did she believe that by hiding the head she could conceal what she'd done?

Many perplexing questions remained unanswered about this puzzling murder, and I still couldn't be sure if Maurice was being completely honest with me; for instance, this shrine I walked about now—these countless flowerbeds—was it dedicated to my grandfather for the love, respect, and gratitude Maurice held for him, or did the torment of a man's guilt inspire it? He'd created such a sprawling work of art in this garden that it served to raise my suspicions about him. Right then and there, I spawned the notion that Maurice must be withholding something from me, and it was disturbing to think this because if that was the case, then I couldn't completely trust him, nor could I be certain that everything he was telling me was the truth. I didn't like this inkling I'd had, for I wanted to believe in Maurice, and it made me feel insecure that I couldn't; but even with the question of his trust hanging over me, I couldn't help growing fond of him, and I wasn't sure if this was beneficial for me.

Looking to the carriage house, I wondered about some of the old man's habits, and being a bachelor all his life, you'd think the second-story living quarters would be quite unkempt. Nevertheless, even at his age, he took pride in his appearance, leaving a clean and tidy impression of himself. There couldn't be much living quarters up above that stable, but he seemed so satisfied and content living up there, though. I pictured him smoking a pipe, sitting in front of the fireplace on a cool night, the collie resting at his feet.

Summer was here and it was a gorgeous day. If I were back in the States I'd probably be playing tennis, swimming, or skiing, but instead, I was left to rehash the problematic questions pertaining to a murder committed so many years ago that gnawed at me, and for a moment I stood at the mausoleum in silent reverence for my grandfather.

The distant song of a bird filled the air, and I walked over to a tree to search for where she nested in an attempt to identify what kind of a bird that it was. Once I traced the location of the bird nesting on a high tree branch, she lost trust in me and took off with wings spread in flight. At the trunk of another tree, two squirrels scampered in a game of chase and then froze while clinging to the bark before shooting upward in a spiraling pattern with tails fluttering.

Moving out into the meadow where a sprawling, wilting willow tree stood alone, I meditated on what Maurice had told me about my grandfather's life as a magician. I became open to thoughts of another magician—the Great Houdini. It's true that these two men seemed to have quite a bit in common, but Houdini had climbed to the top. My grandfather, on the other hand, must have been a late comer in attempting to master the art of magic. If born a commoner, perhaps things would have been different, but I supposed he'd taken up magic as a hobby to entertain friends only to learn from that near-death experience in the coffin that he had a gift, which inspired him to a greater purpose in this life.

Back in college, we girls often traded books, and one which stands out in my mind now is *Exploring the World of Psychic Phenomena*. There was a passage in it covering Houdini's pursuit to contact his deceased mother. Years went by with failure, and finding that most mediums were fakes, he carried on with the certainty that it was possible to make contact with the afterlife.

Houdini and his wife, Bess, had formed a plan: In the event of his death—should he die before her—he promised that if it were possible to come back he would relay to her a coded message which only the two of them knew. This code consisted of a series of words—each word representing a letter in the alphabet, which would, in turn, spell out the message.

Long after his death, Houdini's wife received a communication. A spiritual medium known to make contact with a deceased boyhood friend reported receiving a message through the spirit of this boy intended to be passed on to her. He'd started out saying, "A man named Houdini wishes to convey a message to his wife." After translating the combination of words that followed, she proclaimed that the message brought to her was the one she and her husband shared—*"Bess, believe."*

Given time, this incident came to be controversial as the wife of Houdini later retracted on her belief that Houdini had sent the message, claiming thereafter that she'd been tricked. However, the medium always held to his account that Houdini's message came out through him. One can't help believing that if anyone who'd passed on could've reached out to our present world, it would have been Houdini.

CHAPTER 11

EXPLORING THE CELLAR

Day turned into evening, and without the sun's rays, temperatures cooled down; the encroaching darkness made the earth a different world, and all life outside this house seemed to perish. Dreading the coming of night, I felt very aware that tonight was different from last night, for I knew I wasn't alone in the house; and I not only contemplated the ghostly image of Angela, but I also remembered that noise which woke me in the middle of the night, glimpsing the hall light on and the sound of footsteps on the stairs. Trying to put aside these things and shake this feeling of anxiety I had wasn't easy, as soon I'd be all alone, and I couldn't overlook my own superstitions about what the night would bring.

I attempted to take my mind off my fears by choosing a queen-size novel from the many literary works in the library. Finding a cozy, comfortable padded leather chair alongside a tall standing floor lamp, I'd taken a slightly laid back position and buried myself in the pages of the book. Whenever my mind had a free moment, my thought processes reminded me that this was the room where my Uncle Daniel hung himself, but I put forth my best effort to block this out of my mind. I also didn't want to think about my grandfather's decapitation because I had to sleep on the same floor where the murder had occurred, but my mind kept returning to these morbidly annoying thoughts. In a strange way, I was more conscious and aware of these things tonight than I was the night before, but I wasn't going to give in to them and let them drive me away.

Later, the grandfather clock in the living room chimed at the hour of nine, and it broke my concentration while serving as a reminder that I hadn't heard from Maurice in some time. I thought it unlikely that he'd leave without letting me know he was retiring for the evening and judging by the hours he kept the day before, I expected he would've said his goodnight and locked up by now.

"Madam," said Maurice, startling me somewhat. "If there won't be anything else, I'll be turning in."

"It's been so quiet that I'd begun to wonder if you'd already gone for the day."

"There were a few chores which needed taking care of," he replied in his own reserved manner.

"I meant to ask you, is the maid coming tomorrow?"

"Yes, tomorrow is Wednesday," he said, as if to reassure himself of which day it was, "and I'll have to pick her up."

"What time do you usually have her here by?"

"The time varies, but I should have her here no later than nine o'clock—she's a middle-aged woman named Katherine Loughton, but she goes by Katie. She's from the old school, if you know what I mean, she maintains a steady routine, and I leave her alone to do things as she pleases. Nobody lives here, so it's just a matter of giving the place a general cleaning, keeping it dusted, and every now and then, changing the linen."

"How long has she been coming to the house to clean?"

"I believe it's going on eight years that she's been employed here."

"I'm looking forward to meeting her. Pleasant dreams to you."

It wasn't ten minutes later that I tried suppressing a yawn, but it overcame my resistance. Maybe I was tiring because I didn't sleep well the night before, the time change that came with my trip, or just the reading that made me sleepy. My eyelids were growing heavy, and it became apparent to me that the sandman was paying me an early visit.

Switching off the lamp next to my chair, I placed the book on the table connected with the lamp and rose to a standing position. At the doorway, I reached to flip the light switch connected to the wall lamp, then leisurely paused to turn and to view the space in the room I'd just vacated. I inspected the ceiling while receiving a queer sensation like I was being watched, and this caused me to look to the huge moose head suspended over the library fireplace; it looked back at me warily and with vigilance.

Putting out the light, I moved from the library up to my bedroom sanctuary and before climbing under the covers, my imagination began to run with a sinister impression of what lay ahead in the night. I would've preferred not to reflect things that had happened here, but the house itself was reminiscent to the people who once occupied it. I knelt beside the bed and said the Our Father, and while in prayer, stressed the point for Him to deliver me from evil.

I then got up to lock the bedroom door before getting into bed, and even though I knew the door wasn't going to stop a spirit, it was the only security I had. Thinking about last night when I saw something or someone at my door, the incident caused me deliberation, and as much as it made me uncomfortable to dwell on such things, I needed to. It was important to find out for what purpose this person had come to my room, for if I was to discover the secrets of this house, I couldn't just shut myself up in this room at night. In order to gain knowledge about the past I'd have to face up to these creaks and thumps in the night because, after all, if someone were trying to frighten me into leaving the house, why were they doing it? Awaking in the middle of the night wasn't something I merely imagined, and if they were trying to accomplish driving me out of this house then this was a test of wills I couldn't afford to lose. I simply had to stand firm for if I left Wales without finding out why my grandfather died, I'd always feel as though I'd failed and wonder about my mental well-being.

Rekindling the determination that I'd had, I convinced myself that I needed to investigate any sound that awakened me, for this was the only way I can expect to learn the mysteries of this horrible murder. It boiled down to the fact that I'd come here for the very specific reason of finding out why my grandfather died the way that he did. There was no real need to talk myself into leaving the door open since deep down inside I knew that if I was going to acquire any real peace in this world, I must be steadfast in holding true to my goal. If my grandmother was a homicidal axe murderer and committed this murder without any real motive, then this was something I'd have to accept. Still, I found this difficult to believe, and yet she had to be out of her mind at the time, for there's no other explanation for such a senseless killing to occur.

Becoming restless, I finally got up to unlock and open the door and stayed awake for some time, lying there with my ears perked up to listen for weird noises in the night. Instead of obnoxious creaking sounds, all I heard was this paralyzing silence that held the house captive, and this needling quiet by itself was quite annoying. I remained wide-eyed, looking at the high canopy cover above the bed where I lay, and with due time, sleep overtook me.

The following morning, after a surprisingly good night's rest, I had a light breakfast and then watched Maurice prepare to leave to pick up Katie Loughton. He wore the dark conservative suit and derby he had on the first time I saw him.

Standing at the kitchen door, ready to walk out, he turned to me and said, "I'll be about an hour, miss, is there anything you'd like me to pick up while I'm out?"

"Well, there's a letter I need to have mailed." Having already brought down the letter I'd written to George, I handed it to Maurice, adding, "I hope it won't put you through any trouble."

"Not at the least, and you're more than welcome to come along for the ride if you wish."

Tempted to say yes, I remembered how jittery Maurice's driving skills made me feel and decided to decline the invitation, saying, "Maybe next time."

Standing by the window, the sun shown brightly in the distance as I watched the old Mercedes rolling down the gravel road leading from the house, and all it left behind was a cloud of dust.

With some free time on my hands, I thought how I'd for the most part covered the interior of the house, with the exception of a few bedrooms; now the idea of this immense house built over a cave intrigued me and I wondered where its entrance could be. It seemed logical that the cave Maurice had described should have an opening somewhere down in the cellar of the house. I hadn't as yet seen the cellar but remembered a door giving access to it near the servant's stairs, off an alcove extending from the kitchen, and I went there.

Coming to the alcove, I opened the door and saw how the area at the bottom of the stairs looked dark and uninviting. Though I didn't see a light switch, I knew they wouldn't have installed electricity in the house without running some sort of lighting down to the cellar. The light of day provided adequate light to enable me to see my way to start down, and I held onto a handrail that kept the same slanting angle as the stairs. The steps felt rickety beneath my feet; and dim sunlight from the open cellar door, now above and behind me, showed me how I barely had clearance before hitting my head on the wide, bulky floor joists above me.

Standing at the edge of sheer darkness, a fat support column stood upright a few feet directly in front of me, and I kept thinking that a light switch shouldn't be far out of reach. I went to feel the squared contour of the column in search of a switch, but if there was one it eluded me.

Hearing a faint squeaking sound as the light behind me dimmed, I quickly turned to catch sight of the door at the top of the steps swinging shut, leaving me in the blackest darkness. Thinking how this old place must be drafty, I immediately went up the steps to the door and saw light seeping around its perimeter, more so at the bottom where there was a gap or clearance between the doors bottom and the threshold. I gripped the doorknob for trying to turn it, but it wouldn't give way, and it became apparent that the old latch mechanism must be weak and binding up because it didn't budge to release the door.

I don't believe this, I said to myself, and trying it again without success, I saw how I'd be stuck down here until Maurice returned, which strained my patience.

Uncomfortable about my entrapment in this cellar, I tried to remain calm as I kept feeling this needling sensation running up my spine to my neck, and rounded my shoulders a few times to rid myself of it. My only hope was that Maurice wouldn't be long returning, and with little choice in what to do with the time spent down here, I chose to try and find a light switch, so I'd at least no longer be in the dark.

Carefully descending the stairs to return to the column, I crept forward in the impenetrable darkness with my hands extended straight ahead of me, using a flailing motion so that I wouldn't run into that darn column. Finally catching hold of the solid upright lumber, I ran my hands all about this wide pillar in an attempt to find the box for the switch. Something faintly touched my face, lightly brushing against my cheek to leave me thinking it to be a cobweb, and I leaned away from it while pursuing the search, reaching up and down the rough-sawn timber.

I felt that faint caress again, this time to my temple, and flung my hand at it to keep it from coming into contact with my face, only to then discover it was a rope or cord. Pulling it, I heard a clicking sound as a light bulb extending out from an electrical box connected to one of the floor joists flashed on. Looking over my whereabouts, I saw a cluttered area and a great furnace, which provided heat for the house during the cold months. What other items that were occupying the cellar were impossible to identify because they were covered by either a sheet or canvas. The house's ancient stone foundation appeared solidly intact, and I moved about in a hunched-over manner to avoid bumping my head on the low floor trusses; and I still occasionally bumped my head while moving about.

Curious as to what made these odd shapes beneath the sheet covers, I slowly and carefully removed the sheets so not to disturb too much dust with the idea I'd recover the pieces before leaving the cellar; I then noticed the floor I stood upon was nothing more than dirt. I first unveiled a tall standing hat-and-coat stand, and then uncovered end tables stacked one on top of another, and then a set of padded armchairs. I next discovered an old rocker with a back-support spindle missing and a manikin for dressmaking; a tall hurricane lamp rested safely in the seat of a plump armchair. Taking a liking to the intricate floral design on both globes of the hurricane lamp, I examined them closely while noticing the bottom glass held a fat oval shape, while the top glass was more circular and round; it flared at the top of its crown where I detected a chip by caressing the edge with my fingertip.

Something off in a corner drew my attention and unable to have guessed any of the objects I'd uncovered by their shape thus far, I had no idea what this one could be either. The sheet draped over it took to a broad rounded circular shape, and underneath I discovered a phonograph or old-time record player resting on a table. The most prominent feature about the record-playing device was a tall horn or tuba-shaped cone where the sound projected from. The base or console for the piece was made of wood, mahogany perhaps, and I presumed a protruding crank provided the means to propel and rotate the record so it would revolve. Seeing a bundle in the form of a paper sack lying next to it, I found wrapped inside a collection of music records; the brittle, dried-out paper sack containing them tore easily and the records, numbering maybe twenty-five, were a little unusual in that they were heavier, more rigid, and thicker than those I'd been accustomed to seeing. Like the phonograph, they must have been quite old, and I wondered if the instrument would work to play them, but I wasn't going to do it without first cleaning everything to get optimum sound. Music had changed so much; I couldn't help being just a little curious about what my grandparents listened to for entertainment.

I felt a strange, chilling sensation on the back of my neck up to my scalp, but it soon gave way to a tingling in my nose and nostrils, warning me that I was about to sneeze. I knew it was the dust I'd stirred up, and I managed to temporarily avoid sneezing, but it persisted. Suddenly overcome by the powerful urge to sneeze and unable to fight it off any longer, an uncontrollable blast of air expelled from me as I sneezed.

"A-choo! A-chooo!!"

I turned my face away while extending my hands straight out in front of me to brush them together in an attempt to rid them of the dust they'd gathered. I then moved toward a canvas covering up what appeared to be boxes stacked next to the wall at the rear of the house. Remembering the payoff Pandora got for her curiosity, I thought I may discover something I'd have preferred not to, and removing the canvas to pry further, I at first found difficulty identifying what I'd uncovered. Sighting another light fixture connected to a joist, I pulled the cord to turn it on and now clearly saw boxes and a chest stacked on top of a long black box. Stepping back, I paused to look at this oblong box to notice how it tapered inward at the ends—like a coffin!

Soon realizing it must be one of my grandfather's props he used when performing his magic, I thought it may have been the one Maurice had told me about that he was buried in, but I doubted it. Having no way of knowing what was in it without inspecting the inside, I began removing those boxes that were resting upon it. Glimpsing inside each one as I set them aside, the boxes and the chest contained clothing and having cleared off the top of the coffin, I was ready to have a look inside it.

I paused before lifting the lid to the coffin, speaking out loud to myself, "You've seen too many horror movies."

Uplifting the lid and pushing it back, a patch of black discharged in my face, "Aahhh!"

Falling backward on my rump, I defensively grabbed at and caught hold of the object that propelled at me and discovered it to be a tall black stovetop hat. Shaking my head and grinning, I then scratched and rubbed my nose to prevent another sneezing attack; then readjusting, I came to an erect position on my knees, pushing my hair back before brushing off my backside.

When beginning to sift through the coffin's contents, I came across a neatly folded cape and removed from the box a long cardboard cylindrical tube, finding it held a scroll-like paper inside and slid it out. Uncoiling it allowed me to see a full-color poster or advertisement for "The Great MacKennsey," revealing a picture of a magician dressed in black removing a white rabbit from his hat; the individual in the picture bore a likeness to the man in the portrait hanging upstairs in the living room—my grandfather. For me, I treasured its sentimental value, and I looked forward to showing it to George when I saw him next, possibly then divulging to him the ghastly story of murder as told to me by my mother. I wasn't going to carry our relationship any further without telling him about it because it simply wouldn't be fair to withhold such a thing from him; he deserved to know.

Closing the casket, I restacked the chest and boxes as they were before, and turning, I saw the strange shape of another large object beneath a sheet, leaning against a wall. The form protruding from the sheet had an odd shape and removing the sheet I saw an old-time bicycle, a "high wheeler" they called it. The bike got its name from its huge front wheel; the seat used by the rider nearly came up to my shoulders, and the frame dropped back in a curve to a miniature wheel—a peculiar mode of transportation by today's standards, it really belonged in a museum.

Further surveying caused me to give notice to an unusual bulge or outcrop in the masonry stone foundation, and I wondered the reason for this unusual protruding swell in the foundation's design. Picturing the layout of the house in my mind for locating the room over me, I tried to find myself on the first floor with regards to the geography of the house. I determined that above me was the living room and conjured the great bulge along this outside exterior wall to be the foundation for the huge fireplace, and I guess it had to be massive for supporting it.

Another oddity that took my interest was how four fat upright studs stood vertically in a square layout no more than a meter apart and anchored securely to the floor trusses above. They rested on a concrete pad slightly larger than their circumference, which appeared to be footing, and short boards nailed together near the bottom served as a means of tying them together. Viewing how these studs stood on end, I thought it obvious they were load bearing, and grasping how they aligned with the fireplace, I understood these studs provided added support for the headless statuette, for the sculpture must have weighed a ton.

I'd spent a lot of time in the nostalgic belly of the house, and hearing footsteps entering from the kitchen overhead gave indication that Maurice had returned with the cleaning lady, Katie Loughton.

I spoke first, shouting, "Hello, I'm down here."

Seconds later, I heard the squeaking cellar door open and the sweet sound of a woman's voice carried from the cellar entrance at the top of the stairs, "Hello, Miss MacKennsey, I'm Katie Loughton."

"I'll be up in a few minutes, Katie. That stupid cellar door closed on me when I came down here, and I couldn't get it open again."

"It seems to be working fine now," she said, closing and opening the door a few times to make sure it was working properly, then checking the door handle from the cellar side to be certain the latch operated from both sides. "If you don't mind, I'll come down," and her footsteps were heard as she started down, as she added, "I've seen every part of this house except for the cellar, and I just want to see if I've missed anything."

"Well, do us both a favor and make certain that door isn't going to close before you start down because I don't want to have to spend the rest of my life down here if it gets stuck again."

I have the door propped open as far as it will go, and I don't think it'll close."

She spoke with a slight accent, and when she came into view, I saw a stout, red-headed woman with a friendly face and well-rounded, plump cheekbones.

Glancing about, she smiled, "Well, it certainly looks like a cellar," and let out a short chuckle as she started towards me with her hand extended in greeting.

"I'm very pleased to make your acquaintance, Ms. MacKennsey."

"It's my pleasure. Please, just call me Claire; Ms. MacKennsey sounds far too formal."

"Are you treasure hunting?" she asked with brows raised.

"I guess I was, but I've finished, and now I need to recover all the things I've uncovered in my search."

"Well, here, if you're done, allow me to help you," and the two of us began rearranging the sheets to adequately cover the furnishings, but she almost immediately stopped.

"Oh, this dreadful dust," and she paused, making an unpleasant expression. "I have sinus problems and this dust may be the cause for me sneezing for a week. I can already sense my allergies flaring up, they're like cold symptoms, and I'll be miserable for days."

"Well, I can manage here, Katie. Why don't you go upstairs and I'll be up in a minute, then we can talk some more."

"Wait, I've got some paper facemasks upstairs under the sink that cover the nose and mouth which I've been saving for just this sort of an occasion. The dust may have the same effect on you as it does me, but you just don't know it yet, so I'll have them back here in a jiffy."

"Okay," I said, and while waiting I reminded myself that I wanted to bring up the magician's advertisement, and I also wanted to try the phonograph to see if it still worked.

When Katie returned, she wore a white facemask and handed me one. Putting it on, my voice sounded slightly muffled as I spoke into it, "We look as though we're getting ready to perform surgery."

She giggled and then we began carefully recovering those items I'd just uncovered, moving slowly but deliberately so not to disturb any more dust than we had to.

At one point, she stopped and reared back in surprise, "Oh, my, what a perfectly lovely lamp," she said, referring to the tall hurricane lamp resting in the arm chair.

Standing to the right of the chair the lamp rested in and Katie to the left of it, we spread open the sheet while preparing to cover them up and I said, "I was admiring the detail of its floral design, too."

She touched the petals on the lamp with her fingertips. "The flowers and their leaves, they look so life-like."

We proceeded to cover it up and then secured a sheet over what I thought was the last piece, the coat stand; and then I went to turn out the light at the rear of the cellar, where the coffin and bicycle were kept stored.

"A gramophone," she remarked, referring to the exposed phonograph resting upon a table.

Realizing I'd forgotten about the record player, I returned to her side, "Is that what it's called?"

"That's what we always called it. It's a phonograph, of course, and my grandmother had one like it when I was a little girl."

"I wanted to take it upstairs to try it out."

"If you like, I can carry it up for you," she said.

"No, I'll get it, it may be heavy." Then I had a thought, and lifting the paper sack that was the bundle holding the stack of records, I said, "You can take these records up for me if you like."

She nodded, opening out her arms to me, and I placed them in her grasp. I then moved to retrieve the cylindrical cardboard tube containing my grandfather's advertisement for his magic act.

"Here, I can manage that as well," said Katie, and she took hold of the cylinder.

"I appreciate your helping me, why don't you start up now and I'll be right behind you."

I picked up the gramophone, maneuvering it for carrying it up the stairs, using one hand to tug at the last loose sheet in arranging it to cover up the table the musical piece had rested upon. I managed to pull the cord for putting out the light, while Katie ascended the stairs first, waiting while holding the door open for me.

Making my way up the stairs with the bulky gramophone in my arms, there was only the natural light coming from the doorway at the entrance to the cellar at the top of the stairs. Once I joined her in the alcove, she closed the cellar door, leaving the area, once again, engulfed in darkness.

CHAPTER 12

AN ANGRY SPIRIT

When preparing to place the phonograph on the kitchen table, Katie was quick to say, "Claire, I need to put something on that table first, or Maurice is sure to throw a fit."

Holding the record player long enough for her to put the records aside and spread newspaper on the table, she then gave me a hand to let it settle on the table.

"He probably wouldn't say anything to you, miss, but I'm certain to catch all kinds of trouble if he saw that dusty thing on this table."

"Maurice is quite picky about certain things, isn't he," I asked.

"I'm sure he means well, and in some ways he's a gem, but there's times when he's worse than a nagging old woman."

We removed our face masks to look the phonograph over, and Katie asked, "Are you familiar with these old-time record players?"

"Not really."

Katie took hold of the large cone and swung it from right to left to show me how it swiveled, "This cone-shaped thing comes off," and she lifted and removed the piece, then went to the sink to clean it.

She put the cone-shaped piece in the sink, "It won't hurt to wipe this part down with a damp cloth, but you want to use care with the rest." She went to a closet to fetch a feather duster, and handed it to me, "It'll be almost a miracle if the thing still works, but you never know."

Finishing up with the feather duster by giving the bottom a once over, I then gave particular attention to the needle, picking it clean of foreign matter.

Katie dried off the cone-shaped piece, and commented, "I think I may have come across more of these old records somewhere in the house a short time ago. It seems I saw them in a second floor closet when I was cleaning, and when it comes to me where they are, I'll bring them down to you."

I moved out of the way, allowing her space to reattach the cone-shaped piece to the player, and she turned it until it was straight. "Perhaps we ought to take it to the library; I want to start preparing a nice dinner for you and Maurice."

"Okay," I said, intending to move the gramophone to the library, but I first removed the records from the dusty paper sack they'd been stored in to determine their condition. Examining their aging labels, I said, "I've never heard of any of these titles."

Katie disposed of the paper to begin wiping the records down with a dry dishtowel, and afterwards set them aside. "These records are heavy and rigid, not like the vinyl material they're usually made from."

Maurice came shuffling into the kitchen, leaving a bag of groceries on the counter, then he saw the old gramophone on the kitchen table, "What have we here?"

"I found this phonograph down in the cellar, I was going to take it into the library and try playing it."

Maurice motioned towards the phonograph, "Allow me to carry it in there for you."

Not wanting to get Maurice all stirred up, I let him carry the thing into the library. I walked ahead of him, moving quickly to rearrange a few objects on the desktop to make space for the phonograph, and he set it down.

Situating the phonograph and its cone so it would play out into the center of the room, he gazed at it, "I placed those records and this player down in the cellar years ago. After your grandfather's death and before your Aunt Irene came to live here, the house fell under a period of disorder. Given the uncertainty of the times, no one knew what was going to happen, and the servants dropped out of their regular routine. The help had the run of the house, and I was one of the youngest, so they hardly recognized me as a person of any authority. Anyway, one day a few of them began playing the phonograph, and when they were done with it they left it out and the records in disarray, I hastily bagged up the records and placed them and the player down in the cellar. I was deeply saddened over your grandfather's death, and I suppose that I, much like the others, feared losing my position here, but there was never a time I wasn't loyal to your family. I'm only mentioning it because seeing the old phonograph brings back the memory of those grim, dark days."

He then backed off from the desk, "I'll be outside tending to the garden if you need me for anything." Then Maurice left the library.

Katie soon brought the records in and setting them down beside the player, she said, "You know, miss, you'll have more space on that other table over there." She nodded in the direction of the spacious oblong reading table on the far side of the room that had nothing on it except a lamp with a stained glass shade. Then she added, "In the meanwhile, I'm going to get to my chores, and if I remember where I saw those other records, I'll bring them down for you."

"Are you sure you don't want to sit down and listen to a couple of songs from way back when?"

"I have too many chores to get on with, and then there's dinner that needs tending to, but I expect we'll have some time to chat later."

With that, Katie was off making her routine rounds, and I saw she was right in that I'd be far less cramped using the table on the other side of the room. I carried the phonograph over to the reading table that had two wooden chairs accompanying it, finding the table well suited for arranging the phonograph by comparison to the desk top. In my eagerness to see if I could get it to operate, I turned the crank numerous times, and when adjusting the mechanism that held the needle, to my surprise, the turntable began spinning.

Just as I turned to retrieve the records from the desk, a loud crash erupted against the bookshelves over my head! I ducked and blinked as it sounded like glass shattering, and as debris rained down, another startling crash came nearby. Raising my arms to cover my head from showering pieces that flew about, I winced, stooping down low to protect my head from scattering debris, and another exploding sound of glass breaking prompted me to cringe. Squinting while raising my elbow up to look under my arm for getting a look at what was happening; but another crashing, shattering sound burst just to my left, making me flinch and I firmly shut my eyelids.

My mind racing in panic, not only did I not know what these frightening clashing bursts were, but they kept reoccurring and I didn't know what to do to act in defense of it. I finally caught a glimpse of a dark object coming directly at my face from across the room; I shifted my right arm to block it, and it struck the bone in my forearm with a fierce blow before breaking into pieces! The excruciating pain made me grimace as I sank to the floor in an effort to dodge and avoid whatever it was that kept battering me!

Guarding my face with my arms and hands, I chanced a glimpse at what was attacking me and seeing something black sailing wildly off into a corner, I realized it must be the records! Lying on my side curled up in the fetal position on the floor as the only means of protecting myself, there was no way to avoid them; I took a hit in the leg and another to my hip, and even though they didn't deliver the wounding pain as the one that hit my arm, they still hurt.

Relentlessly pummeled by this barrage of pulverizing bursts, all I could do was remain close to the floor, and as another struck me in the shoulder, I kept my face guarded and my eyes closed. All the while praying for the terror to cease, when one struck me in the cheek of my butt, I wondered how much more of this I can endure, and it suddenly and abruptly stopped. I opened my eyes long enough to see fragmented pieces of records scattered about me on the floor, then raising my head cautiously while hoping that it had really ended; I saw no one else in the room, but there were hundreds of pieces of these black records all about me. I guessed there must have been nearly twenty records in that stack before they began flying across the room at me, and now I didn't even see one remaining on the desk where they'd flown from. It was as though someone kept flinging them forcefully at me, one after another—a vicious, mad attack that seemed never ending.

Bewildered, while stunned by this astonishing event, the underside of my right forearm hurt terribly, and when looking at the wound, it appeared as though the record that struck me nearly cut clear to the bone; there was already some slight bruising around the cut it had made. Having never before experienced such a phenomenally weird occurrence in my life, I rushed to the kitchen to clean and dress the wound, all the while wondering about what had just occurred; as much as I hated to think about the scary notion, it became apparent I'd just gone through a rattling paranormal experience. Not only did this house have a poltergeist, but this entity disliked me tremendously, and that made me fearful that there'd be more attacks in the future. As improbable as it was for me to believe, this seemed the only rational explanation for what just happened. I'd read about encounters of this sort and seen horror films depicting the supernatural, but this is the first time I'd ever experienced a downright frightful event of this kind.

I had no idea about what to do, no one would believe me if I told them of this incident, but it occurred to me that if I told Katie, she'd probably never come back to this house again. Thinking I preferred that she not know, I took a broom and dust pan from the kitchen then guardedly and watchfully returned to the library to sweep up all the shattered pieces from the records; and after bringing the fragments all together in a pile, I used the dustpan to place the debris in a trash bag. Placing the bag with garbage kept outside, I returned to the library and noticed a number of gashes and scars in books and in the wood shelving from the pelting records and this, to me, represented a raging anger. I kept asking myself if it was my grandmother's spirit that had gone on the rampage, attacking me, or was this poltergeist a new spirit. Fearful that Angela wanted to harm me, for I was certain it was her ghostly apparition I'd seen entering her bedroom, and it may be that she resents an outsider coming to her home and tampering with her belongings. If the phonograph and records belonged to Angela, then she apparently had strong ties to these objects; and besides, Angela had a motive for being a restless spirit here, as she was the one suspected of being an axe murderer. As much as I didn't want to accept this, there weren't many other considerations to explain it.

Keeping my wits about me and my awareness peaked, I felt certain now more than ever that there'd be a test of wills, and I wasn't quite sure how to deal with this situation. I was facing off with an invisible and intimidating spirit with strong intentions about having her own way, and she was obviously bent on making it known that my presence here didn't sit well with her. The fact that I had drawn the attention of a paranormal entity made me feel terribly uncomfortable, and she had the upper hand because I had no idea when she might strike again. Downright fearful of what she might do if I stayed here much longer, I didn't like being the focus of this rage, and what worried me most was that she had the ability to move objects. What's going to happen the next time she tries to harm me, am I going to have to be on my guard every minute of the day from flying objects?

Afraid and a nervous wreck too, it broke my concentration when Katie appeared at the entrance to the library wiping her hands with a towel, having no idea that she'd startled me. "I've finished most of the day's duties, Claire, and I wanted to ask you if you'd like to join me for a cup of tea?"

"Sure," I said, casually turning my body to keep her from seeing my bandaged arm.

"Oh, and one more thing, give me just a second," and she momentarily disappeared from view, returning seconds later with a narrow square box which she placed flat on the desk. "Here are those other records I wanted to give to you."

Thinking this was the last thing I needed to see, through the open side of this plain cardboard box I saw what looked like at least six of the same type of records lying inside it. Halfway expecting a mad scene to erupt like before, I stood there with a gawking stare, looking at Katie with what must have been a dumbfounded expression.

"Are you okay, Claire, you look awfully pale, dear?"

"No, I'm fine, I'll be right there."

"Did the phonograph play for you?"

Still afraid of the upheaval and heart-pounding madness repeating itself, I kept glancing at the box containing the records; and feeling awkward about how to respond to the question, I finally managed a smile, "I haven't been able to get it to play."

"Oh, that's a shame, but tea is ready whenever you are," and she went back to the kitchen.

My eyes darting at the box holding records Katie had just placed upon the desk, I'd yet to feel threatened by them, and I moved toward the door staring at it until I'd exited the library. I quickly moved across the corridor to the living room and took the main staircase to the second floor, going to my room to change into a long sleeve blouse for hiding my injury. I used the servant's staircase to return to the first floor and joined Katie in the kitchen, taking a chair at the table while she brought over the pot of tea and a pair of cups.

She poured the tea, "One spoonful of sugar, or two?"

"Just one."

After stirring, she placed a cup before me, "I've always considered it sort of a privilege to work in such a splendid home."

"Unique architecture isn't it," I commented, pulling the cup nearer to me, and then gently caressing my injured arm to ease the painful throb I'd acquired. Just before having my first taste of her tea, I held the cup close to my lips, asking, "Do you have a family, Katie?"

"Yes, I have my husband and three daughters. My husband used to be a coal miner, but he injured his back in a fall while working, and now he's disabled."

After sipping from the rim of my cup, I asked, "What ages are your daughters?"

"Margaret, twenty-nine, Elizabeth, twenty-six, and Jennifer, nineteen."

"Are any of them married?"

"Margaret is divorced; she has two children of her own. Elizabeth is married to a carpenter named Patrick, and they have three children. Jennifer has been seeing a young man, but I haven't heard any talk of marriage, although she's young yet."

She held her teacup with two hands when adding, "Patrick has his own business, but lately there's hardly enough work to keep him going. He's very talented though, and he used to employ three men, but I expect that he'll soon get back on his feet financially."

The more I heard, the more I realized that her family had fallen on hard times, and I wanted to help out without making it sound like charity.

"Katie, ever since I've come up from the cellar, I've been thinking about that old furniture cluttering up the cellar. Most of it is in fair condition, and if you can make some use of it, you're welcome to it."

"Now, Miss, I haven't been telling you my family's problems in order to get you to give me anything. I was merely makin' conversation, and we're doing just fine."

"I know, but that furniture is just taking up space down there, and if somebody doesn't make some use of those tables and chairs they'll one day be no good to anybody."

Believing I was making a point, I added, "You've been coming and caring for this old house a long time, and I'd like you to have them.... Doesn't this son-in-law of yours, Patrick, own a truck?"

"Well, yes."

"Sometime in the next couple of weeks when it's convenient for you and Patrick, I want you both to come to the house and I'll pitch in giving him a hand loading up his truck... If you don't come and get that furniture it's certain to waste away down in that cellar."

"I'll talk to Patrick, and if he's interested in coming to get them, I'll let you know. I'm grateful for the gesture just the same."

Thinking she may have knowledge of the past after coming here and spending so much time in the house, I asked, "Do you know anything about the history of this house?"

"Not very much, some time ago I had an opportunity to talk with an elderly neighbor who spoke about a gruesome murder which occurred here many years ago. I believe he said someone had beheaded the victim in his sleep, and I have to admit I was a bit intrigued when hearing about it, but when I asked Maurice, he'd neither confirm nor deny it. Forgive me for asking, but is it true?"

"Yes, my grandfather was killed in this house. However, because it happened so long ago, I'm having difficulty learning about circumstances surrounding his death."

"How awful, and it's odd that Maurice has never made mention of it, but he may know very little about what had happened. I don't know if I'd want to stay in a house where a murder occurred, not that I want to make you feel uncomfortable about staying here, just that it seems rather ghoulish."

Fidgeting with the teacup while the injury to my arm throbbed all the more, I kept thinking about what transpired in the library and how I'd undergone an attack by those airborne records. Here I had an opportunity to talk with someone who's spent years coming to this house, and I felt the urge to ask if she'd had any extraordinary experiences during her time coming here. I casually placed the rim of the teacup to my lips and asked, "I don't mean to change the subject, but in all your years here, have you experienced anything out of the ordinary?"

Katie paused while looking down at the table and sensing something had occurred caused me to remark, "Something did happen, didn't it?"

She gave a mild shrug as if not wanting to discuss it, but then she opened up and said, "It must have been two years ago, in the late month of November. In those days, I'd occasionally come twice a week and back then my husband John would pick me up in the evenings. He had little patience waiting for me, and I was in a hurry to get things put away so I'd be ready for him when he came. I remember Maurice was overdue for returning from some errand, and like I was saying, I was in the midst of tidying up when I looked out the window to see if my John had arrived. At that moment I saw a man wearing a black hood over his face with holes for the eyes, and I tell you, it frightened the bloody hell out of me."

"A man wearing a black hood," my eyes wavered as I considered the fear she must've felt.

Katie inched forward in her chair to tell more, "I locked myself in the bathroom until the men returned, and when I told Maurice what I'd seen, he looked at me as though I'd lost my screws. Said I'd never return to this place to work again, but one day he came to see me at my home, promising me a small raise and to cut my hours too. I did, however, make it clear that I'd have to be out of here before sundown, and he also agreed to pick me up and drop me off from then on, which John appreciated."

She looked me in the eye, adding, "To this day, I can't look out that window without expecting to see that black hood and those glaring eyes staring at me."

Stunned about this story of a hooded man, I thought maybe it had been Maurice at the window, but that made no sense whatsoever. Why would he want to scare her, then turn around and give her incentive to come back to this house to work? The story also caused me to recall my first night here, when I heard the noise that woke me in the middle of the night, catching a glimpse of the hall light on and a blurred dark image just before the lights went out. It gave me an ominous sensation to think this may have been the same person Katie saw at the window.

"Do you think this man wearing the hood was a burglar?" I asked, in a soft spoken manner.

"Why, I imagine he was, why else would he have been wearing that hood—he looked very sinister with those piercing eyes, as if thinking something terribly wicked. Yes indeed, he may have been some type of psycho for all I know—the world's full of 'em, and just the thought of seeing him gives me chills."

This tale of a hooded man stayed with me the remainder of the day, and it bothered me to think that a hooded figure may be prowling about the premises. Here I hadn't gotten over the incident of a rampaging poltergeist throwing records at me, and now I had this hooded prowler to contend with. Though the story of the hooded man happened two years ago, it certainly shook me up and worried me, raising concern about my safety. Staying in this house alone made me an easy target for such a shadowy figure and more than ever, I felt uneasy about spending the night here alone. The idea of confronting a masked intruder in the middle of the night conjured up terrible happenings in my mind, for Maurice wouldn't hear my screams, and even if he did, what could he do?

If the figure I'd glimpsed in the hallway that first night wasn't Maurice, then it could've been this hooded man Katie described to me, but who was he? I didn't believe this was a ghost or a spirit at my bedroom door that night, for I presumed it was a man of flesh and bone, and this individual must have entered the house by some means. If he had a key, how did he acquire it? I hated addressing these questions, but they remained relentlessly persistent in my thoughts, probably because I believed it was only a matter of time before I'd stumble into him. It was bad enough staying alone in this house without imagining life threatening situations and conjuring up thoughts of me falling into a dangerous predicament that would leave me vulnerable.

I felt I'd made the right decision about not saying anything to Katie about my experiences with the paranormal because I felt certain that she'd never return to this old house once she'd heard that a ghost resides here. After all, she'd not only seen a hooded man at the window but she also had knowledge of a gruesome murder that had occurred here. She had good reason not to want to be in this house after dark, and if we lost her over fear of witnessing a ghostly presence, then I'm sure Maurice would have a terrible time replacing her. There weren't many people who'd want to drive all the way out here to this isolated house for a meager-paying job.

The incident in the library placed strain on me for staying on here at Strathmoor Heights. It got the better of me in that it left me edgy for a few days, making me feel insecure about sleeping in this old mansion, and in my growing apprehension, I dreaded the coming of nightfall. I'd been depending on Maurice to lock up the house at night, but I started checking the outside doors before turning in to make certain the locks were in a secure position. For a time, these wild and unpredictable situations were affecting my sleep, as unseen phantoms began stalking me in my dreams, and I felt as though staying in this house was wearing me down.

CHAPTER 13

A TRIP TO THE ASYLUM

A few days later, still tense and jittery after my experience with the phonograph records, and holding concern for Katie's story of a hooded prowler, I sought a change in plans; I felt I needed a diversion to take my thoughts and worries from occurrences in this house. Thinking I wasn't going to sleep well for some time to come, I believed only by taking more drastic measures could I expect to learn more about the circumstances surrounding my grandfather's death; and I decided to go to the institution where the authorities had sent Angela so many years ago. My thoughts were to go there in hopes that there'd be some documentation or records relevant to the cause for her murdering her husband. If nothing else, they may be able to tell me something about the seriousness of her illness and if it could possibly be passed on through heredity.

The phonograph was on the table in the library where I'd left it and the box of records still on the desk; I had no incentive whatsoever to play those records any time soon, mostly because I felt fearful of the consequences in trying to play the old-time record player. I was afraid there may be a similar replay to the first incident or possibly something even worse, and having difficulty understanding what set off such a violent display, I thought it best not to push my luck. I fully intended to make another attempt at playing the phonograph another time, some other day, but for now, I'd had all I can bear. Pushing myself into becoming a nervous wreck, it occurred to me that experiencing one more crazy thing may be enough to send me over the edge. I needed time to regain my stamina and composure before even touching those records, and I plain and simply had to get away from this house, even if it was just for a day, or even for only a few hours.

For all I'd learned while staying here, I was no closer to learning what triggered the event that ended my grandfather's life. The information I gained thus far had really done no more than to raise further speculation, and this wasn't the least bit helpful. I understood Angela had a bruised face the night of the murder, but there was no way of knowing how or when she acquired this bruise; nor did this prove that my grandfather actually struck her, but if he did, then why? The police thought he'd learned she had a lover, but this was something they'd surmised, and while I uncovered no evidence to substantiate that, I didn't want to spend time concentrating on ideas that merely served to fuel even more supposition. Even if she did have a lover, and their marriage was falling apart, that didn't help explain what happened here—that's no motive for murdering someone in their sleep. It all kept pointing to the fact that my grandmother had a deranged mind and that she'd lost touch with reality, and now I was intending to find out more about the condition of her mind by going to this institution. This was my main purpose for coming to Wales in the first place.

At breakfast, I approached Maurice, "Maurice, do you know the name of the institution where they had my grandmother put away?"

Maurice continued setting the table, his mind in thought as he said, "She was put away in an asylum, but I don't recall hearing much about her after they sent her away. Your Aunt Irene once mentioned that she'd died, but never said anything about the circumstances."

"Okay, but can you recall the name of the institution where she'd been taken to?"

"The name of the place where they sent your grandmother," Maurice pondered the question while pouring me a glass of orange juice, and then he took a kettle and poured himself a cup of black coffee.

He sat down with me before clasping his hands around his coffee cup, and then he took a sip while going into deep thought.

129

"Angela had been sent to the Brookridge Sanitarium located on the outskirts of a city called Swansea, near the southern edge of the country."

"I'm going to go there." I said, waiting to see a response from Maurice.

"Well, miss, I think I can make a few calls and get some information that might be helpful to you in finding it, there's a bus that goes regularly from Cardigan to Swansea. We'll have to find out its schedule, and I can drive you to Cardigan so you can catch the bus there. Considering how long it's been, do you think they'll be much help in telling you anything useful?"

"I don't know, but it's important to me to find out why my grandmother murdered my grandfather in his sleep. I'm counting on someone there to produce records of her medical history that might give some insight into her frame of mind at the time of her incarceration."

"I can understand a person's curiosity, especially given the circumstances, and I hope they can provide information helpful to you. The sooner you put that tragedy behind you and move on with your life, the better off you'll be, because nothing can change what happened."

As soon as we finished with breakfast, Maurice returned to the carriage house to make inquiries by phone for arranging my travel to Swansea for visiting Brookridge Sanitarium.

The following day, we got an early start, Maurice drove me to Cardigan where I caught a bus to Swansea, and I expected the trip to take about three hours. From the bus depot, I took a cab to the institution where I saw a fairly modern building nestled in a clump of trees far back from the road. The ground around the hospital had a peaceful setting, but the structure itself seemed quite cold in appearance, and I wondered how many have come this way, knowing this to be their final retreat in life.

Tipping the driver, I asked him to wait, but before entering the institution, I saw the cornerstone near the main entrance and the inscription etched in it read, 'erected in 1955'. I then went back to the driver, "I was expecting the building to be much older, making me wonder if there may be another hospital with the same name?"

The driver shrugged, "This is the only Brookridge Sanitarium I know of in the area, miss."

I went ahead and entered the building with the impression that I must be at the wrong place. This hospital was far too new and modern to be in existence from the time of my grandmother's incarceration. Through a set of glass doors and into a spacious lobby, I approached a counter where a thin black-haired nurse with a pale complexion sat. She wore a typical white nurse's uniform with a cap and she remained seated while turning her attention to me.

"Yes, may I help you?" she asked, keeping the same plain, unenthusiastic expression.

"My name is Claire MacKennsey and I had a relative who came here for treatment some years ago. I was wondering if there'd be someone who I could consult with about the illness she suffered from."

"Do you know the name of the doctor who last treated her?"

"No. This happened a long time ago, the woman was my grandmother."

"What's the patient's name?"

"Angela MacKennsey. I am Claire MacKennsey."

"If you don't mind waiting, I'll have the head nurse come to the desk, and she may be able to help you." The nurse then spoke into an intercom, saying, "Mrs. Linden, please come to the desk."

I stood waiting for a few minutes, giving study to a modern art sketch hanging on the wall until an older, pudgy-faced, stocky-built nurse appeared from behind the counter, and she made eye contact with me.

"Mrs. Linden," began the nurse at the desk, "this lady's name is MacKennsey, and she was inquiring into her grandmother's illness."

"Do you know the name of the doctor treating your grandmother?"

"Actually, no, but it may have been as far back as sixty years ago when she was admitted for treatment, and I'm not even sure if I've come to the right place. Is this the only Brookridge Sanitarium?"

"I see," said the head nurse, "there was another Brookridge Hospital located down the road from here, and I'm afraid it burned to the ground in the late forties. The fire occurred late at night, taking the staff by surprise, and there weren't many patients who survived. However, even if that hospital were still standing, it's hardly likely they'd be able to recover records on a patient who received care that long ago."

I nodded, "I knew it was a long shot, but thanks just the same."

Exiting from the hospital, I knew I'd made every effort to learn the cause of my grandmother's illness, leaving no stone unturned, and there seemed little chance of knowing her frame of mind at the time of the murder.

I felt downhearted when taking the cab back to the bus depot in Swansea, and having learned their schedule for knowing the time I'd be returning to Cardigan, I phoned Maurice to see that he'd be there to meet me. During the bus trip, I felt solemn, for I really believed there to be an explanation for what went on in that house the night my grandfather died. Still determined to uncover facts for finding out what caused this murder to take place, I believed there had to be answers as to why it happened; there must be, and I knew deep down inside that there was something inside that house that could shed light on why it happened. I hadn't completely lost that ambition and drive that urged me on from the beginning, and I wanted to continue the search; but I felt so lost in how to carry on in this endeavor.

From what I'd learned from Maurice, my grandmother showed no outward signs of mental illness, but a person doesn't just decide to decapitate someone on the spur of the moment. There are few people in the whole world capable of committing such a brutal killing; humans don't do something so monstrous on impulse unless they've been going mad for a long while. However, the only person who can give testimony for this being the case has told me there were no indications she was going out of her mind, but was it possible she could've been going insane over a long period of time without anyone seeing through it. It seemed unlikely she'd be in a mental struggle with her thoughts for a long time without showing outward signs, and it's also possible Angela didn't perceive her mental behavior was changing. Most who suffer from Alzheimer's disease aren't aware of it, and I would think that most individuals with a serious mental problem who are losing their connection with reality aren't aware of it as well. Their not likely to express their engaged in outlandish fantasies in which they can't make the distinction of what is real and what is deceptively delusive.

Maurice isn't a psychiatrist and if he wasn't around to observe my grandmother's abnormal or irrational behavior, why should he have suspected that she had a mental problem prior to the night of the murder. If my grandmother had been going out of her mind, she must've demonstrated strange behavior for a long while, and I was certain that there had to be more to the story. My family surely would've tried to keep her condition from help working in the house because they didn't want to start gossip. There must have been other servants who may have seen something or who knew about the illness the lady of the house suffered from, but wisely chose not to share what they'd both seen and heard. If a woman's state of mind was faltering whereby she required constant care and looking after, more than likely another female would be best suited for the position of being her guardian; they would've entrusted her care to a maid, or seamstress who'd been with the family for a good many years. This may have meant that when my grandmother wasn't herself, either this guardian or a family member would escort her off to a place where others couldn't observe her odd behavior.

Thinking Maurice must've been a young man at the time this murder occurred, he probably didn't know quite as much about the family or my grandmother's mental condition as he thought he did. Even though he knew her to be depressed and that she drank at times, he didn't understand the seriousness of her mental frame of mind. When caught up in despair and depression, where were her thoughts during those periods when she went off by herself, was she caught up in delusions? The one question that kept cropping up in my mind was what happened to the head of the deceased—what kind of a crazed maniac would take the head and for what purpose?

Because it occurred so long ago, I had little expectations in anything new developing for learning more about the circumstances surrounding the murder. I didn't have any confidence in newspapers because no local newspaper from that era was still in publication. At the time of his death, my grandfather had long since lost any notoriety or fame he'd gained as a magician, so except for the gruesome method in which his life had been taken, the story wouldn't have made for a great deal of publicity. Even if a newspaper in London had carried the story, not only would it be difficult to run down, but how reliable could it be in giving me information I didn't already know? I had to consider the possibility that a newspaperman could've sensationalized or embellished the story to increase circulation, and even if they only printed the facts, what would they tell me over what I already knew.

On the ride back to Cardigan, although I'd accomplished nothing, I tried to relax on the bus trip back by taking in the scenic beauty and picturesque countryside of this land I visited. Feeling pressures driving me away from what I'd set out to do here, for all I'd strived for, I wasn't any closer to learning what happened than when I first arrived in Wales. I wasn't ready to give into these annoying frustrations, but clung to the hope that something of significance about this grim murder will turn up. I knew I was letting matters I had no control over agitate and aggravate me, and I wanted to quell the inner anger I felt before I saw Maurice because I didn't want to snap at him. For the moment, he was the best friend I had in the world, and as far as I knew, he was being honest with me. I simply had to remain focused on finding answers, and hold to the goals that brought me here.

CHAPTER 14

STRIKING A NERVE

Maurice picked me up at the bus station, and after I told him I'd learned nothing from the people at the sanitarium, he and I hardly spoke a word on the drive home.

Upon our arrival at Strathmoor Heights, Maurice stopped the car in the courtyard behind the house to let me out, saying, "I'll be in just as soon I've parked the car, miss. I prepared some sandwiches for you on a dish covered by a plastic wrap in the refrigerator."

I used the key Maurice had given me to let myself in the house and placed my purse on the kitchen table. Accomplishing nothing on this trip left me drained, and not wanting the day to end this way, I sought something to give me a lift. I'd hardly eaten anything all day, which drew me to the refrigerator to partake in the sandwiches Maurice had prepared and the spread of tuna fish and mayonnaise tasted good. I had a glass of milk, and not feeling much like sitting still, I began pacing the floor.

Taking another bite of the sandwich, I continued to chew while I walked through the dining room to the entry hall to look in the library. Gazing into the darkness, it wasn't so much that I wanted to test fate by going in there, but I couldn't help flirting with the temptation to do so. The culmination of many things driving me to think about the records and phonograph, I felt teased by the tantalizing thought to attempt playing the phonograph again. The only thing that made me reluctant was that I feared doing so could involuntarily cause a violent ruckus that would throw the house into turmoil. Day would soon be turning into night, and I was in no mood for a nerve-racking disruption that would keep me up all night.

I went back to the kitchen to indulge in eating a second sandwich, guzzling down more milk while doing so, but kept thinking about the phonograph and records. I went back to the library, and this time turned on the light so I could view the room. I observed the phonograph resting on the table across the room and the box holding the records were still on the desk where Katie had left them. Feeling a strong desire to try playing the phonograph again, and yet fearful of the consequences, the fear outweighed the urge, so I exited the room and turned out the light when walking away.

Having not gone far from the door to the library, I turned back and switched the light back on again, for the deliberation wasn't over just yet. Taking a deep breath, the thought of going into that room for the purpose of touching those records amounted to playing with fire. I dreaded the prospect of trying to play that phonograph, but there was a stubborn part of me that was set on pressing the issue, and I went back to the kitchen to have another bite to eat. I either consciously or unconsciously left the light on in the library, as though influencing me to have to return to that room, giving me reason to fight with the idea of playing that darn phonograph. This was not a conflict that I necessarily wanted to win, but I just couldn't leave it alone.

I sat down at the kitchen table and munched on that sandwich, taking another drink of milk, and then I just sat there in a poised, fixed position. Getting up from the table and returning to the library once again, this time going to the desk and pulling the records out of the box so I could view their labels one at a time. The first bundle of records I'd discovered with the phonograph down in the cellar were loosely wrapped in paper and stacked one on top of another, but the records in this batch were still in the original plain paper glove they came in when new. The paper protection had yellowed and discolored from age, and even though the labels were viewable, I did not recognize any of their titles; one of the records I noticed was a reddish color instead of the ordinary black color as you'd find most records to be, and I thought this unusual. Having gone this far and feeling drawn into playing a record, I moved over to the table where the phonograph was situated and sat the records down next to it.

Intent on playing the first record readily available, I inserted it onto the phonograph player, and then cranked the lever. Watching the record revolving on the turntable, I next took hold of the arm holding the needle and carefully placed it on the beginning of the record. A scratchy sound immediately became audible as the music came out of the cone-shaped piece with a fair amount of clarity; and it sounded like music from a concert or an opera. The music had a kind of sound quality as though coming from a tunnel and after listening to it for a short time, I tried another, and it sounded like classical music to me as well. The music was a softly and beautifully played arrangement as a string of violins accompanied a piano to share in the melody and composition. I could understand why a person of an older generation would like the tune because I even found it to be somewhat pleasing to listen to.

At this point, I didn't feel much danger by playing another, and I thought I'd play the one that had a reddish look to it. Taking a second to examine the printing on the label, I found reading it to be difficult, but it looked like the faded title read, "Ma Blushin' Rosie." Exchanging the red one for the last record, I'd sensed the phonograph slowing near the end of the last song heard, so I cranked the lever a number of times before setting the needle in place, and the record began to play. The song sounded a little more bouncy and upbeat than the others, strummin' banjos started things off, and then a male vocalist boisterously chimed in,

Ro-sie, you are my po-sie.
You are my heart's bouq-uet.
Come-out here in the moon-light,
There's something sweet, love, I wanna sa-a-ay.
Your hon-ey boy is waiting,
Those ruby lips to greet.
Don't be so captivated,
My blushin' Ro-sie, my po-sie swe-e-e-et.

The song sounded kind of corny and, of course, romantically old fashioned, but I suppose I wasn't being fair to it or to those who'd listened to it and appreciated it because music has changed so drastically over the decades. This was most likely a jumping, swinging tune in its day and when taking this into consideration, I could understand how the people of that era could be fond of the liveliness it had. After all, this was probably before Bing Crosby's time, and I imagine whoever the singer was must have been a real crooner.

Suddenly, a woman's startling gasping moan blew threw the house—a loud, dull moaning or sorrowful groan that had depth in how it filled the house, leaving me with a bone-chilling sensation that made my blood curdle and my skin crawl! As chills ran all over my body, I wondered what retaliation or repercussions I'd now have to face. I pulled the needle off the record, pausing to listen in an attempt to identify what I'd heard, but there was only silence.

If I was sure of anything, it was that it certainly struck a nerve, and certain the gasping I'd heard was from Angela's spirit, I wondered what it was about that particular song that set her off. Walking from the library across the entrance hall into the living room, I looked up at the second-floor balcony to where I sensed the sound had come from. Rolling my shoulders to throw off the chilling effect the gasping groan had given me; goose bumps were still running up my spine. Here I thought I might've accomplished something by forcing myself to play the stupid phonograph, and now that I'd done it, I didn't know what to think or expect. Had I overstepped my place by playing that old song?

In my pondering, I came to the conclusion that maybe hearing the song, 'Ma Blushin' Rosie', may have triggered the hurtful gasp. I theorized that the song might be a memorable favorite of my grandparents and a reminder of the past for Angela. Unable to arrive at any other explanation for the time being, I tried not to dwell on the experience and went back to the phonograph to put the records away. Placing the records back in the box, I stopped to stare at the old gramophone while thinking about that unnerving gasp, believing that what I'd done had disturbed her, but apparently, it had not enraged her. Still wondering if she'd come after me with a vengeance, bombarding me with objects; but it was more so as if playing these records moved her than shook her up, as though the music touched her in a way that made a sentimental connection.

The incident continued to give me the heebie-jeebies, and standing there, I could still clearly hear that gasping moan in my mind, and I played the eerie sound back in my head. Suddenly sensing a presence in the room, out of my peripheral vision I caught sight of a dark figure closing in! I abruptly turned to see Maurice standing there.

"Oh! Oh, Maurice, you frightened the life out of me," and scoffing at the fear that had overtaken me, I placed my left hand over my chest as though expecting my heart to burst. I leaned against the table which held the phonograph, drawing a breath of air as I regained my composure.

I'd apparently startled Maurice, too, and he was momentarily at a loss for words.

"I didn't mean to scare you, miss."

"I know, but you did, just the same."

"I just wanted to let you know that I'm turning in for the night and to ask if there was anything you needed before I locked the place up."

"No, that will be all for today, Maurice."

It wasn't my intention to be short with Maurice, but his unexpected approach had done little to improve my mood, and after he'd gone away, I heard him turn the latch on the back door. Still trying to calm myself, I took a deep breath of air and then exhaled, and as much as that loud gasp had upset me, I don't think it scared me half as much as Maurice had.

I had this uncanny feeling that by playing these old records I'd awakened something in Angela, as though hearing them rekindled some deep-rooted feelings that remained within her. Still edgy and unsettled, I was in no hurry to go upstairs, so I cleaned up the little mess I'd made in the kitchen before returning to the living room, and still hesitant about going upstairs, I relaxed on the couch, and soon dosed off to float in a dream world....

Some of the oddest noises and strangest sounds aroused me as surrounding activity brought me around to where I heard voices in the trade-off of casual conversation and occasional laughter. A weird consciousness came over me, and opening my eyes before rising to an upright position, I discovered I wasn't alone. The house was alive and abuzz with people as a group gathered, and at first, I didn't even know where I was until realizing I still occupied the couch in the living room. Sitting up, I felt like a sleepy child who'd awakened at a party in the midst of adults whom I didn't know. Although I felt like an outsider, they didn't give me the impression that it mattered, and it seemed as if I was a just another guest. Even though they were complete strangers, they greeted me with cheerful smiles or a friendly hello to make me feel welcome. One elderly woman, well-dressed and with a perky expression, gave me a bright-eyed look with a smirking smile as if pleased to see me and possibly knowing I may be somehow connected to the cause for this event.

I remained on the sofa viewing these people in well-tailored evening clothes, assuming I accompanied them at some sort of dinner party. The room had this gay, happy atmosphere as the guests continued to mingle and engage in lively conversation. Most of the women wore dressy evening gowns, their hair all done up, and they wore necklaces and other forms of jewelry; many of them sipping champagne while conversing. The men were also dressed up, wearing conservative dark suits. I even saw one tall gentleman in a dress suit with tails giving a woman a story about a hunting trip he'd had in Africa, and really piling it on thick when describing how he took aim and shot to kill a charging lion. Some of the males drank champagne too, but a good many of them had tall, slender V-shaped beer glasses, or steins foaming with the brew.

Suddenly I heard the keys on the piano hit a familiar jingle and everyone turned their attention to the pianist, indicating they wanted to join in the fun. Just then, I realized that the individual playing could be no one other than my grandfather, and I saw him across the room at the keyboard with his back turned to me. There were already a good number of people gathered about the huge instrument, watching him and taking in the fun.

One attractive and alluring brunette in a low-cut glittering dress adorned with a knockout diamond necklace leaned on the piano across from him. Her ravishing full-bodied dark hair was worn back to allow her face to show, and her gorgeous eyes had depth and beauty; she beamed with a dazzling smile. Her plump, full red lips helped give her an amorous expression when playfully making goo-goo eyes at my grandfather, and I watched her straightening up to raise her glass in time with the music.

"Bill Bailey," she declared aloud, responding to the musical tune when recognizing it.

The prospect of sharing a moment with my grandfather moved me off the sofa, and I made slow progress drifting though the crowd for coming to his side, but unlike the others, I felt an urgency to reach him. Nothing in the world seemed more important than for me to see my grandfather up close, and as everyone was enjoying themselves, I fell in line with all the others while he played the lively musical notes so well. The crowd kept stalling, as if we were moving in slow motion, and it fast became a serious issue with me to get through. A young servant carrying a tray of glasses brimming with champagne asked to be pardoned when passing me by, and at a glance, I thought he could've been Maurice.

The flirtatious, beautiful woman so happily keeping my grandfather company at the piano began to bob and rock her shoulders up and down in holding to the beat and rhythm of the song. Everyone joined in singing, and I could see him, getting just a tantalizing glimpse of his face as he had a lively bounce in the piano seat, singing with the others,

Won't you come home, Bill Bailey, won't you come home.
I've moaned the whole night lo-ong.
I'll do the cookin', honey, I'll pay the rent.
I know I've done you wro-ong
Remember that rainy evenin',
I threw you out....with nothin' but a fine tooth comb?
Ya know I'm to blame, now ain't it a shame.
Bill Bailey, won't you please come ho-ome.

No matter how hard I tried, I was unable to get around the persons ahead of me to get in plain sight of him; and as more people converged to move in front of me, it seemed improbable that I'd ever get to be in my grandfather's company. I stopped and stood in the background for merely a second before deciding to start pushing and shoving my way through the crowd in a desperate effort to get closer to him. As I started to make headway, the music began dying down and voices singing the second verse of the song were fading out; I knew that if I didn't get through soon, I'd be losing the greatest of opportunities.

It became of the utmost importance to get through to see my grandfather; and then I had a moving thought about the delightfully charming and captivating woman taking a fancy to my grandfather, playing up to him in a flattering, flirting sort of way at the piano, she had to be my grandmother! She looked so happy, and cherishing the thought as if expecting that I really, truly had a chance to talk to both my grandparents and communicate with them, I wanted so much to tell Angela that I'm her granddaughter and that I wished her no harm.

Giving a final hard shove to break through the line of people, I stumbled forward and found the grand piano unoccupied; the room fell into complete silence as the area about me quickly grew dark and dim. Losing this one chance to meet them gave me crushing disappointment; the moment was gone forever, and I'd have given anything to turn back to that gloriously joyful time they shared. Everyone was having such a delightfully wonderful time, but now having fallen into shadows while standing beside the piano stool, I realized the darkness surrounding me didn't mean good things but bad. Having lost that one opportunity to talk to Angela meant that she may still want to harm me, and I felt warned of the impending danger in being here in this house alone. Fearful of what she might do, I sensed her presence, and I looked up at the second-floor balcony to see if she might be standing there staring me down, but all I saw was an ominous creeping mist coming through the spindles and falling down around me.

The creepy crawling mist hung about waist high off the floor, like a fog overtaking the house. I didn't know what to do at first, but something kept urging me to face up to whatever it was, even if it were her spirit. I walked toward the stairs at a slow pace, looking at what lay ahead, and at times glancing upward to see what may be waiting for me up above on the second floor. The fog kept getting thicker, and it moved with me and about me in a swirling motion, as if inviting me and daring me to go up the stairs. I stared warily up the staircase to the crest where dim light allowed me to view the ghostly fog slipping silently downward and toward me, like a foggy mist oozing from the edge of the second floor as if it were water running over in a slow but constant pace. I kept ascending the stairs, turning my head to glance the lone halberd axe on the wall, its threatening wide-angled blade crying to get used. Upon coming to the top of the stairs, I felt reluctant to venture further, sensing whatever force or presence in the house pulling me. I knew that if I didn't stop now, I'd never be able to, and the idea that I may be on the threshold of meeting something evil and harmful to me kept holding me back, but I knew I must face it; I had to—just like the chance I'd lost to speak to my grandparents, if I stopped now, this opportunity could be lost forever too.

Managing to rally the nerve to free myself from the tugging fears, I started down the long hallway, my motion in the smooth flowing mist helped to bring on the appearance of a steady stream of water at my feet. I knew that before long I'd see its imperceptible source and find out what made this house tick. Soon I found I'd regretfully transported myself to the door to my grandfather's bedroom, the one room in the house I hadn't the courage to enter until now, but I still couldn't force myself to open the door to enter it. Standing there facing the door, the fog appeared to be seeping from the door to his room, permeating from the very pores of the wood; it swelled, creaked, and splintered as if the room were a steaming pressure cooker—whatever unknown power that dwelled behind it was fighting to get out!

The door jam started to falter and loosen, and the wall's cracking plaster weakened while moving as it shifted from the pressure pushing outward, and believing the door was on the verge of giving way; I frantically braced my back against it. I could feel the door breathing as it puffed and expelled more steam, surging while pressing against me with ever-increasing strength, but I kept feverishly pushing back. In my futile resistance to restrain and repulse whatever it was that wanted out, I felt like the little Dutch boy with his finger pressing against the dike, as though at any second all hell was going to break loose!

Unable to contain this power much longer, now the house itself began to shake and quake, and terror struck, I started running full out to escape its fury! The door, walls, and everything fell with a thunderous crash, and sensing a roaring fearsome force chasing after me, nipping at my heels as it approached my back, I couldn't run fast enough, and it began to devour me!

I suddenly woke up breathless, as though I'd been running, and holding my hand over my chest, I sat up with the silent cloak of night hanging over the house. I found myself on the sofa in the living room where I'd rested hours ago, but now it was in the early morning hours—in the dead of night.

What a crazy dream, I thought to myself, still holding my hand over my chest, feeling my heart pumping hard.

I got a grip to quell my fears, my heartbeat finally slowed down, and I looked about the living room, surveying my surroundings with the quiet stillness of the night as my only companion. Taking a long deep breath to further calm myself, I didn't know what time it was, and I really didn't care; I just knew I had to stop allowing this house to get the best of me and go to bed. I still had on the dress shoes I'd worn earlier, and they were starting to make my feet ache, so I slipped them off, one at a time.

A faint creaking sound alerted me, causing me to jerk my head to one side for looking behind me, and needles and pins shot from my toes to my scalp with a persistently tingling sensation. All goose bumps, I held a wide-eyed heedful stare as my eyes tried to pierce the darkness beyond the wide doorway at the end of the living room. Holding this pose, I couldn't guess what the noise was that I'd heard; it wasn't as though I'd heard the distinctive sound of a creaking board or an object fall, but I did hear something that left me alarmed. Terribly fearful, I thought the only place in the house where I felt halfway safe was in the sanctuary of my bedroom. At least the door for this room had a lock to give me some sense of security, which was, of course, ridiculous, as though my bedroom really provided safety, but I still felt I had my best chance to find protection there.

My shoes were the only sure thing I could get my hands on to throw at whomever or whatever it was, and I decided to take my only line of escape by making a mad dash for the staircase. I went up the stairs like a frightened deer; never slowing down until I got to the top, then took a two second glance back at the area down below to make certain no one was following me before sprinting to my bedroom door. Pausing for a moment to think about that insane dream I'd had, I looked down the hall to where my grandfather's bedroom was located; I had no incentive whatsoever to see the interior of that room. It was the one place in the house I felt to be off limits to me, but at the same time, I thought sooner or later I may have to investigate there. Deep down inside, I believed I was going to one day have to enter that room, and it may be the last day I spend in this house.

Closing and locking the door behind me, I felt a little more at ease in my bedroom and began to undress. I still recalled that crazy dream, it wasn't like me to remember a dream, but this one seemed like such an insanely horrifying experience that it must've caused me to press it into my memory. Tomorrow I'd resume my quest for information or clues that might enlighten me about my family's past, but for now, I desperately needed rest. Crawling beneath the covers, the comfort of the bedding helped me to sink into a relaxed position and I eventually fell asleep.

CHAPTER 15

THE LAMP

My experiences with the phonograph records had disrupted my sleeping habits, and desiring to get my life back on track, I put the old gramophone and the record collection down in the cellar. Over time, things returned to normal, and as easy nights came and went, I became comfortably accustomed to my life here at Strathmoor Heights. Following through with the routine of checking the outside door locks after Maurice left in the evenings, I felt as though I had lost that sense of vulnerability I had with sleeping in the house alone. Gaining a feeling of security, those things which frightened me in the past now seemed like nothing more than a bad dream; and with time, I felt more relaxed than I had for a long while. I didn't know why I was staying on here, but I was in no hurry to carry on with my life without having learned what happened that dreadful night so very long ago.

The few times I became desperate for recreation, I had little trouble finding a good book in the library or I would take a short walk through the meadow. I'd occasionally stretch my legs by taking a nature hike to explore the outlying land and one afternoon, I spotted deer outside our patch of wooded forestry where the land took to scenic rolling hills. Just this last Saturday, I marched all the way up to a hilly peak, and my eyes followed the Teifi River as it snaked on its way out to sea. I must've been a good distance from the shoreline, but here the landscape was already turning barren, rocky, and rugged.

I'd remembered Maurice telling me a story about a legend connected with these heights, and that there were ruins of a castle on the peak; he'd emphasized not to look for the remains of a stone structure on the high point because the primary construction of the building was wood and all that remained of it were some rolling mounds. I came to find heaps of earth on the peak as he'd described, and while standing there and taking in the view, it reminded me of the folklore.

Long, long ago, a prosperous and powerful landholder ruled over the people that lived in this region, and this wealthy and influential lord desired a young maiden that lived in the village, but she found him repulsive and repudiated his advances. This rejection caused him great embarrassment, and it angered him too, for in his eyes it severely damaged his prominent stature among the commoners. He wasn't about to suffer such a dishonor without exercising his authority; so, to exact revenge, on his orders he had the maiden abducted and held captive.

A squire passing by the village on his steed heard of this maiden's imprisonment, and this young nobleman, who wanted more than anything to become a knight, sought to free her. He discovered that the embittered lord over this land wouldn't grant an audience to a lowly squire, but this did not stop him. Urging some of the villagers to help him set the maiden free, he had little trouble rallying commoners who gathered to give him aid and support, for the lord had made few friends by the stern methods he used to govern over his people.

The squire devised a plan, which he put into motion that same night as he went with a small band of men concealed under a wagonload of hay scheduled for delivery to the landholder's fortified stronghold on the peak. Under the cloak of night, they made their move, pouncing on the guards, and then opened the gates for the mass of peasants who'd chosen to revolt. The squire and the villagers took the unsuspecting lord and his followers by surprise and slain them, while setting free the maiden, and the structure was set ablaze.

The story had a romantic ring to it, and it whether it was true or not didn't concern me, but seeing the remains of this structure in a short outcrop of a stone foundation made me believe there must be some truth to it. The plot reminded me a little of the siege of Troy in the Iliad as written by Homer—how heroic Greeks secretly breached the defenses of Troy when entering by the means of a Trojan horse. Their goal was to rescue Helen, but Maurice never did say if the squire won the hand of the maiden, and so I guess this left one to make up their own ending on how you believed the story ended.

The bright sunny days grew quite warm as time drew closer to those mid-summer scorchers; and in the cool evenings, I'd sometimes take a stroll and gaze into the night sky to admire the starlit infinity. Wistful stars sparkled in the broad, black endless pool that sprawled out across the heavens; and once I enjoyed viewing a meteor shower, perhaps visitors from another distant galaxy. I spent many days hanging around the house, and there were still many things about this grand old mansion which impressed and intrigued me; even things I'd seen over and over again still held my interest, and the place was becoming more like home for me.

George never left my mind either, and there were nights when I yearned for his companionship. I'd only kissed him once, and yet I knew my feelings for him ran deep; still however, I only took time to write him a second letter. In this letter, I told him that if other offers should arise, he should feel free to act upon them. Judging by what mother told me about him, I didn't think he needed any advice; he was certainly no monk, and having never received any replies from my letters, I wondered if he bothered giving me a thought, and I wasn't intending to write him again soon.

One sunny Monday morning, an old gray truck climbed the gravel road to the house, its wheels spewing up dust as it clamored from the road's unevenness, and the vehicle was driven around to the rear of the house. Its passengers approached the house to knock at the kitchen door, and I opened the door to greet Katie in the company of a tall, stocky young man; he had a friendly smile and held a dark brown cap in his hands.

Katie spoke first, saying, "Hello, Claire, this is my son-in-law, Patrick, whom I told you about. I hope we didn't come at a bad time."

"Not at all, pleased to make your acquaintance, Patrick. Won't you both please come in?"

"Nice to meet you, Ms. MacKennsey," said Patrick, looking the place over as he stepped inside. "I have to admit to being a skeptic when Katie told me about this house, but it is some mansion you have here."

"If it's a tour you've come for, Patrick, I'll be more than happy to show you around."

"Ms. MacKennsey," began Katie, "Patrick and I don't mean to put you through any trouble, but he had some free time, so we thought it would be a good opportunity to get that furniture that's in the cellar. That's if you'd still like to be rid of it...I tried calling, but Maurice is never available to answer the phone."

"It's no problem, Katie, but I don't think we should bother Maurice. I'm afraid he may hurt himself trying to help, and I know he wouldn't want anyone making a fuss over him."

"Who's this person, Maurice?" asked Patrick with a slight squint as he looked at Katie. "I've heard you mention him on a few occasions."

"He's like the family heirloom," Katie replied, looking at me with a grin.

I nodded, and then led the way to the cellar. On the way down the stairs, I noticed it felt cool and comfortable in this lower level, leaving me to comment, "Oooh, it feels nice down here, as if it were air conditioned."

After taking a few minutes to sort things out, able-bodied Patrick muscled one piece at a time out of the cellar. First shifting and rocking the furniture out into open space, he would position it in such a way that he could lift and then carry the piece without assistance. Maurice soon showed up and offered to lend a hand, and by then Patrick was ready to move the big arm chair.

I removed the hurricane lamp from its seat, holding it in my arms as they readied to lift and carry the bulky chair. Concerned Maurice might injure himself, I said, "Maurice, I'd feel much better if I was the one helping him tackle that chair—those stairs are steep and it may be too much for you to handle."

"Oh, miss, I think I'm perfectly capable of helping this man carry this chair out of the cellar," Maurice replied with a touch of resentment in his voice.

"I merely need someone to help me with the balancing of it," explained Patrick, and he lifted the chair up by himself, but Maurice was determined to pitch in and came to his aid by gripping one end.

"Do be careful, gentlemen." Then watching them carry the heavy chair up the cellar stairs, I worried for Maurice's sake, as he started up the stairs first in a hunched-over position.

"I think Claire is right, Maurice," said Katie, "maybe you'd better let one of us take it."

"Now, just hush," demanded Maurice with an angry tone.

Katie and I looked at each other, she wearing a smirk, and sure enough, the chair became wedged in the doorway at the top of the steps. It had to be maneuvered and quarter-turned in order to fit through the opening, but it finally cooperated and went through.

"I hope Maurice can make it to the truck without dropping his end," Katie uttered, her eyes turning to the hurricane lamp I held in my hands. "His back will probably be out for a month after that little job."

She then made eye contact with me, "I believe that's all you intended parting with, Claire, and I want to thank you for your kindness."

"Don't you want the lamp?" and I motioned to hand it over to her.

"Oh, no miss, you've been far too generous. It's a pretty piece and, I imagine, quite valuable."

"That may be so, but I'd never consider selling it."

I let the lamp rest on a table they were leaving behind and Katie stood at my side gazing admirably at it.

"I'd want someone to have it that appreciates its beauty, and while it's just sitting down here collecting dust, it would look nice on display in your home."

While Katie idolized it, touching the larger flower emblem on its globe, I felt this peculiar needle and pin sensation on the

150

back of my neck running up to my scalp. Then I distinctly heard softly whispered words spoken in my left ear, "Keep the lamp."

Swiveling my head and neck to ward off the strange tingling sensation, I turned to Katie, "Did you say something?"

"No, miss, but I really don't feel right about your giving me all this."

"I want you to have it. It's my way of saying thanks for having done such a fine job in keeping the house up. And besides," I added, humorously, "the chair it sat in and the lamp are a set, we can't split them up. You don't want me to ask the men to bring that chair back down. It'll kill Maurice."

Katie grinned, "Bless you for being so kind."

I could tell she was grateful, and I then pointed out the lamp's only flaw, "There's a small chip here on its crown."

"Awh, that's nothing, miss, that gives it character," and as I picked up the handsome lamp, she said, "I'll carry it up if you like."

Placing it in her arms, I said, "Now if you'll start up, I'll get these lights."

Seeing her starting up the stairs, I turned to look for the cord connected to the light above me, and the lamp suddenly burst into pieces at my feet!

Startled by the crash, I saw Katie standing on the stairs, shocked while gaping at the remains of the shattered lamp.

"Katie, are you all right?" She gave no response, and I tried getting her attention again, saying, "Katie?"

"It was as if the bloody thing leaped from my hands. Like someone snatched it from me..." She lifted her vibrating palms, staring at them.

Seeing she was shook up and knowing, too well, how she must have felt, I went to her, took hold of her hands, and brought them together; she was a bundle of nerves.

That needles and pins sensation convinced me of Angela's presence, and wanting Katie to go before something else happened, I spoke to her sympathetically, "Katie, it was an accident. Don't give it a thought...I'll clean this mess up. You run along now."

Teary eyed and bewildered, she said, "I'm sorry. I don't see how it happened."

"It's all right, you and Patrick go ahead now, and I'll see you on Wednesday. Tell Patrick good-bye for me."

After Katie left, I looked upon the shattered glass, and then surveyed the dark area about me in the cellar while wondering if I was alone. I picked up a piece of the glass displaying the rose colored petals, and it made me think this lamp must have been a memento Angela relished, and the whispered words I'd heard, "Keep the lamp", were more than just my imagination. Suspecting Angela wasn't far roaming about, and believing my being in this house provokes her, I expected it wouldn't be long before she and I had another confrontation. If she had cherished the lamp all that much, then maybe she preferred it be destroyed rather than allow it to belong to another.

Angela's spirit had, once again, proven the ability to intercede by moving objects, presumably articles that were once her personal possessions. This incident served to remind me of the event in the library, where she'd flung records in the air at me; understanding how she can willingly interact in the present by destroying the lamp here in the cellar, these occurrences made it evident that she may wish to act to destroy me too! Her interaction concerned me in a worrisome way, for it demonstrated a powerful will and a determination so strong that she refuses to let go of the life she once had. This sort of violent intervention meant that she may be able to injure and harm me, and I couldn't help thinking that my staying on here could possibly lead to disastrous consequences.

This was a situation growing more and more serious, for as long as I dwell here in this house and Angela believes me to be an intruder, she's sure to oppose me. Hovering over me was the question, why should she give my presence here any consideration or interpret my being here as a threat? She must be aware of an outsider being in the house, and it's almost as though she keeps watch over me, knowing or in some strange way sensing my purpose for being here is to investigate what events led up to the murder of my grandfather. My impression was that she must be on guard against anyone learning the reason for his being murdered, as though maybe this has always been a great concern for her. Is there something she's bound and determined to keep others from finding out, or is she still influenced by an illness she once suffered from—the diseased mind of a woman who killed in a mad rage—that she's obsessed with the house and those things that were once hers, and she simply cannot stand anyone meddling in them.

Is it possible that the mental problem she had in her former life was so deep-rooted and embedded in the fiber of her being that even after death it still has a hold over her? Trying to understand her mindset left me wondering how to help her, or even help myself for that matter, for I desperately needed to learn what motivated her to commit such a ghastly and horrific murder. Pondering this dilemma further, I felt convinced that the purpose for her restless spirit lingering on in this house revolved around my grandfather's murder—she strives to find a way to correct the past; maybe it's the murder itself she regrets, and she may be bound to this earthly plateau until the end of time because it can never be undone. I wanted to free her spirit and allow her to find peace, but I didn't know how, and if there was an answer or key which could possibly accomplish this, I was in a quandary about how to find out what it was. What made it seem like such a difficult problem to have to deal with was the perplexity and uncertainty of it, and there were times when thinking about it that I wanted to let go and scream.

Should the entity sharing this house with me be beyond any consciousness of time, then she mustn't be able to understand or comprehend that I'm her granddaughter. She only sees me as an outsider upsetting the status quo by tampering in her keepsakes and bringing unwelcome change. I also realized her existence took on more than one form—first I saw her ghostly image coming down the corridor, and now a presence I could not see, yet it could communicate and in a physical sense move objects like what happened in the library. I only wish there was a way I could let her know who I am and what my intentions are.

The incident with the lamp fueled my desire to discover answers locked within the walls of this house, and I suddenly felt compelled to commence a broad search of the premises. I felt much the way I had when first coming here, driven to find something that could expose the cause for the murder of my grandfather and uncover the underlying reasons as to why it happened. I had no idea what I was looking for, but I knew I must give into this strong and overpowering urge to look about in an attempt to find it.

I'd seen almost the entire house, and having no idea how to conduct a systematic search on a house this size, I felt motivated by my instincts, as here within my subconscious was a pressing inspirational yearning. I wasn't sure where this urgency and drive controlling me was coming from, but wondered if there was some supernatural force exerting a power over my mind to make me feel this way; and even though I didn't understand it, I couldn't evade it either. I allowed the hunt to take me to the second story, and checking each door for taking a brief look inside, my search stalled at my grandfather's bedroom door. Something stopped me from crossing its threshold, and it may be that I sense the very essence of his spirit being contained here, waiting for the moment when fate would set him free. I knew one day I'd have to face up to my fears and enter this room, but I didn't have the courage just yet.

Standing with the door open, gawking at the bed—the scene of the horrific crime—I then felt this strange impulse to go down to the first-floor library. Surrendering to this inexplicable guiding force leading me downstairs, I felt an indescribable hint that my answers may lie nearby, perhaps in a book. I started sifting through novels, checking inside their bindings and covers in the hopes of finding a clue, but my efforts were fruitless. Whatever had been guiding me before now left me with the inkling that I was close, that whatever I was looking for was here on the first floor. It could have been a note left behind in one of these books here in the library—maybe a letter of confession Angela had left behind. But which book—there were so many? I knew I was indeed close or at least on the right track, but by some strange intuitive way, I became aware that it probably wasn't here in the library, and that whatever I was searching for would remain elusive and out of my grasp for some time to come.

Giving up the search, I took the comfortable chair I usually sat in when reading. I now felt as though I was lost without this guiding force influencing me and leading the way; and no matter how hard I tried, I couldn't regain the focus I had before. Very much aware that the peculiar thought entering my mind to come back downstairs to the library wasn't my own, I arrived at the belief that this faint tantalizing revelation came through the power of suggestion. I had no idea how to proceed without that fleeting enigmatic flirtation I'd sensed before, but as strange as it was, I came to believe that whatever I've been looking for was nearby and not far out of reach. When first succumbing to this mental compulsion, I was certain that it came from the side of good, or at least I sensed its purpose was to take me to something I expected would help put my mind at ease. The force seemed strongest when I stood at the doorway to my grandfather's bedroom, but why has it forsaken me? Pondering these questions, I thought I'd possibly lost its obscure guidance because I'd misinterpreted its message or ran off course from where it was leading me. I'd lost touch with it and it may never come back to me again.

CHAPTER 16

THE PHANTOM RETURNS

Later, after Maurice and I had dinner that same evening, we sat together at the kitchen table and he selected a bottle of sherry, pouring each of us a glass.

"I watched your father grow up, he and I got along splendidly, and I remember him best as a baby-faced youngster."

Putting his nose over the rim of the glass, he took a whiff before taking a drink and then said, "No more than three miles from here is a small lake where we'd sneak off to go fishing. He was fifteen when his Aunt Irene gave him a stallion, which, of course, from then on took up most of his spare time. Your great aunt used that horse to drive your father to learn, and learn he did for if his grades faltered he risked losing his riding privileges. Irene was a stickler when it came to education and it was the one thing she kept on him about."

He grinned, "I can't tell you how many times she said to him, 'Do you want to wind up like that Maurice?' or ' I'm not going to leave my money to someone who can't manage it. Somebody will just take it away from you', and she'd say it like she meant it. She didn't mean anything against me by using me for an example as she and I got along quite well. However, she knew your father looked up to me, and to some degree, I guess I was a father figure to him, but she wanted him to see me for what I was, and I can't fault her for that. It was very important to her to have the family holdings fall into competent hands, and she was determined to push Winston to his full potential."

We drank, and Maurice handled the bottle by its neck to top off our glasses, "I'm a bit disappointed Winston never mentioned me, but it's no wonder, the busy man he was. He never forgot me around Christmas though, always sending me a bottle of sherry...This is one he sent right here, God bless his soul."

He winked and wiggled his index finger for me to come closer, and then said, "I'll tell you something, it was I who introduced your father to spirits...I can recall when your father and I sat down and had a long talk about the birds and the bees." He slapped his knee and let out a chuckle, "And a dandy conversation it was too because I was by no means an expert on the subject.

"Here in this kitchen, at this very table, we finished off a bottle of sherry together." He slapped the table flatly and laughed, "He got sick as a dog, and I caught hell from his Aunt Irene...Ahh, but we did have us some fun."

I thought Maurice was feeling a bit tipsy by the way he'd become so talkative and animated, but it didn't bother me; I enjoyed hearing stories about my father. Beginning to feel the effects of the alcohol myself, I nursed what was left in my glass by taking short sips, while remarking, "He must have held a special fondness for you, Maurice."

"I like to think so, madam," he replied.

Maurice prepared to top-off my glass once more, but I put my hand over it, "I believe I've had enough, Maurice."

He waved the bottle over my glass and filled his to the brim. "You know, the era I've lived through while staying at this house may be remembered as hard times for many of my generation, but for me they were the good ole days. People weren't so materialistic."

"Have you ever thought about moving into town or going to London?" I asked.

"I have no interest in living in any big city. I'm happy and content with my life here. Everyone living in the city is in a big rush, all the crowds, competition, and crime, who needs it?"

He took a drink then said, "Tell me, if you don't mind my asking, why aren't you married?"

I shrugged, "I've never met the right fella."

"What's the matter with those American boys—if you don't mind my giving you a compliment, you're a lovely young lady of beauty and breeding." He then lifted his glass, adding, "Here's to you, my dear, and may you live a long and happy life."

We raised our glasses together and they clanged.

The liquor we'd been drinking must've had some kick to it, and feeling a little drowsy, I thought I'd better turn in while I can still climb the stairs under my own steam.

"I think the sherry is getting the best of me, Maurice. I'm going to call it a night."

"I'm going to reminisce here for a short while, and then I'll lock up. Is there anything you're in need of?"

"No, there's nothing...Good night."

I left Maurice sitting at the kitchen table and took the servants stairs to the second floor. Entering my room, I went to sit at the edge of the bed, and one at a time, used only my feet to press and push the backs of my shoes off to remove them. Collapsing back on the mattress and blanket, I moved towards the head of the bed until my head found the pillow, then fell fast asleep.

Sometime later, a creaking floorboard awakened me—there was something or someone in the room with me!

Startled but remaining calm and still, lying flat on my back in the bed, I cracked my eyelids just enough get a glimpse of who was there. The light was on in the hallway, and standing off to one side near the foot of the bed was the tall standing silhouette of a man, both taller and huskier than Maurice!

Electrified with fear, I resumed slow and steady breathing to simulate sleep but keeping the slit in my eyes open to try and see the features of this phantom of the night and monitor his slightest movement.

He moved forward and toward me, and moonlight through the window enabled me to see the black hood covering his head! Stiffening, I held my fixed position, restraining myself from attempting to flee, hoping for him to go and leave me, but he remained standing over me, as though gawking. Against the background of silence, I heard breathing through the hood's material; and in the room's quiet somber, I wrestled with the urge to scream!

Unable to endure this maniac's presence another minute, tension brewed as I exercised the utmost self-control in pretending to sleep; and while demonstrating this frozen state, through my filtering eyelashes, I saw holes in the hood for his piercing eyes! This hanging, maddening terror caused my throat to turn dreadfully dry, and it antagonized me because I didn't know if I could scream even if I tried. I stirred in getting ready to let out a shrieking shrill, but my arousal caused him to turn away, and he went out of the room.

The hall light went out, a wave of relief came over me, and deliberating whether or not to follow this hooded figure, an impulse powered me out of the bed to trail him. Making a quiet exit out of the bedroom and starting down the hall toward the main staircase, my heartbeat accelerating, my blood pumping, the fear of an encounter with this menace kept me on edge, but I was determined to learn this individual's identity.

I quickly tiptoed in the direction of the stairs where I heard footsteps descending down into the living room, and nearing the hallway's end at top of the staircase, I peeked around a corner. Rushing in the direction of the balcony where I hoped to gain a more profitable view through the handrail's spindles, I stooped low while leaning forward to get an overview of the living room. Squinting to get a sharper perspective of the room's layout, the white headless statuette, the mouth of the fire place, moonlight reflecting off the piano's glazed surface and my grandfather's still image on canvas all came into focus.

Detecting no sound or movement below, I was afraid I'd lost this hooded phantom, and I ventured down the stairs, swiftly but deliberate in taking one step at a time so as to not overtake the one whom I followed. Finding solid footing on the first floor, I crept catlike in the direction of the entry hall; and suddenly stubbing my toe on a table leg, I fell to my knees in agonizing pain; tolerating the aching in the little toe of my right foot, I resisted crying out in pain.

Hearing a faint sound I could not make out, I froze in a crouched position while feeling my heart pounding from the threat lurking nearby. Not wanting to lose the intruder but fearing he may be on to me, watching from the shadows and observing my every movement here on the first floor, I raised my head to survey my surroundings. Although unable to detect his presence, I still felt vulnerable and held fear of him attacking me.

Thinking I may be losing him, I limped along in a stooped-over manner, ignoring the throbbing pain in my toe; and taking to a gliding motion, I moved into the entry hall where I noticed the latch on the front door was in the locked position. Watchfully rushing down the hall and into the dining room, I saw the kitchen light on and proceeded cautiously past the family coat of arms and throne chair situated beneath it. I heard deep breathing, my lungs held full as I anticipated seeing this hooded man in the light; and carefully approaching with my eyes bulging wide, I saw Maurice sleeping in a chair at the kitchen table.

Now more at ease but somewhat irked by the sight of him snoring, I placed my hands on my hips while wiggling my toes to make sure I hadn't broken the toe that I'd stubbed.

I shook Maurice's shoulders. "Maurice, wake up."

Rattled in his awakening and startled by his surroundings, he coughed to clear his throat before grumbling, "What—what is it, miss?"

I went to the back door and, seeing the door was unlocked, turned to him to say, "Someone was in the house. He must've snuck right passed you."

Alerted and surprised by my assertion, he then looked at me wide-eyed, "Are you sure?"

"He came to my bedroom when I was sleeping and from there I followed him downstairs...He wore a black hood over his face."

Maurice rose out of his chair, his eyes looking into mine, "Do you think he's still here?"

"I tracked him here. I think he went out the same way he came in—through the back door."

"What makes you so sure he came by me through the kitchen?"

"Well, I really don't know, but the latch is locked on the front door."

Maurice led the way back in the direction I'd just come from, turning on all the lights along the way; upon reaching the living room, he looked over the furnishings while I remained in the entry hall.

"I don't see how he could've made it past me without me seeing him," Maurice commented.

"He must've," I strongly insisted, motioning to the front door. "The latch is in the locked position."

"Well," began Maurice, "he may have made his entry through the kitchen without alarming me, but it's possible he left by the front door. I believe the front door latch was locked, but he may have turned the latch to free it so he could open the door, and when closing it behind him, the latch fell back into the locked position."

"Okay, but what are we going to do about it?"

"I'm not sure, but it's very peculiar that a thief would've entered this house and not taken something. Not that I doubt what you're saying, but look at all the valuables lying about this room."

I asserted myself, saying, "What if it wasn't a thief?"

"Who do you think it was?"

"I don't know, but Katie told me she once saw a hooded man at the kitchen window and I'm obliged to think this was the same man she saw. Also, the first night I was here, I was awakened by a disturbance, saw the hall light on, and then heard someone on the stairs...Supposing this was the same person in all three instances and I think it was, then...."

Suddenly I began to think and consider my options and acquired the idea that the uncle who'd committed suicide could still be alive! In giving it further thought, it began making some sense—Daniel may have failed in his attempted suicide and the results of this attempt might have left him disfigured.

"Is it possible that Daniel somehow faked his suicide? I know it's an unlikely theory, but who else could it be?"

Maurice shook his head, and said, "No."

"Won't you at least even consider the possibility?"

"I would if I could, but I'm the one who cut him down, and there's absolutely no way he could've faked his death. I don't know if you've ever touched a dead person, but his limp body was dead weight and his flesh cold and clammy, and the coroner later examined the body. But what would he stand to gain by faking a suicide and concealing he was alive—he certainly stood to lose a great inheritance."

"Then who is it," I retorted, losing patience.

"I don't know, no one lives anywhere near here, and if they'd come in a car, we should've heard it...I can only apologize for my negligence in the matter, and I promise it won't happen again. I'll be more careful about checking the locks in the future."

"Don't you think we ought to call the police?"

"If you insist, I will, miss, but I don't see how it can do any good. It'll take 'em over an hour to arrive here, and after all, technically, no crime has been committed." Then Maurice added, "I fully intend locking up down here and having a look about the premises."

Knowing I must convince him to stay because I expected he'd only injure himself, I said, "Maurice, I don't want you going out there in the dark and trying to apprehend somebody. If someone is lurking out there, they may surprise you, then where will that leave me?"

"What would you have me do then? The only telephone is in the carriage house, and I'd have to go outside to get to it for phoning the police."

"You're not going out there, and that's final. It may be an inconvenience, but I want you to spend the night on the couch, or even better yet, take one of the beds upstairs."

"If it'll make you feel more secure, I'll bed down here on the sofa where I can keep watch."

"I'll get you a blanket and pillow but I do not want you to leave the house tonight under any circumstances."

"Of course, miss, I won't leave the house. I assure you, first thing in the morning, I'll do some checking to see if anything is missing, and if there is, I'll see to it that the police come out and make a report."

I tossed him down a pillow and blanket from the second-story balcony, and he took a comfortable position on one of the sofas in the living room, then I returned to my bedroom and locked my door.

My stamina and stubbornness weakened by the intervention of this hooded intruder, the incident heightened the mysteries of this house, and I lied awake pondering what was going to happen the next time I stumbled into him. The longer I stayed on in this house, the greater the chances were that I was going to encounter serious trouble, for more than ever before, I felt threatened and unsafe staying here. I believed he may have come to frighten me and drive me out of the house, but I wasn't going let this break my spirit and undermine my resolve to learn what happened the night my grandfather died.

The first night I stayed in this house, I caught sight of a shadowy figure in the hallway outside my bedroom, and I now worried for having seen this hooded phantom in my bedroom. It disturbed me greatly to think this individual has the ability to get into the house without detection, making me wonder if he's acquired keys to the house. Maurice must've had people come to the house to do maintenance work, and perhaps this person made a copy of a spare key, or maybe he had some other means to make his entry. He apparently snuck by Maurice without waking him, but if he was a burglar then why didn't he take anything.

Once again, considering Maurice's place in all this, he definitely wasn't the dark figure standing at my bedroom door on that first night, nor was he the hooded man I saw tonight. It hardly seemed likely that he'd be trying to drive me away, but after what just occurred, I couldn't be sure of anything. My mind momentarily ran with an unlikely theory that he and perhaps Patrick, along with Katie, were working together, but that didn't add up either. The coincidence of Katie recently mentioning that she'd seen a hooded man two years ago and now for him to appear again was particularly strange; but while Patrick was similar in size and build to this hooded figure, I thought him too oversized to fill this person's shoes. No matter how unlikely it seemed, this was a possibility worthwhile contemplating, and these thoughts served to fuel my suspicions. Still yet, I hadn't thrown out the improbable idea that my Uncle Daniel, whom I had believed to be deceased, was somehow involved.

There were so few possibilities to explain these occurrences, but the more I thought about it, the more I came to discount a conspiracy between these people. I knew them well enough to form a judgment about their character, and not only did I find it hard to believe they were the criminal type, but there was simply no logic behind such deceit. They've been able to do as they please with the house for years, and they could've emptied out the place the day before I arrived without me knowing any difference; yet the residence has obviously remained relatively the same since people last inhabited it. No, these people weren't deceiving me, nor did it make any sense that my uncle was still alive, for he'd have been an heir to the family holdings, so why would he have remained silent for all of these years?

Deliberating these thoughts even further, I felt certain this stranger wearing the hood was blind to my following him down to the first floor. However, if he knew Maurice and passed through the kitchen on the way out of the house, why didn't he bother to stop and give him a brief acknowledgment, while instead leaving the house without saying a word?

In my estimation of Maurice, I still had this strange inkling or intuition telling me that he knows more about my family's past than what he is telling me; and it's disturbing to think he may be withholding information regarding my grandfather's death. More than anything else, I didn't want to lose my trust and confidence in the old fellow, as he's been ideal in giving me first hand information thus far; yet he may have come to the conclusion that it may not serve my best interest to gain certain information about the past. He was my only link with the past, my only source for learning the motive for this ghastly murder, and if I thought for a minute that he told me anything untrue, then how could I believe any of the other things he's made mention of.

CHAPTER 17

ENCOUNTERING AN APPARITION

As the long summer days passed, I found the event with the hooded man not easily forgotten; and although I had no further encounters with him, I was still trying to figure out how he worked into the mysterious past of the house. While I thought it uncanny for him to reappear after Katie told me she'd seen him two years ago, I was concerned that when least expected, he and I would cross each other's paths. Considering such a confrontation could prove dangerous and even deadly, I tried to mentally prepare myself for that moment. I thought it unlikely I'd have the nerve to unveil his hood to learn his identity, as I'd probably be running to escape his grasp. One frightening aspect about this hooded intruder was that he was the one who seemed to have control over when, where, and if we'll meet again; and I awoke in the middle of the night a few times when conjuring the image of him standing at my bedside staring at me.

Time helped me find the courage to start leaving the door to my bedroom open, but since beginning to leave it open, I didn't sleep so well. I knew certain incidents only occurred after the sun had gone down, and because of this, I spent many nights tossing and turning, waking up wondering if the hooded man may be lurking about the house. However, staying in this marvelous old house helped me to develop a stubborn, hardheadedness, for I was determined as ever to leave my door open and face my fears.

Not sleeping well the night before, I didn't wake up until after ten the next morning; by then the sun had raised high in the sky and its fierce light shown brightly through my bedroom window. I went to it to look upon the sun-drenched world, and as my eyes adjusted to the stinging light, they became drawn to the stone gargoyle standing guard outside my window. I thought its sculptor incredibly skilled to design such a mythological winged creature, and I'd become well acquainted with the detailed features of this carved limestone image.

Stretching and extending my limbs to loosen my muscles, I felt heat from the sun's rays; and turning away from the sun's glaring reflection off the slate roof, I thought it hot enough to fry an egg out there.

I came downstairs by the servant's stairs to the kitchen to find Katie preparing breakfast, and rarely having a big appetite, I thought it odd she'd whipped up a big meal; and I believe she'd done so out of being used to cooking for a lot more people. I noticed her moving about the kitchen faster than normal, and it made think she was disappointed that I didn't eat more of what she'd placed out on the table for me.

After eating, I retired to the library and plopped down in my easy leather chair that I'd covered with a lightweight woven blanket. I'd sometimes cover it because the leather felt sticky to me in the warm weather, but it was unquestionably the most comfortable chair in the house. The searing heat and exceptionally high humidity made me feel lazy, and I sat there fanning myself with a magazine, watching Katie working to dust the furniture with a feather duster. Katie commented, "What we need is rain and they say we're to expect showers this afternoon... Should cool things off a bit."

Curious as to what made Katie scurry about so quickly with her feather duster fluttering, I asked, "What's your hurry, Katie?"

"Gonna leave early today, my sister's coming in for a visit. She lives up in Liverpool, married one of those Englishman, but we keep in touch."

Later that same afternoon, a weather watch began as invigorating winds whipped and whirled, a strong vacuumed current of air leaving the atmosphere unsettled. Flexing tree branches accommodating the turbulent wind merged, leaned, and swayed in a stirring commotion that drew our attention. Standing at the kitchen window watching Mother Nature's fury as swirling gray clouds darkened the sky, I didn't mind seeing the threat of rain, for the hard dry earth and its plant life thirsted for moisture.

"Look's as though there's a nasty storm brewing," proclaimed Katie, tying a scarf underneath her chin for head protection as she prepared to go out the door.

"Yes, it's moving in fast," I replied in acknowledgement as I viewed the dark clouds, and then turned to see her off. "I hope it doesn't get too bad, by the way, where's Maurice?"

"He's in the car, waiting," and Katie grabbed her handbag. "Sometimes the road gets washed out and I think that's why he's anxious to get going."

Walking out into the courtyard with Katie, I saw Maurice sitting in the car with its engine running, and she rushed to take the passenger seat. Brisk, cool winds cutting across the land felt soothing, and I detected a few scattered raindrops while waving good-bye, then watching as the car disappeared down the gravel road.

Whisking, whirling winds picked up velocity, kicking up debris with lightweight, unsecured objects becoming airborne, and as raindrops fell in greater numbers, I sought shelter by returning to the house. Upon reentering its interior and trying to close the door behind me, I felt forceful resistance from an onslaught of wind while attempting to secure the door. At that moment, a cloudburst broke loose with a driving rain assailing the house; hard rain pounding against the windows gave the effect as though some awesome adversary wanted in.

Passing through the dining room while making my way toward the library, I heard the wind howling, a deep echoing thunder rattled the house, and I felt intimidated by the storm's rage. I went over to a window where I saw a blackened sky and raindrops pelted and splashed against the glass, blurring all outside imagery. I turned on the tall standing floor lamp I usually used for reading and took the nearby burgundy leather chair I'd occupied earlier in the day. Thumbing through a magazine to take my mind off the storm's fury, I felt a slight chill in the air, which I welcomed; but a minute later, I began to hear the faint sound of a woman's whimpering.

At first discounting the sound as being part of the storm's whistling wind, but it soon became clear to me that this was a woman crying, and I made an effort to track the sound with my hearing as my eyes wandered. Wanting to ignore this mournful weeping, while hoping it wouldn't go on much longer, and a grisly wrath of thunder rumbled over the house, jolting me. I saw the bulb in the lamp blink off, and then it immediately came back on. As this woeful crying persisted, the wailing wind howled, I prayed the electricity would hold; and for a time I tuned in to her weeping for determining its place of origin, but I could not distinguish the angle or location from where it was coming. The room grew much cooler and goose bumps ran from my ankles up to my spine and neck—the lights went out!

Fear kept me braced in my chair, and swallowing to clear my throat, I wished and prayed for the electricity to come back on; but in fleeting seconds gone by, all hope for light to return died. As the storm moved its furor to full force, the sad whimpering of this brokenhearted female came on strong until her beseeching sorrow touched me and stirred my emotions. It was as if I came to bear some of her agony and heartfelt sadness, and I knew what I heard could only be Angela's spirit languishing in mournful sorrow. I also knew my presence may not set well with her, yet the sobbing and whimpering poured forth, as if aching for someone to reach out to her.

The weeping taunted me until my heart filled with compassion, compelling me to seek out this grieving soul; and as this deeply saddening sound nudged me out of my chair, I felt drawn to the living room where I stood at its center and listened, focusing on this woman's anguish—the sound came from upstairs. I did not want to go up there, but a pressing willingness to ease her distress provoked me while pushing me into trying. I never felt so alienated from the outside world, and keeping watch on the balcony at the crest of the stairs, I kept anticipating someone or something may suddenly appear there. This dreaded notion made me think of the hooded phantom and how this would be the most frightening time to for me to be confronted by him. Nevertheless, I kept short stepping my way in the direction of the stairs. Lightning flashed, a quaking thunder shook the house as the storm moved to an even more violent phase, and I had the dreadful thought that the ferocity of the wind was going to take the roof off the building!

Beginning my ascension upward, an ever-increasing fear holding me back, I took one step at a time; and with each advancing step, I experienced rising apprehension. Without using the handrail to aid me, I moved steadily upward until reaching the halfway point—the crest of the stairs in view—I glimpsed the halberd axe hanging on the wall. My breathing turned over with short, fast strokes while my heart pounded, causing me to hug the handrail with my hip, sliding against it as I moved forward, eyeballing the blade of the axe as I became skittishly heedful.

Nearing the last step, another flash of lightning froze me in my steps, and the following rumble inhibited me as though sucking all the driving determination I had left in me. I pulled myself together long enough to realize that if I didn't investigate, my failure here would only serve to gnaw at me later, and reinforce the irking idea that I may be more like my grandmother than I'd ever care to admit to myself. There was something up there I needed to face up to, and for the sake of my own sanity, I had to know if my grandmother was an evil entity bent on destroying me.

Stepping onto the balcony and staring down the dark hallway ahead of me, I believed with certainty that this grieving anguish came from my grandmother's bedroom. Holding my arms folded tight to warm myself from the cold chill, I moved forward, her persisting despair growing louder as I neared her room. I approached Angela's door from the far side of the corridor, unsure of what I'd find beyond it. Fighting an inner conflict, my conscious mind objected with a cowardly twinge, warning me not to venture one step further, but my spirit clung to the hope that I could win if I didn't give up—I had to go on to save myself.

The fury of the storm reaching its peak, the hall flared from a blast of lightning flashing through the window at its end. The crashing roar of thunder made my heart jump and bracing my back against the wall, my warm breath expelled steam into the air as I focused on the door. Petrified, my widened eyes stared at the doorknob as I listened to her ceaseless sorrowful weeping, and wailing. With the next flash of lightning, I reached for the knob without further hesitation, a freakish high-pitched shrill came with crackling thunder as I turned the handle and burst in!

Standing in the dim gloom of this room that felt like a cold crypt, a hush fell over the house, and I discovered frost on the glass of the french doors. Just as Angela's painting fell off the wall, my eyes caught sight of a veiled black figure at her vanity, rising and taking on human shape! Spine-chilling terror surged through me as I watched the figure turn. I saw a woman's pale face reveal a hateful scowl; cringing in fear as the specter raised its arms menacingly, a sudden flash blinded me as lightning exploded just outside! A tremendous crash came as a huge tree branch smashed through the french doors, and I turned to protect my face from a shower of glass fragments. As the vanity and bed heaved at me, I dropped to the floor, falling away while trying to guard myself from their crushing assault—I thought I'd die!

I remained curled up; shutting my eyes until the room abruptly fell still. In a matter of seconds, the storm moved on and in this still quiet, I heard drips falling from the enormous tree branch that had plunged into the room. Then I heard the song of a not-too-distant bird. Taking a breath of air, I uncoiled and opened my eyes to see sunshine breaking through the clouds, a tapestry of bright rays piercing through the gaping opening where the french doors had hung securely before. Still shaken but managing to come to my feet as I numbly gaped at the aftermath, the great snaking tree limb and its sprawling green foliage caught the sunlight, looking more like a tree than a branch.

The room looked like a hurricane had ripped through it. I saw how the limb had crushed the bed and knocked the dresser to the far side of the room. The flimsy curtains flapped from the fresh, cool breeze, and water droplets fell from the shaking leaves of the tree branch. Looking beyond the damaged french doors, the hand rail of the wrought iron balcony was left bent and twisted, but the extending structure had borne the bulk of the weight of the tree branch and kept it from falling. Where the lightning bolt struck the tree, the limb had split away from the trunk, leaving raw, bare, and badly splintered wood exposed.

A throbbing, stinging pain in my right arm brought me to my senses. An elongated pie-shaped piece of glass pierced my arm, and I carefully pinched the glass firmly with my thumb and index finger before yanking it out. Blood gushed forth and ran down my arm, and the intense stinging pain made me grimace. I took hold of a pillow and shook the pillowcase until the pillow fell out, then I used the pillowcase to cover the wound to stem the flow of blood.

Seconds ago, I feared for my life, and perhaps I'd gone too far by venturing into Angela's room at that particular moment when her spirit mourned. Remembering the angry rage the face held, I noted it bore a striking resemblance to the face in the painting which had fallen off the wall when I entered the room. Feeling fortunate that lightning bolt struck at the miraculous moment it did, there was little chance that lightning hitting that tree just then was a mere coincidence. If the tree limb hadn't crashed through those doors when it did, I believe I would've suffered great harm. The more I thought about the experience, the more it seemed like divine intervention had saved me from a terrible fate. There had to be a force or power directing it, and I only hoped God or some other entity of good had acted to protect me.

Convinced some outside force played a hand in steering that lightning bolt into that tree, I'd like to think I have a guardian angel watching over me, but this occurrence was something beyond my understanding. These thoughts brought me to dwell on another time when an intuitive sensation took hold over me to guide me that day when making a brief search of the house that led me to the library. Even though I uncovered nothing in my search, I felt a guiding presence showing me the way and now, for this to happen, it made me wonder. I didn't think of myself as strong willed enough to go on alone, but perhaps there was a guiding force influencing me to stay on for unlocking the past. I only wished it so.

I thought about Angela, wondering where and when our paths would cross again. How could I let her know I wanted to help her? How could I make her understand I wasn't a threat before she harmed me, and will I be as lucky the next time I meet up with her spirit?

When Maurice returned home, he immediately treated my wound and wrapped my arm with gauze and bandages to stop the bleeding. We made little attempt to straighten out the mess in Angela's bedroom that night, but the next morning, Maurice phoned Katie and asked if Patrick would be interested in removing the tree limb. Patrick accepted the job and soon arrived at the house, strapping on his safety goggles to commence dismantling the tree branch with a chainsaw. Working at a steady pace dismembering the limb, he'd rev up the chainsaw, spewing dust and spraying chips into the air with the loud sound rattling my eardrums.

Maurice and I pitched in, stacking the wood to one side, and we kept the door to Angela's room closed to keep the sawdust confined to this area. Patrick cut the wood into short chunks to make for firewood in the upcoming winter, and with each cut, the limb broke down piece by piece. Working into the thickest part of the tree limb to clear a path to the balcony's edge, we then passed pieces of the tree limb to Patrick, who pitched them down to the grassy area below. Dismantling the bed, we determined the only part undamaged was the headboard, as the bedding's supports were beyond repair, and Patrick cut the damaged foot of the bed in half before dropping it off the balcony. We briefly discussed using the framework of one of the other beds of the same size from another room to replace it. I wanted to reuse the original head board because its intricate wooden carvings made it unique, but we couldn't be certain it would be compatible with parts from another bed until we tried reassembling it.

After the tree limb and old bed were removed from the room, Patrick took off his dusty safety goggles and assessed the damage to the french doors.

"I don't think these doors can be repaired, Ms. MacKennsey. Not only did the tree do major damage to their framework, but weather and time has caused decay. I suggest we do away with these and hang a new set of doors. We can stain the new ones dark enough to match the rest of the woodwork."

"It's completely in your hands Patrick," I remarked. "I hope you don't have trouble finding doors like these."

Patrick replied reassuringly, "Woodwork is my specialty, and I don't expect it will be much of a problem, but I'll get some measurements right now. The worst that can happen is that they'll be an odd size, and if they are, I'll see if I can find a used set of doors that'll fit the opening."

Finding Angela's portrait face-down on the floor, the glass broken, I placed it inside the cabinet where her dresses were stored. I made sure that her portrait remained intact and the frame unbroken, intending to replace the glass and re-hang the picture after we'd fully restored the rest of the room.

Patrick cut the last of the tree limb free from its trunk, then pushing and prying it to one side so it would fall away from the bent and twisted balcony railing. His took a swift, awkward step backward into the room, a surprised look on his face. "Whoa!"

"What is it, Patrick?"

"The balcony, it moved," and he stooped to study the balcony for examining how it connected and hung from the building. "Yes, see here," he knelt without venturing out onto the balcony, pointing to where the wrought iron had pulled away from the building's stone facade—the metal had extracted from the stone holding it and loosened the mortar around it.

Studying the balcony further, he added, "It may have shifted as a way of making an adjustment, and now it's moved all it's going to. After all, it took the impact of that tree limb when it fell and still supported both the limb and me at the same time."

He stood up, and held onto the inside of the door jam as he carefully leaned to step onto the balcony, then for a moment allowed it to bear his full weight. Removing his hand from the building to stand freely on the balcony for a second before stepping back inside, he said, "I don't detect any give to it now."

I gazed at the balcony's damaged and twisted railing, "Do you think it can be salvaged?"

"Well, you can see the bashing the wrought iron took from the weight of that tree limb, but before I can be sure of anything, I need to get a welder up here to have a look and see what has to be done to make repairs for reinforcing it."

Looking over the balcony, he again stood out on it long enough to see what steps he needed to follow to perform work on it.

"Aren't you afraid of it giving way," I asked with concern.

He stepped back inside, shrugging, "It's probably a lot stronger than I can imagine, and may have moved all it's going to for a while. That tree branch must've weighed ten times what I do and look at all the time I stood out there on the porch pitching those logs without it giving way. While it appears structurally sound, much depends on how deep those anchor supports extend into the wall, and years of weathering have taken its toll on it. Considering the time it will take to make repairs on the railing, you might as well start from scratch by replacing the platform. If we have to set up scaffolding and redo all the mortar and stonework where it attached to the building, you may be looking at a costly undertaking."

"Okay, well, when you get a chance, please give me an estimate for the work, and in your bid, keep in mind that I'd like the new railing to have the same style of design. Of course, what's most important is that it's safe and sturdy when you're done—I wouldn't want somebody going out there a few years from now and having it fall down."

"I know what you mean," said Patrick, "and from this viewpoint we have no idea how far those anchor supports run inside this exterior wall. A person would certainly be taking a risk by going out on it now, so I'd recommend keeping off it until I can make an assessment and test it for strength."

"Maurice and I have no reason to go out there, so you don't have to worry."

Patrick then commented, "Long after we're all dust, this place will still be standing," then he went downstairs to begin stacking the wood he'd just cut.

The tree limb had collapsed inward on the foot of the bed, but had done little more than to shove about the other furnishings. Somehow, the vanity and its mirrors survived the tree limb's astounding entrance. I was surprised at how the merry-go-round jewelry box had hung on for the ride and showed no damage whatsoever.

Maurice, by now, had swept all the twigs, leaves, loose bark, and sawdust into a heaping pile on the carpet. We shifted the vanity back into the space it previously occupied, and he said, "After I sweep most of this up, I'll bring up the vacuum sweeper to get all the wood chips and sawdust out of the carpet."

"We've done enough for one day, Maurice, you must be tired. At least the rain cooled things off some, tomorrow we'll finish cleaning up, and we'll see about moving one of the other beds from another bedroom in here. We'll have to make certain the old headboard is adaptable for fitting to it."

Afterward, I went downstairs to give Patrick a hand stacking wood, and when opening the door to go outside, I met him standing there.

"I thought before it gets too late I'd better get into town and see about those doors. We don't want to leave that doorway opening to the balcony exposed to another rainstorm, so before I leave I'll cover the opening with a tarp I keep on my truck."

"Okay, then, I'll stack the rest of the wood."

"You needn't bother, Ms. MacKennsey, I can finish it up when I return tomorrow."

Intending to move some of the logs anyway, I placed them out behind the carriage house where some firewood was already stacked, and the job went on for some time. In the midst of this task, I noticed an entrance door left ajar on the side of the carriage-house building where the door appeared cracked open. This ordinary door was a commonly used entrance separate from the main wide double doors once used to open for horse-drawn carriages. Deciding to peek in, I opened it up wide enough to encounter two other doors at a landing or junction space. I imagined the door straight in front of me gave access to the staircase which Maurice used for passage up to his living quarters, expecting the other door, to my left, gave entrance to the ground floor and stable.

Inquisitive, I stepped inside the entranceway, first trying the door leading to the stairs and second story, but found it locked. Then I tried the other door on my left and opening it, I saw a dark area where the only light was that which came from the sun behind me. As I stared inside, the dim outline of stalls formed, and I noticed a large carriage far back in the rear.

Standing inside the alcove where these doors intersected, I heard a strange sound that drew me back to the first door I'd tried, which led up to Maurice's living quarters. I recognized the sound of a sniffing dog on the other side of this door, as it then began scratching to get out—it was the collie, Shannon.

Suddenly a shadow appeared behind me, I turned quickly to see Maurice standing there holding a tall glass of lemonade in his hand.

"Here you go, Miss, a little something to cool you down a bit," and he handed me the glass. We heard the dog on the other side of the door reacting excitedly to the sound of his voice, and he said, "Guess I'll have to let that pesky old dog out, she'll probably just run off."

He withdrew keys from his pocket to unlock the door, and the dog immediately ran out to begin jumping on both of us. "She's been cooped up for a while," and Maurice raised his hand as if to strike her, but the threat had no effect on the dog's overanxious excitement.

"Get down!" he shouted, and the animal simmered down.

"A-w-wh, she just needs some lovin'," and I knelt to gently scratch her behind the ears.

"She's no house dog, that's for sure," he said. "She's got so much energy, they're natural jumpers, you know. Collies are loyal companions, they're good with children, and what she really needs a home with a family."

"Deep down, I can tell you're a pet lover, Maurice."

When Maurice started back to the house, the dog followed him, and wanting to play, she kept jumping up and down.

"Bah! Get down ya pesky mongrel."

The door was open, and I saw a straight-running set of stairs leading up to his living quarters, but I couldn't bring myself to climb them. It just didn't seem right to invade the privacy of someone else's home just for the sake of curiosity, especially when they'd been so kind and considerate to me.

Returning to the logs, I moved them until they were all stacked. I was fatigued and exhausted afterward and managed to sneak a short nap on the living room couch before dinner. The rest helped revive me, and for the first time since my arrival, I came to the kitchen table with a real appetite.

Following dinner, Maurice changed the bandages on my arm and examining the wound, he saw no signs of infection, as it appeared to be healing well. Not expecting Patrick's return tonight, I hoped he'd have success in finding a set of french doors that would fit the door space leading to the balcony outside Angela's bedroom. I counted on him to return in the morning and install the doors before any more bad weather arrived.

I didn't think about it much last night, but I no longer sensed Angela's presence in the house, but still held fresh in my mind the moment when that tree limb crashed through those doors. If there was a force which oppressed or counteracted the threat she aimed against me, it may have left her bound to another existence in some limbo where she couldn't interact with the present. I might have a false sense of security, but at least for now, I didn't feel as though I had to worry about encountering her. For now, she wasn't a threat to me.

I hadn't written George in a long time and wanting to pour out my thoughts to someone, I wrote him before going to bed that night. This time, I detailed the story that brought me here, and told him everything about my grandfather's death. I confided how I believed I'd seen the ghost of one of my ancestors and also made mention of the hooded man. Writing him helped ease my state of mind, alleviating the pressure I was under, and yearning for him, I asked that he write back at his first opportunity.

CHAPTER 18

THE MAGICIAN'S LAST RITES

The following morning, I woke with a chill. Lying in the fetal position, I discovered my blanket at the foot of the bed and thought I must've kicked it off during the night, something I hadn't done since a child. Patrick arrived early, he'd found a new set of french doors very similar to the old ones he was replacing, and he proceeded to make the necessary modifications to hang them. He used care to keep from damaging the interior walls when replacing the old woodwork as part of the doorjamb.

After extensive cleaning and dusting, Maurice and I started dismantling a bed from another room at the end of the corridor and transported it piece-by-piece into Angela's room. The original headboard from Angela's bed was compatible with it, so we went ahead and used it. Early that afternoon, I rode in to Cardigan with Maurice to do some shopping, purchasing new curtains for Angela's room and a soft pink floral bedspread similar to the old one I'd discarded. Using this opportunity to mail the letter I'd written to George the night before, afterward, I found time to get a new glass for the picture frame for Angela's portrait that had broken.

Arriving home later that same afternoon, Patrick informed me that he'd hung the replacement french doors, also remarking that he'd stained the doors and put a coat of finish on them. He then mentioned he'd left the doors ajar and cautioned me against closing them tightly because they might stick.

When he finished loading up his truck for the day for preparing to leave, he said, "Tomorrow I'm starting a new job in town."

"I thought you were going to bring out a welder to inspect the balcony?"

"I know you're anxious to get the balcony repaired, and I don't mean to let you down, but the balcony isn't something requiring immediate attention. I really need to take this other job while the opportunity is there or else I stand to lose a great deal of work."

"I understand, but can you give me some idea when you'll be able to get to it?"

"It'll be two to four weeks before I can return, but no longer that that, I assure you. You don't have to pay me for any of the work I've done until the balcony's completed. That way I'll be all the more eager to get to those repairs on the balcony."

I insisted on paying him for the work he'd done thus far, having faith he'd keep to his word on getting to the balcony as soon as he could.

The next day, Maurice and I made certain the finish on the french doors had dried before closing and securing them, and then we hung the curtains and finished making the bed in Angela's room. Soon it was much the same as it was before the tree limb caused so much damage, and after replacing the glass in the picture frame, we hung her portrait on the wall.

Late that same evening, I'd taken my usual leather chair in the library and started a new novel. Maurice had turned in early, and I, too, began feeling drowsy. The reading made my eyelids heavy, and when pausing to rub them, I distinctly heard four notes stroked on the piano's keyboard. It grabbed my attention, and I laid the book down to investigate.

Entering the living room, I targeted the piano with my sight but saw nothing or no one there. Continuing to move in the direction of the huge black instrument, I halfway expected a cat or squirrel had found its way in the house and walked across the keyboard, but I saw no such creature in the room. Glancing at the grandfather clock, I noticed it had stopped keeping time to register almost nine-thirty, and in the quiet which held the house, I became aware that I hadn't heard it chime all night.

179

Realizing I'd grown quite tired, and thinking notes heard on the piano may have been my imagination, I decided to turn in. I reentered the library to shut off the lights and saw something out of the corner of my eye: it was a man hanging by his neck from a wooden support beam! He had bulging blood red eyes, a bluish purple complexion, and mussed curly black hair!

Closing my eyes in disbelief, shutting out the ghastly and horrific spectacle, I reopened them after a second to no longer see him there. Believing my eyes were playing tricks on me, I blinked a few times, and then raised my eyebrows while surveying the library's ceiling. The vision lingered in my mind—as did a creepy, chilling effect—but I no longer saw anything there. Glimpsing the moose head hanging over the fireplace, the stuffed and mounted animal with a big protruding nose and huge antlers seemed to be asking me if I'd seen the same thing it did.

Still unsure of what I'd seen and heard, I was aware of the delirium I'd fallen under to momentarily question my senses. Thinking how the last couple of days I'd put forth a lot of effort and energy getting my grandmother's bedroom back into shape, I summed up that I was more tired than I realized. Convinced I'd imagined what I thought I'd seen, and having regained calm and composure, I chose not to dwell on the experience, for I felt I needed sleep. To think about it any further would only serve to place my mind in a paranoid state, and I wasn't going to allow myself to lie awake for hours as I'd done so many other times. I switched off the lights and went up to my bedroom.

Wrestling with the thought of whether I should lock my door, in the end, I took a stance of defiance to leave the door open and climbed into bed. However, there seemed to be no end to the time I lay in bed awake, and I learned how long the lonely night can be. Eventually sleep came, and in it, I took to dreaming.

I found myself standing in the corridor outside my room with everything covered by frost, the length of the hallway stretched out of proportion before me. Attracted to the echoing sound of music coming from the end of the hall, I heard the song "The Band Played On" played on a piano. Lured by the gaiety of notes played on a fine-tuned piano, I stalled when frightened by the flurry of a spirit standing in a doorway. The pale lackluster image was merely my own reflection in a mirror, and the fluttering was nothing more than the motion of the gown I wore. Drawn again to the sound of musical notes, I made my way to the servants' staircase; the music came from the third floor. My curiosity drew me to it.

My gown and robe flowed in a subtle breeze running against me, and in a strange way, I felt as if I was caught up in an Alice-in-Wonderland world filled with exaggerated distortions. Motion came slow in this dreamscape as I started up the dark, twisting staircase. Uneven stairs made the climb awkward and perilous; I looked back with the inkling that a white rabbit may be pursuing me and saw there was no way to reverse course— there were no steps behind me, just an infinite black abyss!

In my endless climb, I detected light awaiting me at the crest of the staircase. As the ballroom came into view, I saw a colorful life-size carrousel carrying on a revolving motion, its horses bobbing up and down as though keeping time with the music. In this curious circus atmosphere, the music took on a more lively rhythm, but remained steady in playing the same tune. Approaching the ride, I anticipated the piano was located on the stage on the far side of this immense rotating merry-go-round. Desiring to see who was performing, I concluded the only way to get to the other side was to catch a ride on the fast-moving carnival ride.

The floor rolled and pitched to the beat of the song, and in the midst of this distortion, the ride slowed down, and the music's pace did too. In my anxiety to see what or who awaited me on the stage side, I stepped forward onto the carousel and caught hold of one of the upright bars. I moved forward and found company with a cheerfully decorated black horse, then gaining hold of the bobbing horse's mane while glimpsing its face. As the music and ride resumed a bouncy beat as if performing in time, the ride took me around to the stage side, but instead of seeing a piano, I saw Angela's bed on the stage. I recognized the headboard and printed bedspread.

This made no sense, and just as the beat of the song picked up, I saw the expression of the horse I clung to changing while turning fearful and wide-eyed as though warning me to get off the ride. I took this signal seriously, and as the merry-go-round kept revolving, I got off at precisely the same spot where I'd gotten on; but for reasons I couldn't comprehend or have any control over, I still sought the music's origin. Seeking to leave the third floor, I returned to the dark rickety servant's stairs; then remembering that the only piano in the house was down on the first floor, I started down the twisting stairs. In my own way, I thought the only one who could be playing the instrument was my grandfather; and feeling the sudden pressing desire to see him, I began to venture there. Continuing my downward flight, the circus or carnival sound in the version of "The Band Played On" grew to a distant echo and the notes from the piano on the first floor became well-defined while growing stronger and distinctly clearer.

When arriving at the second floor, I hesitated before deciding to take the hallway corridor as an avenue for reaching the main set of stairs off the living room. Freezing cold temperatures accompanying me along the way increased in intensity, causing me great discomfort, but I had no choice except to endure its sting. This biting cold made me worried and warily watchful for Angela's wrath; I knew she roamed these halls; and if we stumbled into one another, she may, once again, direct her anger at me.

Scurrying on in my journey down the icy corridor, I heard the tune and melody played on the piano changing while remaining in lively character with that turn-of-the-century era. Notes of a different song revived the gaiety of those golden days as though happier times from the past were being resurrected; there came sporadic laughter in a party atmosphere, and then men and women began to indiscriminately join in song—slightly off key but cheerfully adding lyrics to the upbeat rhythm.

"Hel-lo my baby, hel-lo my hon-ey, hel-lo my rag-time gal.
Send me a kiss by wire, baby my heart's on fire!
If you re-fuse me, honey, you'll lose me, then you'll be left
a-lone;
Oh ba-by, telephone and tell me I'm your own."

Nearing the corridor's end, the accompanying voices faded out on the last verse, and all that I heard now was the pounding of the keys on the piano keyboard. Arriving at the second-floor balcony, I came to view the living room, and I saw a headless pianist in a tuxedo with his hands and arms working the keys, but I kept coming down the stairs, and halfway down the staircase, I stopped and stared at the bizarre sight, preparing to run back up the stairs at any instant.

Turning my head, I saw the hooded man at the stair's summit—in his hands the bloodied halberd axe!

The sheer terror awoke me, and I sat up in bed with my eyes open wide—the convincing horror suddenly became real, for *I* heard the same piece played on the piano downstairs in the living room!

Shivering all over, the moon's dingy glow coming through the window enabled me to see my blanket rolled back at my feet, leaving my body exposed to freezing cold temperatures! The incredible cold was what caused me to shiver, and the clarity of the musical notes played on the piano dancing freely throughout the house left me unnerved too. I didn't dare guess who the pianist was, but surmising it wasn't Maurice, what choice did I have but to investigate, and I threw on a wrap matching my pajamas for combating the cold. Moving barefoot into the hallway, I closed my robe while folding my arms to further guard against the bitter cold. Moving hurriedly down the dark hallway to see who or what was working the piano keyboard, I became wary that the dream was a premonition and cautiously looked back to see what was behind me before making my approach on the stairs.

From my vantage point at the top of the stairs, the living room seemed like a gigantic pit and I gasped, quivering as I saw the piano stool vacant, but the keys dropping vicariously on their own!

Starting down the stairs to have a closer look, the moonlight's misty beam through a window came down in oblong fashion across the piano as it conducted its own play. Stifled and overcome with fear, my legs stopped working while I stared intensely at the keys—exercising method and procedure to compose the bouncy sound I heard. The keyboard finally fell still, and at the stroke of pure silence, a deep rumbling quaked and shook the house!

I braced my back flat against the wall, raising my hand until my right hand came into contact with an object, and I winced when realizing I'd touched the medieval axe hanging from the wall over the staircase!

A sudden surge of air came down the staircase, steadily increasing until a streak of white whooshed past me, rustling my hair and nightgown. The white shadow circled the room, and with a popping sound, I detected something had taken place at the fireplace, and then I witnessed the white shadow streaking while disappearing into a narrow opening. The opening looked to be a concealed panel next to the fireplace behind the white headless statuette.

Expecting more of the unexpected, my eyes glanced to the top of the stairs to see if the hooded man had appeared; and once certain he hadn't, I watched over the room's radius—the still, headless statuette and resting piano keys. Seconds later, temperatures returned to normal, and my filled lungs exhaled. I had a revelation that tonight, destiny had me playing a key role in its scheme; and in order to alter my own course and learn the purpose for my being here, I'd have to venture off these stairs and join in these cosmic events. Certain that God had his hand in this, perhaps my prayers were going to be at last answered, but not without my voluntary participation.

Finding it difficult to move at all, but with my inner self urging me to meet whatever fate had placed in front of me; I managed to get my legs to cooperate and then completed my descent to the first floor. Advancing in the direction of the hidden compartment, next to the fireplace and behind the statuette, I crouched while peering inside where I saw a foreboding and eerily obscure darkness. Hearing a strange buzzing sound, I straightened and turned to focus on the face of the grandfather clock; the hands were spinning backward!

My eyes drawn to the moon's reflection on the piano, I saw the five stick candelabra arranged in the piano's center. Hunting down a box of wooden matches from on top the mantelpiece, I removed one and struck it against the side of the matchbox to ignite its flame, then noticing that only two matches remained in the box. Moving to the side of the fireplace to force the door to the compartment open wider, I extended the hand holding the lit match inside and saw an uninviting narrow set of stone steps leading down and around the outside of the fireplace foundation. Hesitant and distrusting about entering this inhibiting underworld, I knew if I was to learn the secrets of the past, it was essential to face my fears and go forth.

Momentarily moving from the passageway to glance out the window, I saw a thick fog had rolled in; thinking this night had long ago been written on the pages of time—formulated by both the past and present—I didn't believe I had much time to deliberate. Whatever forces making this phenomenon come into being weren't going to wait—I decided I must try; I must act now.

The match I held had nearly burned back to my fingertips, and I tossed it into the fireplace before opening the match box and using a second match to light all five candles mounted on the candelabra. It crossed my mind that I had but one match left in the box, and I held the matchbox tightfisted in my left hand while firmly gripping the candelabra with my right and lifted it off the piano. Together, these five candles made a sufficient, reliable light source; and making my way back to the narrow opening, the candlelight allowed me to see a hanging spiderweb, which pulsated from the fluctuating cool wind escaping this underground passageway. Ducking to avoid the spiderweb, I started down these rapidly descending stairs of rounded stone concealed within the construction of the fireplace in how they took a bend around it. Passing arched stone foundation walls, the way ahead looked much like what one would expect to find leading down to a dungeon in a castle. I felt as though I'd penetrated one of the pyramids and was on the brink of entering an ancient pharaoh's tomb.

A sudden down draft of air came, and with its growing strength, I closely watched the candlelight's flickering, and tried to guard the dancing flames from the wind by encircling them with my hand and arm; but one continued to decline, weakening until it went out. Then I heard a slamming sound, and I knew the panel had shut tight behind me; and with the entrance to the passage closed, the draft dissipated. Thinking whatever force had manipulated me into coming this far must be determined to block my retreat, I watched the remaining candles flames rebound in their brightness as they stabilized.

I held the candelabra upright while descending further down into this steep cavity, and not having the tiniest inkling of what lay ahead in this godforsaken domain, I was somewhat regretting the expedition at this point. Shaking off my fears and still determined to press on, the stairs finally ended, but the pathway I carried on with kept a slight decline, and I saw the stone walls fuse with natural stone—the entrance to the cave! The change to a natural cavern held my interest for but a second, and continuing to venture into this dark infinity while having hair-raising sensations about what lay ahead, I couldn't help the frightening feeling that something was lying in wait out beyond my field of vision.

My eyes navigated by the candlelight's hypnotizing glow that reflected off the walls and ceiling of the cave as my feet went on making steps; and I fell mentally under a numbed paralysis as though I was in a mesmerizing dreamscape. The mere matter of my walk caused the dancing gold flames to quicken the melting down of wax running down the candlesticks and dripping off the brass. Cut off from the rest of the world in this bleak, barren, dormant dimension, I thought I could hear the sound of dripping water; and not far ahead, I faintly saw water droplets falling from a crack in the stone ceiling and landing in a shallow puddle. The water seeped and slowly trickled from an overhead crevice, and I tried avoiding the drops. I tiptoed on stones covered by a slippery, slimy sludge of a muddy green color, and this cold, moist mold gave an icky feeling to my bare feet.

Now marching up a slight incline, walking on jagged stone pebbles covering the floor of the cave caused me pain and discomfort, the space around me began to widen, and the ceiling raised over four meters above my head to where I could barely see it.

"Ouch." I sang out loud with an echo as the heel of my left foot received a stabbing pain from a sharp pebble; and leaning against the cave wall for balance, I brushed the bottom of my left foot free of small rocks; and switching my weight to my left leg, I did the same to my right foot.

Resuming my walking pace, I saw the walls and ceiling expanding even further until they could no longer carry the candlelight's reflection. Bewildered by the surrounding darkness in this great open chamber, when putting my right foot forward, the ground had taken a big dip, and I lost my footing, stumbled, and fell, snuffing out the precious light and fumbling the matchbook too!

Marooned in my blackest, bleakest nightmare, while lost in this blind desolation, my fingers found the candelabra, but all the candles were missing. I reached and searched about me to recover one candle then another, but they were entirely useless to me without a flame; the matchbox mustn't have fallen far out of reach, but where? Rendered hopelessly helpless without the candle's light, unable to see my hand in front of my face in this pitch-black, I began to panic while desperately reaching and feeling about for the matchbox; and caught in this gripping fear of the unknown, my fingers were finding nothing but pieces of stone. My very life depended upon my finding that matchbox— I'd never find my way out of here without it. A strong feeling of doom came over me, and as tears flowed from my eyes and ran down my cheeks, I tasted their salty wetness on my lips.

Unable to find the matchbox, I felt a draining, heart-sinking sensation, and I begged out loud, saying, "Please, God, help me…Please…"

Suddenly, a blinding white light shattered the darkness, and I winced while squinting at the dazzling divine prelude of a vivid brilliance such as I've never seen before! Having commenced from a far corner and engulfing the entire area before me, this pure, bold light touched my senses, warmed my heart, and showered me with love, curbing my fear and filling me with wondrous awe.

An astonishing fire burst forth from this corner with a roaring fury—red, amber, and bright yellow serrated flames danced and spit! I beheld within this blaze mystifying imagery taking on form and shape—a swirling, glimmering glitter fused around a body of blue in the shape of a head or a man's face! I became absorbed in reverence as the mouth of this face opened, and it spoke to me in a masculine voice, saying, "In your pursuit to discover what your heart desires, look to the beast. For beneath him is where your answers lie...."

The face blended into the flames, which gradually began to die down; and as the fire's brightness decreased in intensity, just before total darkness engulfed the area around me, I saw the matchbox and snatched it up. Overwhelmed by the vision I'd just witnessed but once again alone in this blackest pit, I reminded myself that I had only one match left, and it was the key to finding my way out of here. Getting a grip before carefully opening the box, my fingers were my eyes, as I made certain I didn't have the matchbox upside down so not to lose that last match. Now carefully taking hold of the match firmly in my grasp, I stroked it against the side of the matchbox and a flame ignited.

Exhaling a sigh of relief, my whole existence seemed to revolve around this single flame; and snuggly holding one of the candles on an angle in my hand, I proceeded to light it; the candle's wick took the flame, and after dropping the quick-burning match, I stood the candelabra upright, planting two other candles in their holding places. Using the lit candle to start their wicks to flame, I then set the lit candle in the center of the candelabra; and believing three candles were adequate to light the way, I firmly gripped the candelabra and came to a standing position.

Feeling more at ease but wanting to get out of this cavernous place as soon as possible, I took a moment to press into memory what I'd both just seen and heard and somehow connected the image I'd seen to my grandfather; I actually believed the head I'd seen in the fire was that of my grandfather's. I replayed in my mind his aspiring words while speaking them out loud, "In your pursuit to discover what your heart desires, look to the beast. For beneath him is where your answers lie."

Even though I wasn't sure what the words meant, my inner soul brimmed with the hope that I'd eventually be able to discern their meaning; and before deciding to launch my exodus, I felt drawn to the corner where I'd witnessed this miracle. There I saw what I perceived to be a large knotted bundle or garment resting on a flat stone; the garment appeared bundled in a circular fashion and stained with a dark substance. In moving to further examine what I'd found, I placed the candelabra on the ground, making certain it was secure so that it couldn't fall, then I proceeded to move closer to undo and unfold the cloth material. As I did, I became jolted when its contents became exposed—a white skeletal head rolled off the stone to my feet! Cold hollowed cavities for eyes were in stark contrast to the almost pure white curvature of a smooth cranium; the skull appeared longing to be unveiled while the eerie dental work carried a wide sinister grin as if glad to be liberated.

"Oh God! Oh my God!" I said, scrambling to distance myself from the object.

Momentarily stunned by the features of my discovery, I realized the skull belonged to my grandfather. His skull had been resting here ever since the night of his murder, and I immediately thought how its rightful place was in the mausoleum with the rest of his remains; only then can he find true peace. Now considering the grim prospect of transporting the object, I took the cloth I found it in, spread it out, and then nervously rolled the skull into its center. Closing and securing the corners before knotting them to make it easy to carry, and with this pouch dangling from my left hand, I clutched the candelabra tightly with my right hand and lifted it. Now my eyes began to search for an exit and I saw not one, but two nearby openings, one larger than the other, but I sensed that neither were the passageway I'd entered from.

To get to the larger opening—a wide oval-shaped hole—I had to climb a mound of rubble, so I chose to take the other way, and my surroundings made me feel like I was trapped in a maze of tunnels. My worst fear was not seeing something to cause me to stumble and fall into a deep pit too steep for me to climb out of; also, such a fall would cause me to lose my precious candle-light, so I had to move slowly and deliberately with each short step taken. My efforts soon took me to a few stone steps leading up to a steep, winding wooden staircase—I was back inside the house again, but I had no idea of my location within the realm of the structure nor did I know where this staircase was leading me to. With each turn in the narrow rickety stairs, my worst worry to consider was meeting up with the hooded man; all the while gnawing at me was my morbid cargo—a human skull!

The vigorously long, hard climb took me steadily upward; and making a turn, I caught a glimpse of something squirming on a step—a black hairy rat stuck its head out of a hole, showing its teeth while snarling!

Springing backwards to avoid this vicious creature, the candle's light snuffed out as I extended my hands and arms out-ward to catch myself from falling down the stairs. I barely kept my balance while hanging on; trapped in this wretched darkness with this awfully big rat, I lost myself and began frantically pounding at the enclosure around me with the candelabra while hanging on tight to the garment carrying the skull. I desperately kicked and flung the candelabra about me in a mad rage, and when ramming the piece solidly against the wall, a panel burst open, and I plunged head-first forward into a dark room to fall on the floor; belching out of that passage with a cloud of dust, the panel closed just as fast as it had opened.

At first confused by my unfamiliar surroundings, dim moonlight from a nearby window enabled me to focus on the room's interior; and from my position on the floor, I focused on a big four-post bed—the very site of the murder! The skull I carried had escaped the garment and rolled out onto the floor; it lay in arms reach at the edge of the pale moonlight, partly in the light and partly in shadow, and those gaping dark eye sockets peered at me as though to say, "Don't forget me." Gripping the loose, weightless garment I'd carried it in, I rose to my feet; and setting up the garment in an effort to hold it open close to the floor, I moved to nudge and maneuver the skull back into the garments fold then left the room hurriedly.

Carrying the skull inside the garment like before, my worst fear was encountering the hooded man, and I remained warily watchful and cautious of coming upon him in the dark of night. I didn't understand why my fear of coming into contact with this phantom was greater now than ever before; maybe it was that I felt most vulnerable at this particular moment or because of the skull I transported; but in the dead of night, walking through this dark house, it only seemed the fitting way of fate or destiny for us to meet. I scurried down the hall to the servant's staircase, moving quickly down the stairs to leave the candelabra on the kitchen table. Reaching the back door off the kitchen, I opened it and saw a crawling ghostly fog awaiting me as it beckoned me, daring me to venture out into its mist.

Stepping out of the house, my feet made contact with the cold, damp cobblestone as I waded into the night's dense fog; and starting in the direction of the flower beds, an uncomfortable feeling haunted me like the sensation that I might fall prey to someone or something unseen lurking about out there. Unable to see the carriage house out back, I watched how my movement disturbed the night's swirling fog; and hearing the repetition of a strange muffled sound, I turned, and my eyes widened in an attempt to penetrate the fog—I was being stalked—but I couldn't return to the house just yet because I knew that whatever was out there was between me and the door I'd made my exit from.

Hearing something behind me, scared but clinging to the idea that I had such a little ways to go to reach the mausoleum, I kept moving. I turned around to look back and my dancing, watchful eyes couldn't see anything, but my instincts told me that a predatory creature was on the prowl, sizing me up. I only wished I had a weapon or some means to defend myself because I felt so very vulnerable; I just had to try to get into that mausoleum and accomplish placing my grandfather's skull inside the sarcophagus with the rest of the remains of his body.

I told myself I had to keep going—I must try for the sake of my grandfather; it's the only way he can find a lasting peace away from this world.

Suddenly startled by what looked like a fair-sized animal closing in and moving toward me, I balked before realizing it was the collie, Shannon, and I felt relieved to see it was her. Kneeling to gently caress the short hair on her long nose and then massage her behind the ears, I immediately became hopeful that she'd accompany me to the mausoleum, and starting off together, she remained at my side. The flowers soon came into view; the night and this nasty fog dulled their beauty, as they seemed to be in a dormant sleep, appearing blunt and lacking of life and luster. The murky fog drowned out my view of the area ahead, but I kept following the path, and soon I saw the dim outline of the mausoleum; and when finally approaching its door, I was terribly disappointed to notice the collie had abandoned me.

I soon met the mausoleum door with awe and surprise, stunned to find it open to me! Extremely alarmed and edgy about this unexpected situation, I felt unwelcome, and my eyes scanned its dim interior until focusing on the crypt or burial vault, then I cautiously entered. Placing the garment used to transport the skull on the floor, I then went to the far end of the burial casing where I expected the head should rest; and getting firm footing, I leaned while extending my arms and braced the palms of my hands against the lid of the casing while pushing hard, but the stubborn lid held firm and wouldn't budge.

Questioning whether I possessed the strength to move it by myself, but hard-pressed to try again, I braced my legs and feet while leaning to push and apply all the strength and leverage I had in my body. Taking a deep breath and shoving again with all my might, this time the stone lid made a short dull grinding sound as it dislodged from the position it held. Trying once more, this time it shifted slowly, the sound of stone grinding against stone was awful, and I finally managed to slide it to where I had it angled open sufficiently to allow me to put the skull in. I gathered up the garment carrying the skull and lowered the dangling cloth down into the black chamber to where it settled with the rest of my grandfather's remains.

Changing my position by moving to the other side of the sarcophagus to where I extended my arms and firmly applied pressure from my pushing palms to readjust the stone lid, and it moved slowly until finally shifting back into place. With the remains of my grandfather whole, I believed he can now find peace. A little exhausted from the task, I took a deep breath before walking over to the entrance to the mausoleum; and turning to gaze upon the stone sarcophagus once more, I thought I'd finally accomplished something by coming here to this estate.

Suddenly hearing something directly behind me and drowning in fear from what it could be—my mind would not accept or comprehend what it might be—I lost consciousness and blacked out.

CHAPTER 19

COMPANY ARRIVES

A cool, wet sensation running across my forehead revived me, and as life flowed back into my body, I detected another's presence. Opening my eyes, I saw flames dancing and went into a fighting rampage to gain my freedom!

My arms and shoulders immediately pinned down; I heard a familiar, reassuring voice saying, "It's all right, Claire."

It registered that the voice I heard was George's, and looking into his eyes, I fought him no more but clutched him tightly; my delight showed in how tears filled my eyes, and I said, "Oh George, I don't think I've ever been so happy to see anyone in my life!"

Realizing I was on one of the sofas in the living room, a warm fire raging in the fireplace projected a soft glow reflecting off his face, the ceiling, and the room's furnishings. George sat on the edge of the sofa cushion, leaning over me to say, "Everything's going to be just fine now. I'm going to take you away from all of this."

After his gift of a kiss on my cheek, we hugged again, and I said, "You will not believe what I've been though tonight."

His eyebrows rose, "You look like you've been doing excavation in your night gown."

"I must look atrocious, but you're not far from it."

He gently wiped off my face and forehead with a damp cloth, "You look pretty good from this angle—you still have the dimples you had as a teenager."

His eyes scanning my torn, disheveled, soiled gown, giving study to how revealing it was, his gaze and expression told me he was envisioning me without any clothing; blushing, I closed my robe and raised my knees upward toward my chin while wrapping my arms around my legs.

Seeing how banged up my legs were, with scrapes and small cuts, he wiped down my legs, ankles and feet, commenting, "Where'd you get such little feet?"

Viewing the fire while trying to put together in my mind the night's sequence of events, I must have had a faraway look in my eyes as I stared without responding to the question. Watching the tongue-like serrated flames dancing in the fire helped to conjure in my minds eye the moment when I saw my grandfather's face when I was down in the cave.

"Why don't you try telling me about these adventures you experienced tonight?"

"There's an opening to a secret passageway over there, next to the fireplace behind that statuette, I found it tonight after awakening to the sound of the piano playing."

George nodded in the direction of the grand piano, "Is that the piano you heard?"

"Yes, George, and that passageway leads beneath this house to where there's an entrance to a cave. I've gone through it, and I witnessed the visitation of my grandfather's spirit; it was the most amazing and astonishing thing I've ever seen in my life."

"We're talking about the grandfather you wrote me about— the one who got axed and decapitated in his sleep?"

"Yes...He left me words to help me find the answers to what really happened the night he was killed, and George, tonight I discovered his skull. I found it in the cave, and wanting to join the skull with the rest of his remains, I carried it with me out to the mausoleum...Had you given me some kind of warning, I may not have fainted."

"Claire, this is where I found you, only a few minutes ago, right here where you are now."

I sat up on the sofa, looking at him in disbelief. "You weren't the one who came up behind me in the mausoleum?" I placed my hand over my mouth.

George's eyes turned to the fire and then back to me, as he said, "I had to bribe a cab driver to drive me out here in the middle of the night, and I paid him like four times the normal fee. Trying to find this place after dark and in this fog was quite a challenge, and nearly impossible. The driver misjudged a curve in the road and skidded into a ditch about ten miles back and I had to walk the rest of the way here.

"Anyway, when nobody answered the front door I came around to the back of the house and knocked again before letting myself in. It seemed a little weird to chance entering the house without being certain that I'd come to the right place. Still, when no one answered my knock, I decided to try to find you, and kept calling out for you as I came from the kitchen toward the living room. I thought I heard someone go out the front door just before finding you stretched out here on the sofa in front of the fireplace. When you didn't respond to any gestures I made, I went back to the kitchen to dampen a wash cloth, and here we are now."

I removed my hand from my mouth, "If that's true, then how did I get here?"

"How about the caretaker?"

"Maurice, no," and I shook my head no to affirm my answer. "He couldn't have managed carrying me from the mausoleum to here."

"Okay, before fainting, you'd gone to the mausoleum, and what do you remember after that?"

My eyes wandered, not focusing on any one thing as I resurrected in my mind what I remembered, and explained, "The door was open to the mausoleum when I got there. I managed to shift the lid to the burial vault, and just after placing the skull into the chamber, I heard something behind me and I thought...I'm not sure what I thought, but then I blacked out."

I squinted when looking at him, and asked, "You didn't start the fire in the fireplace?"

"No, I did not... I wish I'd come here sooner, Claire, but I just couldn't get away, and when receiving your last letter, I believed you were in danger, so I hopped on a plane to get here as fast as possible."

Leaning back, I rested my head against the sofa's arm cushion, "Well, at least you're here now. Thank God."

George came close, placing his right hand against my cheek and turned my head so I'd face him, "Tomorrow we'll try digging up some answers, but for now, put it all out of your mind."

His fingernails lightly stroked my neck with a caressing touch, and my eyelids fell shut. I drew a deep breath and exhaled with a sigh, "Mmmm, you're putting me to sleep George."

George continued gently messaging my neck with his soothing fingertips, and when reopening my eyes, I saw a wanting desire in his gleaming eyes; he pulled me toward him, our lips met in a most sensual way, and my heart melted—the magic of love was here and now. I fell into his arms, his hands pressing firmly against my shoulder blades as he pulled me to him, and we kissed again.

Logs on the fire crackled as we embraced, and sensing what we shared was real true love, my heart felt light and brimming with a burning, sensual desire. I felt a tingling flutter within myself, like a tug at my heartstrings, leading to a quivering throb, and looking deep into his eyes, I saw in them everything I've always looked for and wanted. We cuddled, snuggled, and stirred; and compulsively wanting all of him, we kissed long and deeply; such a fire ignited to possess me.

Breathlessly kissing as we fondled, I felt susceptibly vulnerable to these driving desires, and my heart and soul overflowed from a dynamic passion I've never experienced before. I confessed in thought to being emancipated and lost control, clutching him with ever increasing aspirations.

"Oh, George."

Temperatures rising, he fondled my breasts firmly and caressingly through the gown's flimsy, silky smooth material; my nipples grew hard and inflamed from an inherent propensity. The provocatively stimulating tenderness gave me spirit, and I temptingly indulged myself, femininely flaunting myself for more. Unable to quell this building, burning hunger and enticement, I removed my gown and laid back, showing an alluring, seductive innocence, and he came to me, kissing my neck and shoulders; and then his moistened mouth administered warm suction on my bulging breasts, which drew a moan from me.

Aching for more loving affection, I anxiously unclothed him; we fell together in a lofty rapture, and I latched onto him, kissing the perspiration riding on his shoulders. He touched me with such feeling and depth that while engrossed in this enduring friction of sweet flesh, we forged a smooth penetrating rhythm and our hearts soared in a splendorous love that erupted in ecstasy.

A half hour later, I lay quietly next to George, and unable to keep from reviewing what I'd experienced in the cave, I recalled the words my grandfather gave me: "In your pursuit to discover what your heart desires, look to the beast. For beneath him is where your answers lie."

Noticing dim sunlight coming through the window beyond the piano, I stood and threw on my robe, "It's nearly sun-up—I don't want Maurice to ever catch us like this, George."

George sat up and took hold of my hand, "I came to convince you to leave this house, Claire, the past is something you can't undo, and you need to accept that." He then added with a tone of warning, "What if something had happened to you when you were down in that cave, who'd have known where you were?"

"I can't leave now, George, I told you I saw my grandfather's spirit and he left me with words to help me learn the truth."

Showing no enthusiasm, George turned his head.

"Don't you believe me?"

"Can you blame me for questioning such a fantastic story?"

"Don't you see, George, peace can never come to this house until the truth is known about my grandfather's murder. I believe there's more to his death than just a mad woman's execution of her husband in his sleep for no good reason, there has to be. However, if that is what happened, her blood flows through my veins, what's to say that I won't someday do great harm to someone I love?"

"I don't doubt for a minute that you've seen these things, but I believe you're the victim of a plot—you've been tricked, and I'm willing to bet that this kind-hearted Maurice Addison is the one orchestrating the whole thing...It's not clear, just yet, what his motives are, but I intend exposing them."

"George, I don't want you mistreating Maurice, and unless you can prove what you're saying, I'd like you to at least treat him politely...Until we've made other arrangements, you'll have to sleep here on the sofa. I'll leave a note on the kitchen table for Maurice, explaining who you are and that you'll be staying with us for a while."

As I turned, George's hand latched on to my arm, "I know it's important to you to find out why your grandfather died, Claire, but as I've said, I've come here to take you back home with me. I'm due in Houston, Texas, to complete some corporate work in three weeks. Wouldn't you say that's time enough for you to determine whether or not you can uncover the facts, am I not being fair in asking you to leave with me in three weeks?"

"I don't want to make a promise I may not be able to keep."

"If you haven't learned what you've came for by then, what makes you think you can ever learn the motive for your grandfather's murder? You're talking about something that happened decades ago, and look at all the weeks you've already spent here searching and come up with nothing. Now, I've come a long way to be here with you, and I not only think that what I'm asking is fair, but I believe I deserve an answer here and now." At first hesitating, I thought George made his point well; but knowing I may later regret agreeing with him, I said, "Okay, I'll leave with you under one condition. If within this three-week period, should I uncover strong evidence or any significant clue bringing me closer to my goal, I'll have to stay on."

"Who's to decide whether this so-called evidence is pertinent to your grandfather's murder?"

"George, I'm not going to quibble with you. I can't promise anything—I'm sorry, but that's the best I can do."

Starting up the stairs, I turned when hearing George say, "Claire, I'm glad I came here...This is some house."

Feeling much safer now that George had come, looking down on him from my place on the stairs, I saw him rummaging through his suit case to remove a flashlight. He tested it by projecting its strong beam at me as he watched me ascend the stairs.

After tossing down a blanket and pillow, I returned to my room; and because I was very tired or possibly because George was here now and I felt more secure, I managed to fall fast asleep. Hours later, in the early afternoon, Maurice helped George settle into a room two doors down from mine. George behaved rather grumpy, and at first, I thought it may be because he'd lacked sleep after his overseas flight. It was no surprise to me for him to be suffering from jet lag, for a long plane trip to a different time zone can make for a difficult adjustment. He later made his suspicions obvious of Maurice, and as much as I was hoping for the two of them to hit it off, George made it clear that he had no wish of getting to know Maurice on a personal basis.

I took George on a tour of the house, and in playing his escort; I showed him those places where I encountered strange happenings. When I took him to my grandmother's bedroom, he saw the painting of her hanging on the wall; and he paid me a compliment by mentioning I resembled her, for she was indeed an attractive woman. I then took him to the connecting door leading to my grandfather's bedroom; and although he didn't say anything pertaining to the fact that this was the scene of a hideous murder, it was naturally the first thing anyone would contemplate. I appreciated him withholding comments as we glimpsed into it.

When coming down into the living room, I took him over to the portrait of my grandfather and introduced George to it, saying, "This is my grandfather, Charles MacKennsey, George."

After taking a few minutes to admire my ancestor, I took him by the arm to lead him in the direction of the fireplace; and after a brief investigation, we found the panel to the passageway behind the statuette sealed tight. George made use of a fireplace poker in attempting to open it and pried on the stubborn door, but it appeared the only way it would give way was by applying more force, so he used the poker to chew a hole for gaining a hold. His efforts were annoying to me because I didn't want to see the well-concealed panel defaced, sprung, or damaged.

"George, stop," I insisted. "Please, stop. I'm afraid you're going to leave the door permanently damaged, and it's important to me to leave this house much the way that it was before I came."

He continued persistently working the poker, using it as a wedge between the small door and side facing of the fireplace; and growing increasingly irritable, and concerned that the door would break before it gave way, I raised my voice, saying, "I don't want it damaged, and that's what's going to happen if you don't stop."

George relaxed the pressure he had on the poker, "I thought you wanted to open this up to explore the cave once more."

"It's not so important that we have to tear the place up to do so. What we're looking for isn't down there anyway." I then gently tugged on his arm, "C'mon, I want to show you the courtyard and mausoleum."

Leading him away, we held hands when going through the house and out the backdoor to the courtyard; George seemed amused by the gorgeous array of flowers along the pathway leading to the mausoleum.

Arriving at the glass encased structure, George tried the handle on the door, but it wouldn't budge. He came close to touching his nose to the glass, cupping his hands around his eyes to shut out the sun's glare so he could clearly see the resting place of my grandfather.

We strolled about the garden for about twenty minutes; and when we returned to the house, I asked Maurice if he had a key that would unlock the door to the mausoleum, but he said no. It seemed we had one more unsolved mystery.

In the early evening of that same day, George and I had gone up to my room, and there we spent some time working on the riddle my grandfather left me.

"How does it go again?" George asked, lying on the bed stretched out comfortably on his back with his legs crossed, using his left elbow and arm to prop his head up.

"Here it is," I tore off a piece of stationary from a note pad on my dresser and handed it to him. "I wrote it down earlier this morning while it was still clear in my mind."

201

George read it out loud, "In your pursuit to discover what your heart desires, look to the beast. For beneath him is where your answers lie..."

I stood at the window looking out, thinking about the words while trying to understand their meaning.

George's arm relaxed as he placed the paper in plain view in front of himself. "Do you have any idea what "beast" he may be referring to?" he asked. "Is there anything around here that fits the description of a beast?"

"The only beast I can think of is my friend perched out here at the edge of the roof," I said, referring to the gargoyle.

"What is it, a bird?" George replied, coming to the window to have a look.

"My first night here, I caught a glimpse of this gargoyle in the moonlight, and it nearly scared me out of my wits—for a moment I thought someone was really out there on the roof looking in."

I felt a sudden, strong tug as George pulled me toward him and onto the bed. I fell forward and on top of him as we rolled over; then I came to settle in a less compromising position, and we playfully wrestled until he pinned me.

There came a knock at my bedroom door, and outside my viewing angle, I could hear Maurice saying, "Pardon me, madam, but dinner is ready."

While George nibbled at my ear, Maurice stood at my door, and I said, "Uh, Maurice, George and I would like you to join us for dinner."

"No," George whispered in my ear.

"I'm afraid I can't, miss, I need to run into town to stock up on a few items."

Wanting to converse with Maurice, yet pinned under George's weight, his annoying, persistent tickling of my neck and ear caused me to let out a silly giggle.

Angered by this frustration, I squirmed to get out from beneath him but couldn't, and I spoke in an urgent demand, "Let me up! I want you to let me up, George—now!"

Sitting up, thinking Maurice had gone now, and allowing these feelings and emotions to come out further, I spoke assertively, "I want us to control our affections in front of Maurice from now on."

"Why, Claire. He must know how I feel about you."

He placed his hand affectionately on my arm and I moved away, but before walking out of the room, said, "I prefer it that way, George. I mean it."

In the upcoming days, George and I spent a great deal of time together; much of it was shared in long walks, and I once led him up to the high point on top of the hill to share with him the view of the river snaking its way out to sea. We had chicken I'd cooked in a picnic basket provided by Maurice and brought a blanket, which I spread out for us to have our lunch on in the sun-drenched outdoors. We took time out to lazily stretch out on the blanket in a comfortable pose, and while holding his gaze, I told him the story of the legend concerning the landholder, the maiden, and the young squire who'd rescued her.

As we prepared to eat, I looked in the basket, and asked, "Do you want a leg or a breast?"

With a rather unassuming, coy expression, he looked at me, "Are we referring to the chicken you've prepared?"

I smirked, raising a brow, "Yes, I'm talking about food."

"In that case, I prefer the breast." Then he placed his hand on my outstretched leg as he remarked, "Perhaps later I can have some leg for dessert."

I removed his hand from my leg and recoiled as I continued setting out our meal, "You are quite persistent, but this isn't the time or the place."

We nibbled through our meal, taking in the view while enjoying a soft breeze; then later we continued on our hike and discovered a lake—very possibly the same lake where my father and Maurice used to go fishing years ago. This tranquil lake and the wooded area around it were picturesque, and the still water mirrored the surrounding landscape, a visually stunning panorama.

Standing together on a rocky ledge where the land met at the water's edge, and while taking in this scenic view, I suddenly recalled a past incident when I experienced the most embarrassing moment of my life. I got this outlandish impulse and without giving it another thought, I suddenly gave into it to push him off the rock, and he splashed into the water. The water wasn't deep, and when he surfaced and rose up to a standing position, he had a confounded look of surprise on his face.

George pushed his drenched hair back, his expression turning to anger; and he asked, "What did you do that for?"

I pointed my finger at him, "I've owed you that for a long time, George Tallin."

George tilted his head as though confused, "What did I do to deserve that?"

"If you think about it long enough, it'll come to you."

Briefly thinking it over, he remembered the time when during a party at my parent's house I'd fallen into the swimming pool; and lifting his hands, arms and shoulders up in the air, he got this stupid boyish smirk on his face when remarking, "I never pushed you into the water. I don't think I even so much as touched you."

I couldn't help grinning, and my eyebrows rose, "Uh-huh, there, see—you know what I'm talking about. Just the same, the reason why I fell in the water was because of you."

"Okay," he said, coming to the ledge and reaching for my hand, "help me out of here."

Having just begun to laugh uncontrollably at his situation, I backed off from the water's edge, "Uh-uh, you're not pulling me in there."

Placing his hands on the ledge, he pulled himself out of the water and hopped up on the rock with water draining from his clothing. Seeing the ease with which he'd managed to pull himself out, I knew he'd have only one thing on his mind. I turned and began running from the lake, but unable to gain any real speed because I was laughing so hard, he caught up to me in no time. He lifted me up in his arms and began carrying me back toward the lake, wearing a deadly serious expression on his face.

My capture subdued my laughter, and I tried to get a serious face while confronting him, "Now George, you know it was your fault I fell into our pool that time, you may as well have pushed me. Now put me down or I'll never speak to you again."

He came to stand at the rock's ledge, holding me loosely in his arms.

"George, I'm warning you, if you drop me in the water I'll make you pay for it—I swear I'll make you pay. I don't know how or when, but I'll get back at you for it if you drop me."

All of a sudden, he gave me a gentle pitch, and plunging into the water, I caught my breath as my eyes bulged.

When my head came up out of the water, I placed my hands on my hips, staring at him angrily.

At first, we just stared at each other, and then George burst into laughter, "I'm not laughing at your being in the lake, but if you could just see the look on your face—if looks could kill..."

I broke a smile and then began laughing with him, and then I reached up for his hand, but he waved at me as if in a gesture for me to give him some room, saying, "I'm coming in with you." After removing his shoes, socks, and shirt, he dove in with me and we swam for a while before he coaxed me into going skinny-dipping to give time for our clothes to dry, something I thought I'd never do.

I couldn't believe what he'd coerced me into doing, but we we're having so much fun at the time and it seemed so natural too; we shared such a great time together. I would've died had someone come along and caught us in such an embarrassing position, but at the time, it didn't seem as though we were doing anything wrong.

CHAPTER 20

HOPE DWINDLES

The days passed quickly without my discerning the words left to me by my grandfather's spirit. I'd begun to have concern that I'd never accomplish what I'd set out to do here—that I'd leave the past unaltered, and my grandmother's soul would remain walking the corridors of this house for the rest of eternity. These things, along with my grandfather's death and the purpose for his spirit's return to this earthly plateau, left me restless and gave me sleepless nights. It was my failure to establish the meaning of his words which caused all this to stand unchanged, and I took it to heart. How could I be so close to grasping the answers I yearned for and yet be so far away in learning the truth that would allow my ancestors to find an eternal peace?

In my mind, I wanted to believe that maybe my grandfather had found peace when I discovered his skull and placed it in with the rest of his remains in the mausoleum; and in a way, it did bring closure to his earthly life. However, the fantastic image of his face as I'd seen it just before discovering the skull gave me a message to help guide me in learning facts regarding his murder, and I believed he'd tried to reach out to me on at least one other occasion. There was the time I felt a guiding force leading me down to the library in search of something. I didn't know what it was he tried leading me to or why; but for some reason, when I went downstairs, I felt as though I'd misinterpreted the place where this force meant for me to go. Because I wasn't able to grasp what it wanted me to know, I lost this mental telegraphic link or communicative transference.

I don't think I imagined this strong fixation explicitly leading me to an area at or nearby the library; but the only thing I was absolutely sure of is that it wasn't my grandmother's spirit leading me. With her, I distinctly felt she desired the past be left alone and undisturbed; and after the incident with the flying records, and having faced that angry specter in her bedroom, I hoped never to encounter her spirit again. There was no doubt in my mind that harm would've come to me if lightning hadn't struck that tree at the moment when I entered her room; and that incident, too, made me believe that my grandfather may have interceded on my behalf and may have saved me from her wrath. That was the very thing I couldn't understand, for the murder destroyed her life and left her terribly miserable, and yet there was no way to console her; she didn't want any meddling interference.

Living with an uneasy turmoil for being unable to discern my grandfather's message, I went inside myself, searching for answers, but they proved elusive. Still, this inward spiral I put myself in made me depressed, and during the night, I restlessly roamed about the house.

One Wednesday, Katie arrived with Maurice, and I introduced her to George, saying, "Katie, I want you to meet an old and very dear friend of my family's, George Tallin. George, this is Katie Loughton."

"Pleased to make your acquaintance, Mister Tallin." She then turned to me, "Patrick asked me to mention that he'd be coming today to make repairs on the balcony. He wanted you to know."

Katie then went about doing her chores, and soon Patrick showed up with an assistant. They had a bigger, bulkier truck this time, and Patrick almost immediately asked that I come outside to take a look at the new wrought iron spindles and railing he'd transported to the house. When I came outside to look in his truck, I saw wrought iron already assembled in three sections that appeared ready for attachment to the existing balcony; the two side sections were shorter in length than the main cross-member that would serve as the centerpiece.

"This is Elliott, my welder, and if you think this wrought iron will do, we're going to check the old balcony to see if it's stable first before securing these pieces. However, if we find the balcony is not secure, we'll have to come back another time to replace the platform before erecting the railing."

"I think that wrought iron looks fine," I said in acknowledgement about the design of the assemblies he'd brought. "It's not exactly the same ornamental style as the old one, but it'll certainly do."

The two men entered the house and greeted George with a nice hello before going up to the second floor to begin their work. They were up there for a while before I went up to see how things were going; they'd already removed and cut away all of the old railing by the use of a cutting torch and tossed the metal pieces off the balcony to the ground below. Only the old platform remained, but it appeared strong in that it supported the two men at the same time.

"How's it coming along?"

"You can see the balcony is supporting the two of us," said Patrick, looking at the man assisting him. "What do you think, Elliott?"

Elliott, who was older and perhaps more experienced in these matters than Patrick, commented with a soft-spoken voice, "There's no doubt that the tree limb falling on it weakened it. The platform has a sort of belly in it, and maybe part of that sag is from the years it's had to carry its own weight up here." He got down on his hands and knees to examine the mortar that had cracked and loosened where the supports anchored to the building. "There are inverted L-shaped brackets bracing the underside of this platform which rest against the house and give the balcony's framework much of its strength to support weight."

I remembered seeing the two L-shaped braces reinforced with a decorative scrolled piece of metal he spoke of when I was looking up at the balcony from ground level, but that still didn't answer the question as to whether the balcony was secure.

Then Elliot added, "The only way to be absolutely certain that this balcony is sound is to remove all the stone around these main supports and install replacements. After the stonework is finished and the mortar has dried, we can start from scratch building a new framework and platform, but I don't know if all that is necessary."

"So what you're saying is that while it's a good indication it can support the two of you now, the only way you can guarantee that the balcony isn't going to fall down at a later date is by doing total replacement." In agreeing with that assessment, I asked, "What would you do if the balcony was yours—if this were your home, would you replace it, or just put up a new handrail?"

"I think I'd just put up the new rail," Elliott replied, "and we can anchor additional support fasteners with the new hand rail for giving the balcony added strength. To install them, I'll have to drill holes completely through these walls, on each side of the doorway, and run long bolts through the walls to tie-in the handrail with this exterior wall." He stepped inside to examine the smooth interior walls on each side of the door opening, and gave attention to where the bolts would extend through the wall. "Fastening the handrail solidly to the building here on each side with bolts will give it more load bearing strength. You'll have a bit of doctoring-up to do on these interior walls after the anchors are affixed, but that won't amount to a major repair job."

He then looked at Patrick, "The only problem is that I didn't bring the hardware attachments needed to fasten the handrail solidly to the building, and it will be couple of weeks before I can come back to install those anchors. I usually keep those attachments on the truck, but I just ran out of them the other day, however, in the meanwhile, we can go ahead with putting up those three sections that make the handrail."

"Well, I have confidence that after the work is finished Patrick can patch up the interior walls satisfactorily for me, and it appears unlikely the balcony will come down before you come back to attach the handrail to the building."

Standing on the balcony, both men held their hands out in a gesture to show the balcony was sturdy and doesn't appear to be going anywhere; then the men resumed their work. Within a couple of hours, they erected the wrought iron handrail, welding the pieces together in addition to using the same techniques to attach it to the base of the balcony. This in itself seemed to make a difference in strengthening the balcony, although it didn't actually gain additional holding strength in how it clung to the building. To accomplish that, they'd have to anchor the handrail to the building's exterior wall, and before leaving for the day, they assured me they'd be back soon to complete the work by installing those attachments.

As time passed, I expect George grew bored staying at this old house, for he showed restlessness, and one evening when he sat down to play the piano, I got the impression that his mind was elsewhere. I'd heard he could play fluently, and it took him no time at all to compose something out of the existing sheet music situated above the keyboard. While flipping through the music, he put together some notes that weren't familiar to me, but they were catchy tunes arranged in a medley. I sat down on the sofa listening and as his fingers danced along the keyboard, there seemed no doubt that he had a knack for playing the piano. Without playing any of the songs from beginning to end, his fingers danced along the keys in a talented way that was pleasing to the ear. He may not have even known I was in the room listening, but without realizing it, he was entertaining me with pieces of these old songs.

He began playing a stylish turn-of-the-century melody that must have been a romancing tune in its time, and I sank back to rest against the sofa cushion while listening. I felt the urge to ask him the title of the song, but remained still while my ears took in the sweet rhythm of the piano keys. After running a long sweeping verse with his fingertips, he surprised me as he began singing out loud,

"I wonder who's kissing her now.
Wonder who's teaching her how.
Wonder who's looking in to her eyes."

Grinning, I finally spoke up, "Just when I was about to ask, a penny for your thoughts. Are you thinking about one of your old girlfriends, George?

His fingers smoothly and rhythmically pranced across the keyboard as he remarked, "Not at all, and you needn't read anything about the lyrics to that old song to make you think otherwise. I'm just messing around here, if you want me to stop playing, I can."

"Actually, I like the way you play. It's entertaining and I'm enjoying it, I just hope you're not thinking about an old flame."

His eyes didn't leave the keyboard, "Well, I'm not... I take it you're not musical?"

"Not at all."

"Come over here and sit down next to me, we'll do something together."

I took George's invitation and came to sit down next to him on the piano stool, and after only a few minutes of tutoring, he had me playing notes and recognizing the tune; I laughingly said, "Chopsticks."

He nodded while smiling, and together we kept up the repetitive rhythm of the silly duet, making it sound pretty good for the simple tune that it was; then the clanging chimes of the grandfather's clock rang on and on until it broke my concentration, and I stopped playing. The interruption made by endless chimes rung by the old clock brought me to see the time was nine o'clock.

"It's only nine o'clock, but it sounded like it chimed twelve times," I said.

"I thought it chimed thirteen times," George said with a trace of cynicism. "Maybe it's the ghostly hour."

"I suppose I can't blame you for being cynical, George, but if you'd seen the things I have you wouldn't be able to joke about it."

"This is it for me, anyhow," he said, preparing to get up from the piano.

"You're turning in already?"

"No, I have some documentation to catch up with, we've got to leave here in a few days, and I have some paperwork that needs to be completed. Before you know it, we'll have to start packing in preparation for our return trip home."

He kissed me tenderly and hugged me, "C'mon, you can help me set up an office in the library, you can be my secretary."

Now I was the one whose mind was wandering, because I knew my time here was running out, and for the remainder of the night, I moped around while watching George examine a spread of papers. I soon grew sleepy from the boredom and said good night before going off to bed.

In the wee hours of that following morning, the sun had only just begun to rise, creating a soft glow on the edge of the horizon. I awoke only a short time ago, and unable to sleep, I aimlessly walked about the house until coming downstairs to sit at the kitchen table. Pondering the time slipping through my fingers—George wanted to leave in just three days, and I did not expect to find the answers I needed by then. My will and determination weakened by the thought of leaving this place without knowing what triggered the terrible tragedy that nearly destroyed my family—its cause possibly being the very key to my own sanity.

To pass the time, I poured a drink from a previously opened bottle of sherry I'd found in a cabinet, after having another, the alcohol began having a dulling, melancholy effect on the senses. I merely meant to take a nip to relax before trying to return to sleep, and had nearly finished a second glass. Soon feeling mellowed out, I became so caught up in thoughts about my family and things that occurred here that I was oblivious to George coming to join me at the table, but there he sat, watching me.

"Do you want to talk about it?" he asked calmly, turning off the flashlight he carried and placing it upright on its lens so it would stand on the table.

I stared at my glass, "Talk about what?"

"Whatever's keeping you up, what's making you drink?"

"You know, George...I feel as though I'm letting my family down by not staying on to learn the meaning of my grandfather's words. I'm not only failing them, but I'm letting myself down too."

George clasped his hands in front of him, "Claire, you know if there was anything I could do, I would. I'm not trying to be funny, mind you, so don't get me wrong, but it's too bad your grandfather couldn't be more specific about where we're supposed to look to find this thing, whatever it is."

I took a drink. "What if my grandmother did go mad and her illness can be passed down through heredity...Maybe, I've only imagined the things I've seen, did you consider that?"

"There's absolutely nothing wrong with you. I think, perhaps, you'd have been better off if Edith had never told you about this place and the murder of your grandfather...Once we've gone from here, you'll forget all that's happened and put this behind you."

His eyes glanced down at his hands, then at me, "You know, I haven't yet given up on the conspiracy theory...Isn't it kind of odd that nothing strange or out of the ordinary has occurred since I've arrived? I'm your protector, I'm your watchdog, and I'm not going to let anything happen to you."

Coming around the table, he kissed me affectionately on the forehead, "Please, don't stay up too much longer."

Left alone in the darkness of the kitchen, I saw George had left his flashlight standing on end in the middle of the table. Determined to finish off the rest of my drink, which was only a couple of swallows, but already feeling the affects of the alcohol, I slumped to doze off, falling asleep with my head resting on my arm.

I don't know how much time had passed before George returned to the kitchen, helping me to a standing position; he whisked me off my feet and took me into his arms, and then carried me up to bed. When he gently placed me in bed, I tried to get him to keep me company by hanging onto his neck, but he reached around and undid my hold.

Now holding onto his hand, I said, "I know you like me, but do you love me?"

Wearing that same boyish smirk, his eyes wandered, "I think we need to continue this conversation another time, now get some sleep."

As I watched him slip away toward the door, I remarked, "You coward."

I really didn't want to bring up the question of whether he was in love, and being that he hadn't voiced his feelings for me, curiosity, along with the melancholy I was feeling, made me vulnerable to bringing up the question. The first night we were together here, he found it easy to express himself; but ever since, I've been wondering if our relationship had become one-sided.

Placing the left side of my face against the soft pillow, I soon fell off to sleep...

CHAPTER 21

THE ANSWER TO THE RIDDLE

In those remaining days, George spent most of his time in the library finishing up paper work he needed to have completed before his trip to Houston, and it was just as well because I felt moody and depressed. To get to the truth about my grandfather's death was of utmost importance to me, and I was prepared to stay on at this house until I discovered all the facts behind this dreadful incident. However, I was having trouble finding the words to break the news to George. Bound and determined to unlock the riddle my grandfather left me, I ran it through my mind uncountable times, but the meaning of those words proved elusive. No matter how much thought I poured into this seemingly vague phrase, I could not perceive its meaning. The key to understanding it was the most confusing part for me, as I wasn't sure what he referred to as "the beast", although certain he must've spoken of an animal.

The night before we were supposed to leave for returning to the states, George came to my room and knocked at my door before entering. Upon his entrance, he saw I hadn't made the slightest attempt to pack my possessions, and while I couldn't leave Strathmoor Heights at this time, I also knew I couldn't persuade George to stay here any longer.

"Claire, haven't you done any packing, I wanted to leave first thing in the morning. We have to catch a flight scheduled to take off tomorrow afternoon from London."

"I'm not going."

George wore a look of concern as he leaned against the dresser and folded his arms, saying, "I thought I had your word that you would leave with me, so when did you arrive at this decision?"

"I know, George, but I can't leave here, not until I've learned what happened the night my grandfather was slain...I know you find it difficult to understand, but I must stay, and it's that simple."

"Claire, all the untold secrets surrounding his death were buried long ago with your grandparents. How can you expect to solve a murder that happened all those years ago, what makes you think you can do better than the detectives who investigated it at that time?"

He was obviously perturbed, as he then added, "You could stay on here for decades and you may never find out why he died. You've got to stop living for the past and start making a life of your own."

"I've made up my mind, George, I'm sorry but I'm staying."

"I want to help, but I don't know how to, and you know I have to leave in the morning, there are people depending on me to be in Houston the day after tomorrow...I can't help thinking that if you stay on here at this place, something's going to happen to you. Now, please, don't do this."

"I appreciate your concern, and I want to leave with you, but I can't..." I looked at him, adding sorrowfully, "Please try to understand, I just can't."

"Well, I can only say I'm sorry you've changed your mind, but suit yourself."

George left the room, obviously angry that I wasn't going.

The next morning, George pleaded with me to go with him; and although I felt tempted to leave with him, I refused, and then I watched on as he took a taxi for Cardigan. He would've had a great deal more leverage and influence over me if he'd just said three simple words—I love you. Those three words would've been all he'd needed to say, and I think I could've put this whole thing behind me and left Strathmoor Heights for good. Whether he knew this or not, I couldn't say, but I couldn't tell him that this was the only thing keeping me from going with him; he had to say it freely on his own.

As the day grew old, I once again found myself alone in the house; but instead of occupying myself with turning up clues to my grandfather's murder, my thoughts were for George. I already missed him terribly, and I believed him to be right; how could I find evidence from a murder which occurred so long ago? I was asking the impossible.

After night fell, I lay in bed wrestling with the question of whether I should've left with him. Although I wanted to share my life with him and my heart ached for his companionship, I'd become unsure of his thoughts and feelings—where did I go wrong? I kept thinking I should've done something different, maybe if I'd held back in giving him my love—surrendering to him the first night he came—he may have thought me different from the other girls he'd known who might have thrown themselves at him. When I fell weak and surrendered to him that first night, I lost whatever mystery I had captivating him; I may have also lost his respect and at the same time any chance of us finding lifelong happiness together.

Unable to help myself that first night he came because I fell under emotions telling me I was experiencing true love, I now blamed myself for having ruined everything. There's nothing I can do now—you can't make someone love you if they don't, and I felt like crying because I believed I'd lost him, thinking I'll never get a second chance. I loved him so much; I guess I always have, and it hurt deeply to think this love affair was already over before it really began. Restless in my longing for George, in grappling with my dark despair, I began to roam about the house in my nightgown; and when coming down to the living room, I switched on a table lamp, and then I became drawn to my grandfather's portrait. Standing before his image, looking at the beseeching silent reverence in his eyes, I confessed to being afraid of letting him down, for my will to find out the meaning to his words was weakening.

Missing George so, if there's such a thing as heartbreak over someone, I was experiencing it now, for the urge to cry swelled within me and tears ran down my face. It soon came to me that the only way I could contend with this loss was to sit down and drown in my sorrow with my foolish heart, and remaining on the first floor, I went to the kitchen. Rummaging through the cupboard for a box of tissues I'd recently seen, in my search, I rearranged the contents on a shelf, coming across two bottles of liquor. Pushing them out of the way, I accidentally knocked something off the shelf, and it fell to the floor. Looking down, I saw what had fallen was a cylindrical-shaped object and then realized it was the flashlight George had left behind. Picking it up, I pressed the button on its handle grip to see if it would work—it didn't, as the fall had apparently jolted the bulb or something internally. After slapping the flashlight against the palm of my hand, I tried it a second time, and it worked for helping me find my way through canned goods, but I suspected Maurice must've moved the tissues elsewhere. Resorting to moistening a dishtowel to wipe the tears from my face, I then thought a drink might calm and relax me enough to think about trying to return to bed and to sleep.

Avoiding turning on the light thus far for reasons unknown to me, I turned my attention to the cupboard again to reach for the bottle of sherry, of which I easily recognized its label. Fetching a goblet from the next cabinet, I carried the bottle, glass, and flashlight over to the kitchen table; and after uncorking the bottle, I began pouring, only to discover it merely filled the goblet a short way. Raising the rim of the glass to my lips, I finished it off in two gulps. Thinking I'd try whatever liquor that still held a place in the cupboard, I rinsed out the goblet and went to get the remaining bottle, which I found to be a half-filled bottle of scotch. Filling the glass one-quarter of the way with the well-aged scotch, I placed the bottle within arms reach in front of me.

My eyes well adjusted to the dark, and having no need for the flashlight, I switched it off before placing the glass to my lips and sipping the scotch, then immediately turned a sour expression. Scotch was definitely not my drink, as it was not compatible with my taste buds; but debating whether to give it a second chance, I glanced at the goblet and then turned my eyes to the bottle. Staring at the bottle, I discovered something oddly familiar about its label, which displayed the side view of a medieval-styled lion standing erect on its hind legs, a forked tongue slithering from its mouth. Examining the illustration of the lion got my mind clicking—there was indeed something about this lion's characterization which served as a reminder of an object I've come across either in or around the house, but I wasn't sure where or when that was. My meditating started nurturing an idea as I reflected back on the riddle.

"In your pursuit to discover what your heart desires, look to the beast. For beneath him is where your answers lie."

Swishing the scotch around in my glass before taking a sip, the taste of it reminded me of mouthwash and I returned a sour expression, but still swallowed it down. Not wanting anymore scotch, I turned my attention back to the bottle's label, in my mind wondering while trying to scratch at the surface of what was behind the image of this lion. Holding the bottle in my hand and studying the illustration on the label, my eyes squinted as I asked myself, *What is it about the picture of this creature I find so intriguing?*

I leaned back in the chair with my eyes unconsciously scanning the room, and I left the bottle resting upright on the table. Now I began to think out loud, saying, "Somewhere in this house I've come across something in the likeness of this beast— *beast!* The king of beasts....KING OF BEASTS!" Then it came to me that I must've come across a lion in a similar form, but where and when?

Getting up from my chair, I began to pace; and though I couldn't fully imagine to what end my thoughts were leading me to, I turned my concentration to what medieval objects I may have come across in the house. There was the halberd axe hanging from the wall off the staircase, the suit of armor standing in the entry hall, but what else?

Inclined to believe that I'd seen something in the dining room, I ventured there and turned on the light. My eyes scanned the room until drawn to the Tudor style throne chair, and then suddenly hitting me like a bolt out of the blue was the family coat of arms above it! Done in the elaborate design of a ferocious lion holding a staff and embossed shield symbolizing royalty, I raised my hands up to it and laughingly said, "It was right here all the time!"

With this tumultuous emotion taking hold over me, I wished George were here to share in my joy. I'd never actually pointed the ornamental object out to him, and he'd never taken much interest in the house's furnishings or fixtures, so it's no wonder that we'd overlooked the thing.

Standing on the ornate chair, I rapped my knuckles against the coat of arms hard metal surface just as if I was knocking on a door, but I couldn't tell whether it had a hollow space behind it. I then made an attempt to pull it off the wall and found it to be quite heavy....*But what if I'm wrong and nothing's there*, I wondered, and from my elevated position on the chair, my arms had the leverage needed to hoist and raise the heavy metal plate. The job proved quite strenuous, and I nearly tripped when stepping down from the chair to the floor, then leaving it resting upright on the floor and leaning against the wall.

Looking back at the space the coat of arms formerly occupied, the outline of its shape clearly pronounced by how the last few times the room had received coats of paint they'd painted around the metal plate. I experienced an exhilarating and enriching moment when seeing I'd uncovered the great secret of this house—this shielded coat of arms had concealed a hollow recession in the wall, and wedged within this basin lay an exposed book!

Ecstatic about my discovery, my mouth unconsciously gaping wide open as my hopes soared, the book cover showed age, and a little fingertip pressure was all it took to dislodge it. Seeing how loose plaster and dust had collected on its outer cover, I blew it away and then wiped off its cover with the train of my nightgown. I felt a sense of urgency, optimism, and excitement when opening it; and in doing so, I learned I had my grandmother's diary in my possession. Her maiden name was Angela Wright, she was eleven years old when she began writing, and I could hardly wait to take the book up to my room to begin reading it.

I first let the book rest on the dining table while I carefully re-hung the coat of arms, and once I had the object in a stable position, I placed the diary under my arm and shut off the dining room light. Glowing with renewed vigor and the joyful hope that I'd soon have answers to all my questions, I went through the kitchen in the direction of the servant's stairs, stopping to retrieve the flashlight to light the way ahead. Holding the diary in my left hand as I ascended to the second story, I noticed the stairs felt cold beneath my feet.

I almost felt giddy when starting down the corridor, looking at the book in wondering what secrets it held, and then that darn flashlight went dead. Stopping to turn my attention to it, I slapped it against my hip in an attempt to get it working again, but it refused to produce a beam of light. I shook it while trying the switch again, and an intense, ominous chill alarmed me to the eerie notion that I wasn't alone; looking ahead of me, I saw the faint glow of a glimmering mist floating toward me—already gaining form and figure! Unable to take my eyes off this ghostly manifestation approaching me, I felt threatened and backed up until my shoulder blades came into contact with the hallway wall.

Shivering from fright as this presence rapidly fused into the illuminating shape of a woman, I could make out facial features and fearfully concluded she must've seen me. My only certain line of escape was the way I'd come—the stairs—and I dropped the flashlight while rushing back through the door and onto the stair landing; glancing the dark descent of the stairs, I clutched a firm hold on the diary I held in my left hand and dropped back to the edge of the landing, my left foot feeling about for the edge until dropping to the first step.

Bracing against the outside wall, my right hand clenched the handrail as I turned to face her; terror gripped me as this luminous figure was already upon me, and cringing while humbling before her, a clinging ice-cold hand clamped my right wrist with a biting hold!

Fearing for my life, I released my hold on the handrail, panicking while fighting to pull my arm free from her, screaming, "Let me go! Let go!"

Finally jerking my hand away, the momentum threw me backward, and I tumbled down the stairs!

Hitting ground level hard with my head in a dizzy spin, I hurt all over, my back and hip joint especially; and I glanced at the stairs to see the descent of a luminous glow! I found the diary lying beside me and grabbed it while scrambling to get on my feet, but in my excitement, I slipped and fell to the floor; she was nearly on top of me when I used the diary to shield myself, and her image vaporized into thin air!

Having seen this with my own eyes, I concluded that her seeing the diary was what must have repelled her. Then taking a second to examine the book's cover, I further realized that there must be powerful and enlightening information in this diary in that there must be something in it that she doesn't want known by anyone.

In trying to get up off the floor, I learned I must've sprained my back; and slowly coming to my feet, I limped in my climb of the stairs. Warily watchful of the way ahead, when I came to the second floor, I saw the flashlight I'd dropped; and stopping to pick it up, I found it worked, and continued down the hallway to my room.

CHAPTER 22

THE PUZZLE PIECES FALL IN PLACE

Entering my room, I closed the door, locked it, and turned on the light. Arranging pillows on the bed to give me back support for taking a comfortable position, I immediately began to delve into my grandmother's diary. Spinning through sorted bits and pieces that opened her life up to me, in my opinion, she seemed quite normal but in some respects a little more vain and self-indulgent than most people. However, I may have just gotten this impression by her writing style and in how the words and their meaning came across to me. Someone else could've read the same thing and interpreted it entirely different. I skipped over much of it because it wasn't pertinent to my reason for intruding upon what had once been her private world.

Angela described her mother as a woman who closely watched over her and guided her with regards to what men she should and should not consider as a compatible mate. Often receiving stern warning to be choosey about the men she spent her time with and not to run off with the first likely bachelor; she also encouraged her to go after a man with money and a high social standing. Her mother probably felt strongly about this because she'd fallen for and married a somewhat useless and deceitful character—a charlatan and a con man. Though her father must've had a likeable side for he was loved by his family, he was a miserable failure and wasn't even much good as a swindler. Her family depended a lot on her mother's parents for support, and because of her father's conduct and his inability to conform to the rules of society; Angela experienced some ridicule from people who knew her family.

As I skimmed over the pages, I interpreted her writing as showing signs of maturing, and learning early on how men took an interest in her, she also understood she could easily manipulate them. There were many men she merely used, but at age eighteen, she became deeply infatuated with a man named Thomas Wesley. The attraction didn't last, and there were others whom she became romantically involved with, but she had little interest in carrying on a lasting relationship with any of them.

She later became drawn to a rather affluent gentleman named Charles MacKennsey, and there were many passages made about the events they shared; and Angela made mention of how these golden days were her happiest. She saw Charles as a prominent, well-bred man of a sophisticated nature, well tailored to fit her needs in what she sought in a man. Their age difference mattered little to her, but the fact that he was wealthy did, and her mother encouraged their association to grow. Angela took into consideration that he made her laugh and expressed how he tried in every way to make her happy before saying yes to marrying him, and of course, her mother was pleased with Angela's choice. At first I wasn't entirely convinced she loved him; but the more she came to know his patience, understanding and devotion, the more love blossomed. His charismatic personality seemed to reinforce their love; and within the next year, the stork came, carrying Daniel. The birth of this child gave new meaning to her life, and she enjoyed spoiling him; the more rotten he became, the more she amused herself by bringing him up this way.

Placing great emphasis on her son's life, she devoted herself to raising him the way she wanted to and never allowed Charles to correct or punish him. At first having trouble understanding this, I later came to grasp from her writing how she relished giving Daniel the rich life she never had. Sensing in her words that Charles had taken a back seat in her life, I came across a passage where she made mention of how she and Charles were drifting apart, as Charles found interest in his magic. She made mention of some of the long trips he'd taken, but she seemed to care little about what Charles did with his life then; she only wanted to take pleasure in pampering their son.

As Daniel grew older, he came to take advantage of his mother in a number of different ways; she caught him in lies but made excuses for his behavior. He worsened with time, hurting her with insolence, and she didn't know how to deal with him. More and more reminiscent about those happy days with Charles, Angela made an effort to rekindle his love and discovered he'd changed—he'd become independent and his new passion was with his magic. She managed to have her way with him though, and not only regained his love, but she, too, fell in love all over again with Charles. She began to travel abroad with her husband, and they sent Daniel off to a private school.

Charles became quite successful at his magic, and as his popularity and fame grew, they began to entertain influential people from all across the globe—these were wonderfully happy days for Angela. During this period, as Daniel came through his teens, he got into serious trouble; and Angela tried to help him by leaning on Charles to bail him out. She detested the individuals he ran with and blamed them for instigating the problems Daniel fell into. Danny had begun to drink, and Angela thought he'd outgrow the habit, as though this was just a spell he was going through. There were nights he became violently destructive, and it appeared from her writing that she'd get in the way as Charles tried to control him and set him straight. Angela tried giving Daniel help and guidance the best she knew how, but it seemed he'd only cooperate with her when he needed something from her; usually money served to quell his rebellious ways, but she had no idea what he did with the money, and she really didn't care to know what he did with it.

Angela had only then begun to see how her son lacked discipline and how he defied authority; so many schools had discharged him that finding one that would consider taking him became difficult, and she worried about his future. She feared he'd end up like her father, an unreliable misfit with the inability to make anything useful of himself, but she wasn't about to give up on him. She then made mention of how Daniel injured himself in a horseback-riding accident and how the painfully severe injuries had to be treated with morphine, which had a surprising effect in how it relieved his suffering. Daniel had a nurse and one of the housemaids aiding him in his recovery, but when treatment didn't bring about the timely results Angela sought, she took over his care. When the pain he endured demanded more morphine than what the nurse would give him, he'd beg for more. Without anyone knowing, Angela administered the amount needed to quell his suffering—sometimes doubling what the doctor pre-scribed—to entirely remove the pain and bring him to a state of euphoria. The change this miracle drug brought about in him was amazing; it even seemed to altar his personality, bringing out a humorous side she'd never seen in him before.

In her diary, Angela made an entry to the effect that she felt relieved to see him coming around and thought he was going to be all right. However, Daniel's situation soon took a turn for the worse when the doctor discovered he'd acquired an addiction to the drug, which resulted in his hospitalization for an unspecified period of time. From what I read, I didn't think Angela grasped how serious my uncle's condition was; as she merely held hope that he'd one day mature to a fine young man. From time to time, she compared Daniel to her irresponsible father, the swindling charlatan; but the difference between her father and Daniel was significant, no matter how much her father failed at making something of himself, he still had the love and devotion of his wife and family in that he was a sympathetic character. It seemed as though everything she'd done to raise Daniel in a good, wholesome way and help him find happiness in this life only served to give the opposite results. Up to this point of read-ing, she was blind to seeing what she made of her son. I sensed she was living in denial for how her son had turned out, and I at least held an idea that she may have been turning to alcohol dependency as a way to adjust to life.

Daniel never completely got over his addiction to morphine, and she shied away from her son after seeing the brutal and devi-ant person he'd become. From time to time, he'd fall back on it or used alcohol as a crutch between those times when he'd try to fight the urges that came over him—he'd fallen into an endless spiral of drug dependency.

Charles put his energy and concentration into his magic, and he thoroughly enjoyed entertaining people; then the time came when Charles dreamt up his scheme to have himself buried alive, and Angela cried out that he was losing interest in her. Her words told of a longing and a need for a man's touch; at times sounding deprived and love starved, she desired sexual pleasures, and when a strange man showed interest in her when she was in town, it sparked an idea to cheat on her husband. However, asking herself if her love for Charles was worth gambling with over an affair, and after all their love had endured, she could not throw it away, for he meant more to her than anything in this life.

Sexual fantasies continued plaguing Angela's mind; this arousing quirk made her desperate for companionship, and fearing she was going out of her mind; it seemed her very existence depended on her finding love. When she confided in her old family physician about these bizarre and impure thoughts her mind had been manufacturing, he believed she had an overactive gland causing it and suggested tests. Unable to cool this ravenous desire down, and seeing it growing to an extreme, she tried to draw her husband's attention, knocking herself out planning a big Valentine's Day party. When Charles decided it was more important to participate in an out-of-town séance than to partake in the party, she became furious. She described herself getting drunk the night of the party, flirting and throwing herself at male guests. Some reacted in an innocently playful manner, but between the lines, she seemed to hint that something more had happened; and further reading revealed a sharper, more detailed picture.

Daniel had been there to witness his mother's conduct at the party and later went to her bedroom to bring her a mixed drink. Wearing only a snuggly wrapped but revealing robe, she sat at her vanity brushing her hair; and as talk about the party ensued, she paused and drank to quell some of the embarrassment she admitted to. Daniel took the hairbrush to stroke her hair, and caressed her shoulders; she suddenly lapsed into a weak state of mind—desiring a man's touch while wanting to gain the love of a son who never returned or showed her love. Angela fell prey to a confusing but stirring emotion that overtook her; succumbing to sensations of loneliness and the stimulating effects of the strong alcohol, she yielded to an incestuous wickedness which she shared with her own son!

Appalled by the unnatural act, at first I couldn't believe it, but as I read on, Angela expressed deep sorrow and regret; however, what sprung to my mind was the strong suspicion that Daniel may have placed a drug in the drink he'd brought to her bedroom and served to her. As the thought remained fresh in my mind, I read little to quell the notion or convince me otherwise, for I'd begun to form an impression of Daniel; and this, along with Angela's depiction of what occurred, I'd come to the opinion that she wasn't in total control of her mental faculties at the time of the incident. She didn't understand what she was doing, as though describing a person who saw what she did in segments or a broken patchwork of frames, and out of touch with reality. The alcohol she consumed over the evening probably intensified the strength of that drug, and it would've made it difficult to distinguish the taste of whatever it was he'd placed into her drink.

Angela was completely crushed, miserable, and burdened with guilt—not only for what she'd done, but also for having been unfaithful to a husband whom she truly loved—and she never realized that fact more than she did now. In her inability to comprehend her behavior, she was unable to completely account for things as they happened, confiding how she had lapses of memory. Trying to repent, she later saw in her son's eyes that the act they'd participated in permanently damaged their relationship as mother and son—he never looked at her the same way again. I continued reading while considering Daniel's lifestyle, suspecting he must've had access to a variety of powerful drugs which would render a person helplessly incapable of being responsible for their actions. It also occurred to me that this may not have been the first time he'd used this method to victimize a female.

Weeks later, her family doctor died, but not before telling her she was pregnant. Angela, now totally devastated, never received confirmation if whether her doctor had been correct in his diagnosis, that an overactive gland had been what was driving her desperately to find sexual pleasure. The test results no longer mattered; nothing did. She became deeply depressed, and did not dare reveal or confess to anyone about anything pertaining to her condition for fear that it may expose the incestuous act she committed with her son.

A scandal unfolded, stemming from the flirting she had done the night of the party, and though she made denials about seeing another man, she could not hide her guilt and shame. Charles suspicions grew, but when it came time for her to give childbirth, he pledged his love at her side. Angela almost died giving birth to not one, but two boys—*Siamese twins* —and a few days later, a long surgical operation separated the twins with one fairing well, while the other would carry horrible life-long facial scars!

The following page was blank and so was all the pages that followed, but between the last page and book cover in the back, I found an envelope. Inside it, I found a note Angela must've written sometime later, and while I recognized her handwriting style, the writing appeared shaky as the words expressed great anguish. The note described how Charles had discovered the diary and in his anger, he struck her and the blow bruised her eye. Daniel arrived home in crazed drunkenness that fateful night, and seeing his mother's bruised face he flew into a rage. Storming up the stairs, Daniel stopped to yank the halberd axe free from the wall, and then charged up the rest of the stairs like a madman! Angela went to stop him, and when seeing the eerie mind-bending sight of a headless corpse on Charles' bed, she fainted.

The pieces rapidly falling into place, I realized she'd taken blame for a murder to protect a psychologically unbalanced son—carrying her guilt, shame, and self-persecution into a mental institution where she spent the remainder of her life. Daniel lost his senses that night; a sociopath disoriented with life and his mind further eroded by drugs and alcoholism, he must've came home higher than a kite, out of his mind with drugs and who knows what. After murdering his father as he lay sleeping, he then took the head down into that underworld of passageways for whatever reason. Perhaps when the shock wore off, his mind blotted out his crime, and although Daniel may not have been able to remember committing such a horrible murder, in his mentally disturbed state of mind, he may have had flashbacks, which haunted him and ultimately drove him to suicide.

I now began to see with some degree of clarity what made Angela's spirit linger on in the present—to protect and keep secret this carnal sin. She tried frightening me in an effort to drive me out of this house, bombarding my mental faculties with illusions—the ballroom party and red dress were mere reflections of her guilt and shame; the rage she showed when throwing the records, and the image of the young man hanging in the library was a last-ditch effort to scare me off. Angela probably never meant for me to find this document; leaving this writing behind as a way to express the guilt and the shame she'd carry with her to her grave, venting the dreadful unhappiness she knew. Her life completely destroyed, she would never divulge what she and her son had indulged in; nor would she allow her son to go to prison for committing murder, at least not while the authorities can hold her accountable. If she felt somewhat blameful for the monster he turned out to be, then she must also have faulted herself, and by accepting the responsibility for his actions, she was persecuting herself for everything that happened in the past; she must've thought that this was the only way.

Placing the note back in the envelope the way that I'd found it, and closing the diary, I then placed it on my pillow; I now understood many things. I knew how and why this murder that devastated my family came about, and in having revealed what happened so many years ago, I discovered why the facts behind it remained so shrouded in secrecy. I now had an explanation for why the authorities never found my grandfather's severed head, and I knew my grandmother wasn't insane, but a woman totally dedicated to her son, which she'd brought up miserably to turn out to be an instrument of evil.

Now at last I'd solved a final mystery, as I had knowledge pertaining to the identity of this phantom that lurked about the property. Somewhere on this estate must be my father's brother, a lonely individual, deprived of a normal life through no fault of his own—*the hooded man!* In forming this conclusion, I came to the belief that he must live with Maurice in the carriage house, and behind that mask may be a gentle man. He must've been the one who carried me in after I'd blacked-out in the mausoleum; how I wished that George were here with me now to hear this news, and still digesting information learned from the diary, I felt a great weight lift off my shoulders in that no more would I fear these phantoms of the night.

I walked triumphantly from my room out into the corridor; the bad dream was over, and now I could move forward to once again relish life. More than anything else, I wanted to tell Angela to forgive herself and I went to her room to further ponder what I had learned. She had in fact allowed her mind to accept that she'd fallen weak to an illness brought about by an overactive gland as diagnosed by her physician rather than see Daniel for what he was. The only way to live with what she'd done was to fault the illness for the sin she'd committed with her son, for to think her son would drug her while contriving such an evil idea was inconceivable to her. Angela could never believe that Daniel had slipped a drug into her drink just before giving it to her, as like in so many past instances, she sought to put blame elsewhere to serve as an excuse for her son's actions.

The more I thought about it, the more I firmly believed that Angela's writing described her being drugged by a son who, because of his upbringing and how drugs and alcohol distorted his perception of the world, bore strange, warped, and twisted concepts about life; a capacity for wickedness and profanity had become engrained in his personality. Throughout her son's entire life, she saw in him in the character of her father; but somewhere along the way, her son deviated from the ways of her father. Maybe because he'd been spoiled rotten to the core as a child, and whatever other damage that was done had been brought on by the effects of his habitual drug use and alcoholism; but no matter how you looked at it, his mother couldn't see to accept the truth about her son—he'd developed into an evil, wicked adult.

I believed Angela's tortured soul had paid the price for her sin. After going into that sanitarium sane, all of those many years spent institutionalized, such an environment must've driven her mad, which may help explain the multiple facets her spirit took on. First there was the ghostly manifestation I saw of her in the hallway; then there was the incident in the library with the flying records, and the time in the cellar when she let her presence be known whereby she snatched from Katie's grip the hurricane lamp which then came crashing onto the floor; and in both of these instances her spirit was invisible. There was the time I heard her crying and bursting into her room, I saw a sinister figure at the vanity; and tonight, I saw her again as a ghostly manifestation on the stairs, and recalling her clutching icy hand caused me to place my left hand on my right wrist where I felt her biting grip. The other strange experiences and imagery was perhaps no more than an illusion she created in my mind—a ploy to drive me out of the house.

These were all acts of a woman spiritually bound to this house, whose wandering, unsettled spirit remained steadfast in concealing immoral and unnatural behavior she'd had with her son on one regrettable night. Unable to understand her conduct and conceive how or why she allowed herself to be part of such a sinfully corrupt deed, she must have gone into herself; and in wondering how her life came apart, she couldn't leave the past alone. The painful shame, regret, and crushing guilt she lived with for the remainder of her life must have consumed her mind and soul, compounded by the hideously horrifying murder of the only man she ever loved. With her dear Charles gone, what did she have left in this life except to dwell on the past, and in a way live and exist only for remembering those golden days they'd once shared together?

In her room, I came to the french doors to open them for the purpose of allowing the night's cool air in, the new finish caused the doors to stick for a second, but then they gave way to opening. Now having more thoughts of my last living blood relative—the hooded uncle who roamed about the premises—I knew he must be out there somewhere; and watching over me in the night was his way of being close to his niece.

I looked to the carriage house, and a thought occurred to me as I spoke out loud to myself, "He must live there, and poor Maurice has been trying to keep his existence from me."

The treetops bobbed from a gentle breeze, and then came a moment when through the rustling foliage I thought I caught a glimpse of a shadow crossing the courtyard. Never forgetting for a second that the balcony may not be safe, I assured myself it was by remembering it supported both Patrick and his assistant, who must've weighed easily three or four times what I weigh. Hanging onto the door jam with my gown fluttering in the breeze, to get a better view of the area down below, I slowly but carefully placed my weight on the platform, and I didn't feel the platform budge whatsoever.

I again saw the shadow drifting across the courtyard, then disappearing by blending into the gray darkness near a tall, lanky evergreen located at the building's corner. Having gained confidence that the balcony was safe and sturdy, I stood on my toes and leaned out over the new wrought iron railing to get a better view.

My heart jumped as the balcony shifted; I lunged for the building, but my fingers fell short as the balcony sank beneath me, and I screamed!

The metal structure made a deep screeching bellow as it pulled out from the stone and became airborne in a furious updraft; doom struck me as I heard a thunderous crash—a whip-lashing, bone-jarring jolt tore into me, and I saw black!

When finally coming to rest on my back in a dazed consciousness, the impact from the fall knocked the wind out of me, and I involuntarily faltered in my efforts to draw oxygen. I was dying from my inability to draw air in and feeling powerless to help myself, I agonized until my collapsed lungs suddenly opened up to draw in air!

"My God!" I said out loud, trying to catch my breath as the wrenching, pounding pain in my ribs and leg made me beg for mercy; and I felt myself rapidly falling into shock! Barely holding onto consciousness, I thought how Angela had gotten the last laugh; but in my clouded vision appeared a tall, dark figure, and not caring who it was, I only knew I couldn't stand this mounting, overwhelming pain much longer.

I caught sight of a hood covering his head, and as his hands reached out to me, I saw a badly mangled left hand with some fingers missing. Lifting me up with difficulty, he carried me off in the direction of the carriage house. The black silky mask seen so detailed and muffled breathing so close, I gave into the impulse to pull the hood off and saw a horribly gnarled and ghoulish visage—the right side of his disfigured face had no cheek; the jaw, gums, and teeth lay exposed, giving a monstrously grimacing expression! I fainted and fell limp in his arms.

He gently laid me down in front of the broad, bulky doors of the carriage house and falling in and out of consciousness, I felt him take from my hand the mask and then dimly watched him enter the carriage house. My stomach churning, I thought I was going out of my mind from the terribly intolerable pain; but then seeing the headlights of a car as it came up the drive, it came to a stop, and George stepped out from a cab. He saw me and rushed to kneel at my side at the same time Maurice showed up holding a blanket, both their faces holding concern for me.

"Addison, you did this to her!" George said.

I immediately dug my nails deep in George's arm and grimacing from the excruciating pain, I said, "Get me to a doctor, George, I'll explain later."

They carefully loaded me into the back seat of the cab with my left leg feeling like someone was beating it with a sledge hammer; and falling in and out of consciousness, it seemed like it took forever for us to get to the hospital. Eventually arriving at the emergency room, a nurse on staff gave me an injection for the pain, and I learned my left leg was broken in three places; they put it in a cast and tightly wrapped my badly bruised ribs.

Later, when I had my first opportunity to speak to George, he came to my bedside and took my hand, "I knew something like this was going to happen to you, I just knew it."

I replied by nodding yes, "I know, but there are some things I need to explain to you, I just don't feel like going into it right at this moment because of the shape I'm in. Tomorrow I'll tell you all about what I've discovered," and I managed a smile.

"Claire, I'm so sorry for having deserted you. As soon as I left I had the gut feeling you were going to get hurt somehow, and I was in the London airport preparing to board the plane when I realized I couldn't leave without you."

Squeezing his hand tightly, I asked, "What was it exactly that made you come back to me?"

"I felt like such a jerk, my conscious wouldn't leave me alone."

"Was that the only reason?"

That boyish grin appeared on his face, and he brushed back strands of hair from my eyes, "No, I came back because I care, I do love you, and I returned to ask you to marry me."

We kissed, and I placed my cheek against his hand; and shortly thereafter, the head nurse came in and ran George off, enabling me to get some much-needed rest.

The next morning I explained to George how I carelessly received my injuries by venturing out onto that balcony. If I'd gone out there after they'd attached the handrails to the building, this would've reinforced the entire balcony and greatly reduced any chance for it to collapse. It was a short-sighted mistake on my part to go out on it, and no one else is at fault. I also told him that I'd found my grandmother's diary and gave sorted details of its contents; I revealed to him the hooded man's identity, but withheld my grandmother's act of infidelity with her own son. In my mind, telling George what my uncle had done wouldn't have achieved anything, and after all, nothing can change what occurred so long ago.

I understood the incest I'd read about suggested that my uncle may possibly be my true grandfather, but this is something that no one can prove or disprove. I'd do anything to altar the past and undo the murder of Charles MacKennsey, but that's something that can't be changed; and if he isn't really my grandfather, there's simply nothing I can do to change that fact either.

David Gatesbury

Still yet, I'm going to go on thinking this wonderful man was my grandfather, and I'll always go on believing it. What happened was in the past, and regardless of my genetic makeup, I am who I am and the product of a gene pool that I had no say in; but I wouldn't be the same individual unless things came about as they did.

CHAPTER 23

THE SPIRIT IS LIBERATED

For two days, my entire body was sore and stiff; I could hardly move without receiving shooting pains. During my hospital stay, I thought about what all had happened at Strathmoor Heights and gave special consideration to the uncle whom I now knew existed, wondering if I could do anything to help him. George used a special mail service to get his corporate papers to Houston on time, and we discussed what we were going to do when the hospital released me. I'd talked him into spending our last night in Great Britain at the MacKennsey estate. The doctors were reluctant about letting me go, but we emphasized we had to get back to the states, and they allowed me to leave after four days, telling me my leg should remain in the cast for a period of six weeks.

Arriving early in the evening back at Strathmoor Heights, I'd learned to use crutches and they were helpful in aiding me to get from the cab to the steps leading up to the front entrance of the house. George obliged by carrying me up the steps and across the threshold; he brought me into the living room and placed me gently down on the sofa.

"If you're still determined to spend the one last night here, you'll have to get used to the idea of bunking down here on the sofa. I'm not about to attempt those stairs with you in my arms, and I'm not going to allow you to risk climbing them using crutches."

Maurice came from the kitchen, drying his hands on a table cloth as he stood in the doorway, "I've been wondering when you'd arrive, I phoned the hospital earlier and they informed me you'd be released this afternoon. Katie and I worked to prepare you a nice dinner, and after you've eaten, if you'd like to have a long talk about Alex, we can."

"Who's Alex?" asked George, not knowing that Alex was the name of my newfound uncle.

"Alex is Miss MacKennsey's uncle whom she met the other night. God knows how or where you found Angela's diary, but assuming you've read it, you must have learned a great deal. Finding it in your room, after reading the inscription on the inside, I brought it down and left it there on the mantelpiece."

Seeing the book's binding on the mantelpiece above the fireplace, I said, "The only thing I can't understand is why you couldn't tell me about him."

Maurice came forth into the living room to sit on the opposing sofa, and said, "Perhaps it would've been much simpler for everyone if I had, but I couldn't... At the time the twins were born, only one of them stood a chance at having any kind of a normal life, and as fate would have it, they chose your father to be the fortunate one. When your grandfather died and Angela was sent away, Irene became the children's guardian. As much as she tried, she could not stomach Alex's disfigurement and she wanted to have him put away.

"You see, I felt indebted to Charles for taking me in when I was a young lad, and it seemed the only way Alex stood a chance at having any kind of a life would be if someone stepped forward and volunteered to take him in. At the time, there was no one, and I coaxed Irene into letting me raise him. It seemed the humane thing to do because if I didn't care about what happened to him, who would...While Winston stood a chance at living a rich, full life, Alex had absolutely no future, the outlook at the time was to have him shut away in an institution.

"I took charge of bringing up Alex, and though he sees me as a father figure, he knows he's a MacKennsey and is aware that you're his niece...Getting back to your question of why you weren't told, I simply saw it in everyone's best interest to leave things as they've always been—even your own father didn't know.

"Originally, I thought you'd come and see the house your father was raised in and then return home, I had no idea you'd stay so long. Alex and I both were delighted you did, for you did more than bring life back into an old house, you gave him and me purpose in that we had someone to look after...As it is, we mustn't have done such a good job, but I assure you, our intentions were quite to the contrary."

"Is it possible for me to at least see Alex? I want to apologize for having pulled off his hood."

"There's no need for that, my dear, he was a bit embarrassed, but he knows you had every right to be curious about who was beneath that hood...I'm afraid Alex wouldn't know how to behave in the company of strangers, he's lived such an isolated life."

"Was there ever a time when the boys were allowed to be together?"

"Your Aunt Irene was very strict about keeping them apart, however, once when your father was very young, he climbed the steps of the carriage house. I imagine he wanted to see me, and when opening the door to enter my living quarters, his eyes fell upon Alex. I'm afraid the episode nearly frightened the life out of your father, but Irene convinced him it was only a dream... Needless to say, he never ventured going up those stairs again."

"I feel so badly, Maurice. I want so much to help him."

"Miss, he lives a good, peaceful life here, and as much as I wish for things to be different, I've learned long ago to accept him the way that God made him."

"But in this day and age, couldn't plastic surgery help?"

"You know, I've often wondered, but it isn't very likely...I have this veterinarian friend who's befriended Alex. He has a farm not far from here, and a number of years ago when Alex and I visited him, Alex injured his hand in a piece of farming equipment while it was operating."

The mangled hand made me think of the mysterious affliction my father had—his paralyzed hand, practically useless for no apparent reason.

"Anyway," Maurice began again, "we've often talked about Alex's chances for getting help. However"—Maurice spread the fingers of his right hand apart and brushed them against his cheek—"because there's so much tissue, nerves, muscle and tendons missing from his face, so many vital things of importance, the outlook isn't good. A colleague of his, a surgeon, examined Alex and determined it would take many painful operations before achieving noticeable improvement. If I thought he had half a chance, we'd try, but in the final analysis, these operations would take years. If just one in the series of operations wasn't successful, it might be a huge setback; any failure could mean that it may not work at all. It would be devastating to his mental being to give him hope of having a normal life and then see these operations not take hold; to me it would be downright cruel to put him through those circumstances and then experience failure. Well, I think you see what I'm getting at, until the day comes that his chances are far more favorable, I'm not going to subject him to scrutiny by the medical community; and it's not likely that day will come anytime soon.

"Alex is a gentle, reserved individual and hardly a young man anymore. He's content with his environment here, and having met few people in his life, he's lacking social interaction with people. He's never gone to school or had any experience with the outside world to speak of, so he has no idea what he's missed, but I've taught him to read and every now and then he enjoys a good book."

I had a thought and interrupted Maurice long enough to say, "I don't mean to be impolite, but it's likely that he'll out live you. What then?"

"I intend to stick around for a while, but since you've brought it up, again, I'm fortunate to have my friend, the veterinarian. He's a compassionate person and the same age as Alex—maybe a few years younger—and they get along splendidly; Alex often assists him with injured animals he's taken in. He's a widower and retired, and he's already made it clear he'd look after him when I'm gone."

Maurice stood, "If that will be all for now, I need to see about getting dinner ready."

Gaining a clearer understanding, I understood Maurice had done a fine job looking after Alex for all these years, and as much as I wanted help, it obviously wasn't my place to interfere.

Now I felt as though there was only one thing left undone, as I wished there was a way to communicate with Angela and convince her to move onto her next plane of existence. If something didn't come about to make her see that she couldn't change the past, she would be bound to an existence of eternal torment. In her realm within the boundaries of this house, she has no idea how much time has passed or how many years have gone by. One way or another, she continues to act in time periods spanning her own life without understanding she is apart from this world and caught between the past and present. The tragedies in her life keep her imprisoned here, locked between the shadows of the here and now and whatever other form of existence await us in the afterlife. We were leaving Strathmoor Heights tomorrow, and this was one great disappointment I'd be taking with me, but I had no idea how to reach her or get through to her. How could I?

Sometime later, long after we'd had dinner, George and I returned to the living room. He built a fire to quell the night's chill, and we cuddled up on the Persian rug in front of the fireplace, his head lying against pillows and mine resting against his chest. The flames of the crackling fire danced before my eyes to place me in a calm, relaxed state that made me sleepy, and my eyelids fell shut.

A short time passed as I dozed in peaceful slumber, then I heard the faint sound of a woman's weeping.

George must've heard it too, and it caused him to stir, as he nudged me, "Do you hear that?"

"Yes," I replied in a soft whisper. We both sat up to listen to what sounded like a woman crying.

"Where's it coming from?" George's eyes wandered.

"My guess is from the upstairs. Help me up."

George assisted in taking me to a standing position, gathering my crutches, and handing them to me. I made my way over to the window behind the piano to see raindrops falling steadily and pelting the window pane as the soft weeping continued.

Our conversation carried on in not much more than a whisper, as George said, "I hope you're not going to tell me that's your grandmother I'm hearing."

"Who else? It's her, George, believe me."

George moved casually in the direction of the stairs. "Why don't I just go up and have a look around?"

"No, George, wait, I have a better idea." I gazed at him from across the large black body of the piano. "Maybe we can get her to come to us. I want you to play the piano."

His eyebrows rose as he looked back at me. "You want me to play the piano?"

I nodded yes, and George came over to the grand piano and sat down. He then began working the keys to play a musical tune, and after playing only a few notes, I motioned for him to stop. I moved around to the keyboard to stand next to him, leaning on my crutches while pointing to the music on display above the keys, "How about this piece?"

George read the title, "The Band Played On." He looked up at me, remarking, "It's not my style, but if you're serious in thinking it can bring her to us, I'll try."

He began playing once again, and I indicated to him that he needed to play louder and step up the pace a bit.

Glancing up at the second-story balcony, I gave him encouragement, "That's good, keep it up."

I moved to the mouth of the fireplace, taking notice of the diary displayed on the mantelpiece, and glancing upward at the crest of the stairs, I saw nothing.

A minute later, she appeared, but not in black, as I'd expected, but as an illuminated, transparent image in a flowing white gown, and it was as if the dress reflected her mood. She must have been expecting to see her husband, Charles, playing the piano because she was no longer in tears.

George ceased playing and came to my side, speaking in a quiet whisper, "My god, I don't believe it."

"Angela," I said, pulling the diary off the mantelpiece and holding it out in clear view. "I know that you're deeply troubled by the past, but the truth has now been exposed—there's no need to go on persecuting yourself."

I leaned over to drop the diary into the flaming coals, and then spoke reassuringly to her, "You must go from this place—Charles forgives you, and he's waiting for you. Go now."

George and I stood together watching as her image at the balcony rail slowly faded and then disappeared. The moment warmed my heart, as I was certain her spirit was no longer a prisoner of this house. She was now free at last, and a feeling of accomplishment washed over me.

"Incredible!" George appeared moved and awestruck by the ghostly manifestation he'd just seen. "She was beautiful and she looked a little like you—she really did."

The book burned slowly. I used the poker to disturb the curled, flaring pages that flamed up, watching them change from orange to red, and then to bluish-green, before changing into black ash and, eventually, into dust.

George saw I was teary eyed and putting his arms around me, sharing this experience brought us closer together. We looked at each other and then kissed. I spent the rest of the night cuddled in a cozy position with him in front of the fireplace, awaking the next morning the same way.

We were packed and ready to leave by 8:00 a.m. Maurice, now wearing his derby, stood ready to drive us to the bus station.

On our way to the car, I hesitated. "Oh, there was something I'd meant to take with me."

"What is it?" Impatience colored George's tone, as perhaps he expected me to say that I'd changed my mind about leaving.

I turned to Maurice, who was preparing to lock up the house. "Would you mind if I took a memento?"

"Anything," said Maurice, "anything you wish. After all, the house and everything in it is yours." He grinned, adding, "I just hope it's not the piano or the grandfather clock—something that weighs a ton."

"There's a music box in Angela's room, on her vanity."

George halted Maurice from moving. "I'll get it." He moved quickly in the direction of the house, "It'll only take me a minute to get the thing, please get in the car."

"It's a merry-go-round, George, you can't miss it."

"Just get in the car. I'll be back with it in only a minute."

In no time, he returned from the house carrying the jewelry box to place it securely in the trunk. We were soon on our way, and later, after arriving at the bus station in Cardigan, George went to purchase our bus tickets for London.

It was time to say our good-byes, tears filled my eyes, and my heart grew heavy when seeing Maurice standing there, hat in hand. He took my hand in his and held my gaze, "If you only knew how much it hurts to send you off in such a banged-up condition…I've done a poor job taking care of you."

"I did it to myself, Maurice. I never should've chanced going out onto that balcony, but I'll heal up." Then I kissed him gently on the cheek, and said, "I'm going to miss you."

George returned, holding the tickets in his hand. "We should be getting along now, Claire, they're boarding the bus."

Holding his hat at his side, Maurice stepped back. "Such a fine couple the two of you make. I want to ask you to take good care of her, but I know you will."

Holding his hand out to George, Maurice said, "It was a pleasure to have met you, Mr. Tallin. I wish you a safe flight home."

George shook his hand. "Thank you, Maurice. I'm sorry if I gave you a bad time."

"Oh, that's alright, you owe me no apology."

"You'll get a bottle of Sherry before Christmas, Maurice, I promise," I said.

Maurice grinned, "And you'll be in my prayers. Well, you'd better be off now before they leave without you."

Hobbling on my crutches as we neared the bus, I heard someone call out, "Hey, wait!"

Pausing at the door of the bus, I turned and saw Maurice coming our way carrying the merry-go-round jewelry box in his hands.

"You nearly forgot your memento." He handed it over to George, and then we boarded the bus.

From the seat I occupied next to George, I waved to Maurice for the last time as the bus pulled out of the station. We both sat quietly as George held the jewelry box in his lap, appearing deep in thought.

"What are you thinking about, George?"

"The old guy, Addison."

"You do like him, don't you?"

"I had my reservations at first, but after what I saw last night, I suppose seeing your grandmother helped lift any suspicions I had about him. He's all right."

"He's a good old soul, George. I'm gonna miss him a lot."

George placed the miniature merry-go-round jewelry box in my lap, and while examining it, I lifted its lid and wound it up. After closing the lid, it played a jingly version of 'The Band Played On'. I rested my head against his shoulder and watched the merry-go-round revolve. Its tune reminded me of the night before when George played the song on the piano, and we stood in the living room together viewing Angela's spirit watching us from the second-story balcony.

The memory warmed my heart and gave me a sense of gratification. George must've been thinking the same thing too because that's when our eyes met, and I felt the special attachment we had for each other. The song serenaded us, and somehow it seemed as though the entire world was smiling. In the moment, we embraced, kissing with such fire, feeling, and emotion that I held no doubt in my mind that he really, truly loved me. My spirit soared, and in my heart, I held a certainty for the future we'd share together.

THE END

CPSIA information can be obtained
at www.ICGtesting.com
Printed in the USA
LVHW110246240522
719593LV00010B/37